Sinai Gold

Image of diamond drilling cores showing rock type and mineralization from below the surface in the Sinai Peninsula

SINAI GOLD

A NOVEL

"The road to the promised land runs past Sinai. The moral law may exist to be transcended; but there is no transcending it for those who have not first admitted its claims upon them, and then tried with all their strength to meet that claim, and fairly and squarely faced the fact of their failure."

C. S. Lewis

BY

JEFF LELEK

STEAMBOAT PRESS

COLORADO

SINAI GOLD
Copyright © 2021 by Steamboat Press

PUBLISHED BY STEAMBOAT PRESS

This is a work of fiction. Names, characters, businesses, places, events, locales, and incidents are either the products of the author's imagination or used in a fictitious manner. Any resemblance to actual persons, living or dead, or actual events is purely coincidental

Printed in the United States on acid-free paper.

Contents

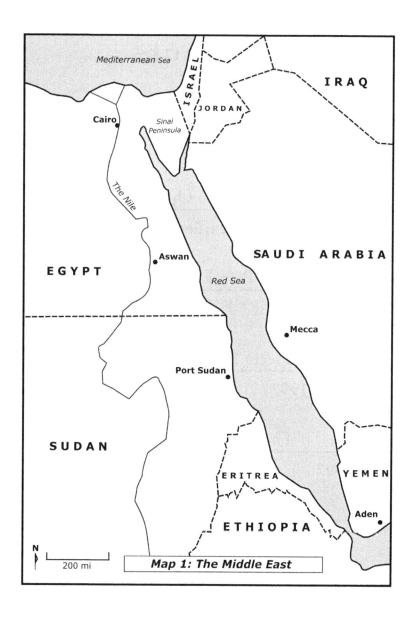

Map 1: The Middle East

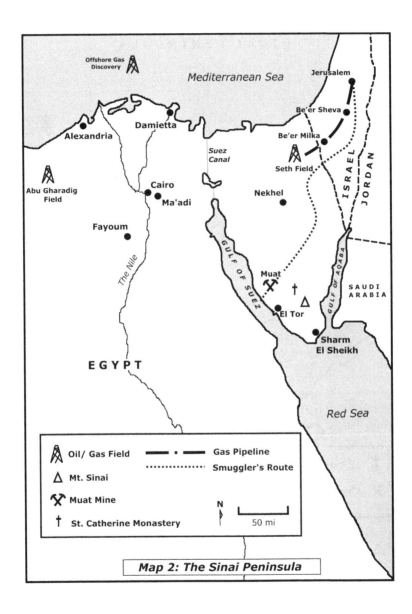

Map 2: The Sinai Peninsula

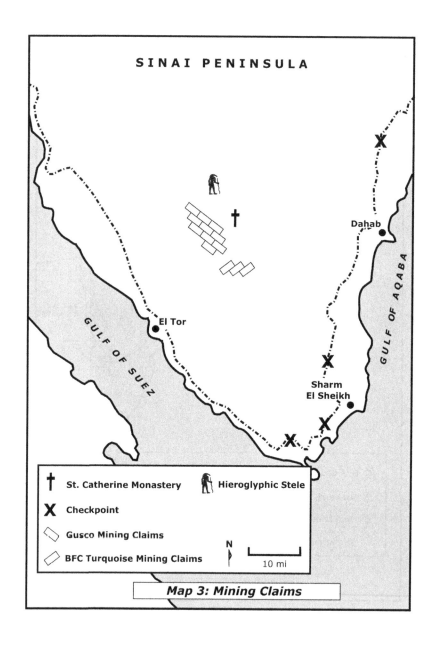

Map 3: Mining Claims

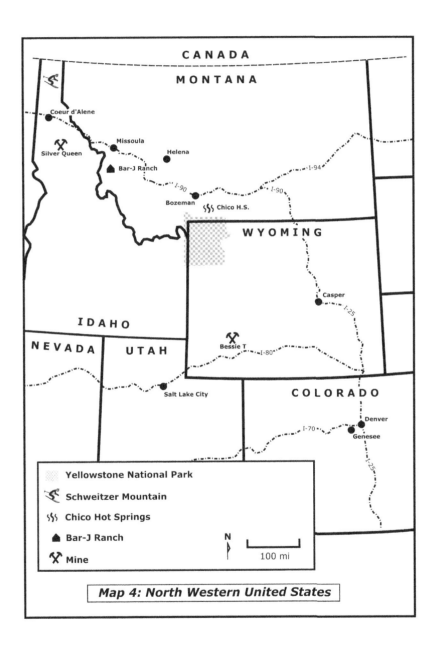

Map 4: North Western United States

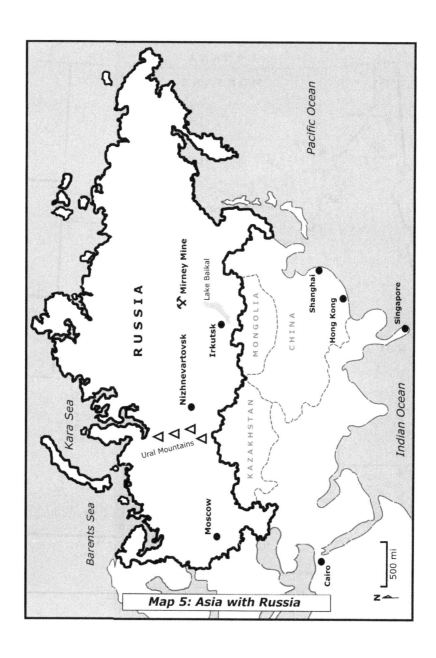

Map 5: Asia with Russia

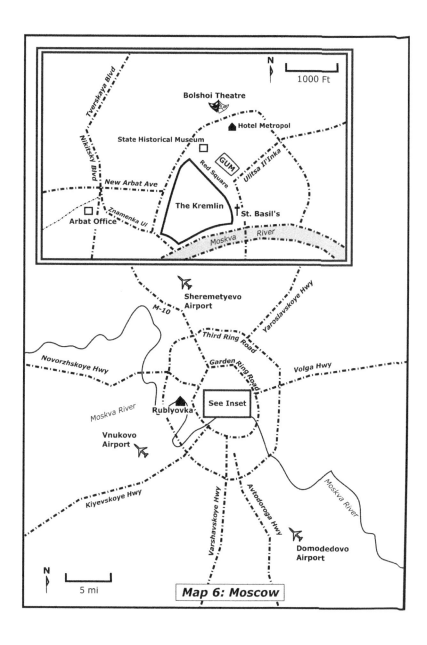

Map 6: Moscow

MAIN CHARACTER LIST

JAKE'S INNER CIRCLE
Jake Tillard – *Geologist*
Augusta (Gussie) Tillard – *Jake's daughter*
Marv Tillard – *Jake's father*
Libby Joyce – *Jake's girlfriend*

UNIVERSITY OF MONTANA
Dr. Don Hynde – *Professor of Geology and Department Head*
Dr. Rocky Winston – *Professor of Geology*
David Li – *Master's Degree graduate student*

WASHINGTON D.C
General Richard A. Radisson – *Deputy Director of the CIA, Operations*
Stan Kawinski – *CIA Operative*

DENVER
Janet Robinson – *Chief Geologist for Pimple Creek Enterprise*
Peter Owens – *Chief Negotiator and Contracts for Pimple Creek Enterprise*
Flo - *Libby's secretary*

RUSSIA

Boris Oblonsky – *Russian Oligarch and head of BFC Co*

Viktor Popov – *right hand to Oblonsky*

Roman Novikov – *Chief Geologist BFC Co and Russian mine fore-man for Egypt venture*

Denis Morozov – *Lead engineer at diamond mine in Mirny*

Marat Bragin – *Chief lawyer / accountant for BFC Co*

EGYPT

Salah el Gindi – *Jake's partner in Cairo*

Mohammed – *The Bedouin from northern Sinai*

Abu – *Mohammed's Bedouin cousin*

General Mohammed Latif – *Egyptian State Department*

Dr Hassan Barakat – *head of Geologic Surveys, Egyptian Mineral Resources Authority*

Hamdi Hamoud – *El Tor police chief, Southern Sinai*

Ahmed al-Houthi – *Yemeni hashish smuggler*

Chou Zhou – *Chinese miner at Muat Mine*

Osama Foda – *defacto head of NOFORTH (No Foreign Thieves)*

Dr. Harold Jones – *University of Chicago Egyptologist*

CHINA

Wang Yong – *Chinese COO for Lim Family*

Liu Ling – *right-hand woman to Wang Yong*

Philip Lim – *head of the Lim family empire*

Chou Lim – *dead father of Philip*

Feng Lang – *head of Feng Shipping in Hong Kong*

Preview
1997

THROUGH the peephole, Jake saw the ugly face of Viktor Popov. He had to open the door but was understandably reluctant. Taking the metal security chain off the guard, he turned the doorknob and let the killer into his hotel room. It was the middle of the night.

"Change plan. Must leave now," said Popov in heavily accented English. Jake had grown to dislike this huge, barrel-chested man with gorilla-like arms, pudgy face, and Brezhnev-like eyebrows.

"I thought we were to act normal. My flight isn't until late this evening."

"Flight changed. Come now. Bring things," replied the Russian.

"But you need to tell me why Viktor."

"Boris will tell why. Come now," replied the Russian.

Jake didn't have much to pack. In five minutes the two men walked through the lobby of the Metropol Hotel and out the revolving door to a waiting black limousine. Jake assumed they would check him out of the hotel at some point. From the back seat of the car, Popov said something to the driver in Russian and they sped down Teatral'nyy Proyezd past the Bolshoi Theater, turned right on Ulitsa Il'inka, passed the onion domes of St Basil's Cathedral, and crossed the Moskva River with a view of the Kremlin fading in the rear. Gazing out the limo window, Jake deciphered Cyrillic signs as they raced southwest on Leninskiy Prospekt. He had never been down this road, and did not know he was heading to Vnukovo International Airport, which handled much of the private business jet traffic.

"Will Boris be on the plane?" asked Jake. "How will I get through immigration?"

"I don't know," said Popov, who turned and looked out his window.

Jake gave up on Popov and settled back in his seat. A half hour later the car passed through a security checkpoint and cruised along airport taxiways towards a waiting Gulfstream IV. Jake climbed up the airplane steps as Popov handed his bag to a ground worker for placement in the hold. Boris Oblonsky was waiting for him in one of the front seats.

"What the hell is going on Boris?"

"I am sorry to be rude Mr. Tillard, but I am afraid the authorities are looking for you. If you don't get out of Russia now you will be in Lubyanka Prison by the end of the day. You're wanted by the FSB, as well as the Border Guard Service and the local Moscow police."

"They're all looking for me? Why?"

Shocked, Jake dropped into the leather seat.

"It's unfortunate, but you are wanted for murder," replied Oblonsky.

"Murder. Those men in your office? But I didn't kill them. You know that. You have clout. Why didn't you tell them I didn't do anything?"

"Because your fingerprints are on the gun that killed two of them."

"But I didn't pull the trigger," screamed Jake, slowly coming to the realization of what was happening. "You son of a bitch."

"Don't be upset Mr. Tillard. It's not so bad. Lucky for you I have connections. I am able to get you out of Russia tonight. Immigration is no problem. My plane will fly you to New York, and from there wherever you want to go."

"You are a bastard."

"Many would agree," Oblonsky smirked, his bodyguard looking alert and standing just behind him.

"But this is not right," protested Jake. "You're a son-of-a-bitch."

"Nevertheless this is how it is. I must leave now. I am taking a big risk helping you like this. It would be unfortunate for you and me both if you were found to be on my plane. You need to get out of Russia now. We'll talk by phone next week. Good luck today, my friend,"

Sarcasm permeated the air. Boris Oblonsky stood up and with his bodyguard departed the plane. The flight attendant immediately raised the steps, closed the door, and the Gulfstream taxied towards the runway. Jake could not rationalize what had just happened. He sat back in his seat, preoccupied with his situation, and stared forward without seeing the pretty flight attendant. When she asked him again what she could bring him, he could not get out any words.

An Inkling of an
Opportunity

1993

(four years earlier)

MOST people climb Mount Sinai in the pre-dawn hours in order to see sunrise. This is precisely what Jake, Libby, and Gussie did, choosing the more strenuous route known as The Steps of Repentance. Established in the sixth century, some 2,500 stone steps ascend to the 7,497-foot summit, from where the three watched with a dozen others as the new day dawned.

"Will you look at that," said Libby, as the sun breached the horizon, and the small crowd collectively exhaled.

"This is something I've wanted to do for years," said Jake. "But I'm glad I got to do it with the two girls I love. Makes it even more special."

"The sun goes up so fast," said Gussie a minute later. "Why does it do that, and then slow down?"

"It doesn't, that's just an illusion," said Jake. "The earth always spins at the same rate, so the sun travels across the sky at a constant speed. It just seems faster when it's near the horizon."

"I don't know. I think it really is faster," said the ten-year old, causing Jake to laugh.

"Not everything is as it seems," Jake said.

"What does that mean?"

"You'll find out as you get older my dear daughter."

Jake thought about her growing up and felt sad that too soon she would be off on her own, finding her way in the world. He opened his backpack and took out the light breakfast and juices he brought, which they eagerly consumed before heading back down, reaching Mohammed and their horses six hours after starting the hike.

"Did you enjoy the walk?" Mohammed asked. The Bedouin had been more than happy to stay and tend the horses, not understanding why foreigners wanted to climb a mountain in the dark. Mount Sinai was remote and it astounded him that so many *khawagas* came to climb it so early in the day.

"It was spectacular," answered Libby.

"Something everyone should do once in their lives," added Jake.

"It was a long way up," said Gussie. "I don't understand why we did it in the dark. We could have seen the same sunrise from our camp, around a campfire, eating one of Mohammed's breakfasts."

Mohammed laughed, having expected those answers from each of them. He helped them onto their horses and guided them away from the mountain, towards the monastery of St. Catherine.

The ride today was the longest yet on their four-day trek. Mohammed finally stopped to make camp just as they lost sight of the monastery. Each night they had camped somewhere different, with new views of the mountains and desert. After their long day, the group was thankful for the grilled kofta, pita bread, and baba ghanoush they had for dinner. As they ate and watched the fire grow smaller, Mohammed sang songs in Arabic, lulling them under an incredible skyscape of stars. There was no moon, and it was as dark as they had ever seen it when the fire finally died. They woke early the next morning as the sun once more peeked above the horizon. The Bedouin was always first to rise; Gussie always the last. This morning, Libby woke up before Jake.

"*Sabah al khair Mohammed*," said Libby, crawling out of her sleeping bag and shaking out her long, chestnut brown hair.

"*Sabah al ful*," replied the Bedouin. It was unusual for a Bedouin to accept someone as forthright as Libby, and spend time with her like he had. But Mohammed was not your average Egyptian, having dealt with foreigners most of his life, and having been field partner to Jake for several years.

He regarded the woman with curiosity. Libby was tall and lanky with a great figure, tanned skin, and an intelligent-looking face that drew people in. Mohammed had heard Jake talk about her for three years now, but had not met her until recently. Although Mohammed found her quite attractive overall, he thought her eyes were her strength. He loved the way she stared into his own eyes without letting go, holding his attention while she asked him endless questions and sought to understand him. It was an intensity that he saw in few people. After four days in the desert, Mohammed knew what Jake saw in the woman, and wondered why his friend had not married her yet. Being a Bedouin, he knew it was not his place to question such a thing.

When they were all awake and had their morning coffees in hand, Mohammed asked them to take a short walk. A hundred yards to the west, at the base of a small embankment, lay a pile of drill cores which the Bedouin had seen on an earlier trip. He had little idea what they were, but thought Jake would find them interesting. Indeed he did, getting very excited when he picked one up. Libby, being a geologist herself and a part owner in three Western US mines, also recognized their significance. She and Jake bent down and picked through them, inspecting some and dropping others quickly.

"You know what these are, right Jake?" asked Libby, clearly excited.

"Yeah, they're diamond drill cores from someone doing mineral exploration. Pretty cool finding this in the middle of the Sinai. I remember rocks like this back in school, but haven't seen anything similar since then. This is all hard rock stuff, nothing to do with oil and gas."

"Right. These guys were probably looking for metals. This is my forte, and I like what I'm seeing. Let's try to separate out some representative rock types, OK?"

"What are these things?" asked Gussie, who had been very patient so far.

The ten-year-old was extremely cute, a bit precocious, clearly intelligent, and prone to ask lots of questions. She was tall for her age, taking after her father. Jake gave the girl wide range, her curiosity moving her to explore her environment and learn at a rapid pace. Libby thought it amazing how Gussie had recovered from their shared experience being kidnapped a couple years ago. That ordeal had lasted weeks, when they were held in a remote house in the woods of Montana. The child had played a large role in saving them both, using a small mirror to signal passing aircraft where they were being held captive. Libby had been greatly mistreated and almost raped, but the psychological trauma impacted Gussie as well. Good counseling and a great father had brought her back almost to normal.

"They are cores that another geologist cut years ago, Gussie," said Jake. "Someone like me or Libby paid to have a rig drill into the ground and pull these out, exploring for something like gold."

"Did they find any?"

"Well probably not," said Jake chuckling. "I don't see any mines nearby, so they probably didn't get much encouragement."

The two geologists spent twenty minutes picking through the small mountain of cylindrical cores, each about two inches in diameter and from six inches to two feet long. The pieces were all mixed up, having fallen out of the wooden trays which originally kept them organized. They had been cut by prospectors at some unknown time in the past, brought up from below the surface by a drilling rig turning a diamond-studded bit shaped like a donut on the end of drill pipe. By the size of the pile, Libby estimated the rig had drilled down at least two or three thousand feet. Or maybe this pile came from multiple, shallower, boreholes. In any case, she picked out what she thought to be representative samples of the different rock types, as well as some pieces that were obviously mineralized. Like Jake, she had a Master of Science degree in geology from the University of Montana. But Libby had specialized in economic geology, the study of ore deposits. From her background, she knew that the green tinge in some of the cores indicated copper, possibly associated with gold or silver. They reminded her of rocks at her Bessie T mine in Wyoming. She strained to see some native gold in the core, but came up short. She was certain, however, that other pale green core was a chlorite-laden rock typically associated with greenstone belts, notorious for harboring economic minerals. Off to one side, she and Jake created a much smaller pile of the cores they selected.

"I think this is good enough," Jake said. "We've got a piece of every rock type. Now what do we do with them?"

"We get them to Denver," replied Libby, hardly able to contain herself. "Mohammed, after we leave tomorrow can you please come back and get this small pile. Keep it safe, and I'll ask Salah el Gindi to get it from you."

Salah el Gindi was Jake's partner in his gas venture, and would likely be involved if anything developed from these mineral cores. He lived in Cairo and knew how to get things done in the country.

"Yes, Miss Libby, I will do that," he said, looking over at Jake for his concurrence.

Libby could never get enough of the Bedouin's face, which was ruggedly handsome and dark complected. His eyes had great depth, which she imagined reflected his sixty-some years of countless adventures in this most inhospitable of environments. Libby knew he had fought alongside both Egyptians and Israelis during several of their wars. She knew he had killed people while saving others. Jake had mentioned Mohammed to her several times, clearly with respect and admiration for the tall man. He said he could not have done the fieldwork he did without the Bedouin. In four days of interacting with Mohammed, she had also become a fan.

"So why are you sending these to Denver?" asked Gussie.

"To see if we can use them to find something the other guys missed."

"Why would they have missed something?"

"Explorers do all the time," answered Libby. "Most of the time when a geologist finds something worthwhile, the area had already been passed over many times by others. It's the smart ones who finally find what is hiding underground."

"What do you think is hiding?"

"Probably nothing but maybe gold and silver," Libby said laughing.

"OK. Can we eat breakfast now please," Gussie said, taking Mohammed's hand.

They returned to camp, cooked their last meal of the trip, and reminisced how wonderful the four days had been. The ride back to the starting point was spectacular and uneventful. Mohammed had procured wonderful Arabian horses for their outing from a local Bedouin village, where they began and ended their journey. They exchanged the horses for a Chevy Blazer the three foreigners would drive back to Sharm el Sheikh. Mohammed would stay with friends in the village before dealing with the cores, and then head back to his home in the northern part of the Sinai.

"*Massalama, habibi,*" said Jake as he embraced his colleague. "Thank you again for everything. I'll contact you in a couple months when I visit the gas field. I'll have some work for you."

"Goodbye my friend," answered Mohammed simply. "And goodbye Miss Libby."

When Gussie came to say goodbye, Mohammed picked her up and threw her slightly into the air. Then he held her hands while singing a local song and doing a little dance, his tan robe swaying back and forth. She giggled, holding his hands and dancing with him. Mohammed finished the song and crouched down so he could look her in the face. He smiled broadly and gave her a high five.

"*Massalama,* my little one. Come back to the desert and I will show you something wonderful again. Something that very few people ever see."

Grinning, Gussie teased, "Sure Mohammed. What will I see next time?"

"You must return to find out."

Gussie gave Mohammed a thumbs up sign and smiled. With that, the Bedouin turned and walked away, joining his brethren.

The drive to Sharm was quiet, each of them reliving the past few days under the shadow of Mt. Sinai. Mohammed had made the desert come alive, pointing out things they never would have noticed without him. A lizard here, a water hole there. A Nubian Ibex, the largest animal in the Sinai, and one that is hardly seen anymore. A desert tortoise. This area was one of the most arid places on earth, but still presented life when you looked for it.

When they arrived at the hotel, they went for a quick swim in the sea, then dressed in fresh clothes for the evening. After dinner and after Gussie went to sleep, Jake joined Libby for a drink at the pool bar. The weather was balmy, a gentle breeze blowing jasmine-scented air past their table.

"You love it here, don't you Jake?"

"Yeah, I guess I do. I spent six years of my life here." He paused, as he decided how to continue. "Paula was still alive, and we were living the expat dream. It was all good. Camping in the Western Desert, diving in the Red Sea, softball every Thursday, parties at any excuse.

Unimaginable trips around Egypt and overseas. We did safaris in Africa, junkets to Europe, trips to Oman, India, and Thailand. The kids all played together. We felt very safe, and we were very spoiled. What was not to like? I'm sorry it's over."

"So why did you really quit Reacher Oil? You could still be living that life, no?"

"The best thing I ever did was quit Reacher and go off on my own. After Paula died in the car accident, living in Cairo became challenging. Gussie missed her mom and there were memories of her everywhere. When Reacher had their huge redundancy program, I knew it was time to go. But I was the one who pulled the plug... I knew I could find a gas field in the Sinai, and Reacher didn't have the staying power for exploration in Egypt. They couldn't handle the risk. I got partners and lined up money, drilled the discovery well, and the field should start producing gas to Israel next year. My only regret is the trail of destruction left behind, especially the toll it took on you, Gussie, and Layla. I've had my share of misery, but the kidnapping was one of the worst things in my life. I'm truly sorry that happened to you because of me. I think you and Gussie have mostly recovered, but I'm not sure about Layla."

"She was a Moslem woman Jake. I know when she was your housekeeper in Cairo, and then when you brought her to the US as Gussie's nanny, you treated her with respect. When we were kidnapped, she could understand everything the men said, while Gussie and I could only understand what they said in English. They did not treat her well, and I think it was very hard on her. After the rescue she went back to Cairo and I doubt she got any decent counseling like we did. Do you keep up with her?"

"You know I tried to convince her to stay in the US with us, but she needed to be with family. After she went back I tried to keep in touch, but our first and only meeting did not go well. Her family has taken over, and the last thing they want is me in her life again. I don't blame them."

"Well, that's all over Jake. Layla will work it out, as Gussie and I have done. I'm amazed in spite of it all that you still love the place and the people here?"

"I absolutely do. I'll love the place till the day I die. And you know it's because of the people. In spite of the poverty, the Egyptians are kind, funny, and so hospitable. They have a universal affection for children, which we experienced firsthand bringing up Gussie here. We never worried about her being kidnapped or abused. It's part of the cultural charm I love."

Libby looked into his eyes with that intense stare and knew he was telling the absolute truth, at least as he saw it. He was happy to have his gas field being developed in the Sinai, and she felt sure he would be glad to have another project here as well. Libby loved this rugged man. His face was rough, his skin tanned and almost leather-like, his muscles toned. His mustache made him look like a rancher. She knew his childhood in Montana was stereotypically western, his parents being true cowboy types, especially his mother. When they were young, Jake and his brother both had long lists of chores each day, but after those were done the boys were allowed to play on their own. No forest was too dark, no river too wild, no mountain too steep. There were broken bones, scrapes with friends, and encounters with animals. It was an upbringing much different than Libby's in Michigan, and one that made her a bit jealous.

CHAPTER 2

SINCE returning to Cairo, Jake based himself at the Mena House Oberoi hotel. It retained the ambiance of an old British colonial hotel, elegant and charming, with overstuffed furnishings, marble, and polished antiques which had made the journey to Cairo decades ago. There were just enough mashrabiya screens, oriental carpets, and tea pots to remind clients they were in the land of pyramids and camels. In the past he could not afford to stay here, but loved dining in the sophisticated Indian restaurant or merely having a coffee by the pool. Since his gas discovery, venture funding had allowed him to travel more extravagantly. The Mena House was now his go-to hotel in Cairo. It was not at all convenient to the Egyptian General Petroleum Corporation offices or anywhere else he did business, but he put up with the commute in order to enjoy the exotic atmosphere in the shadows of the great pyramids. Gussie loved the pool and the costumed doormen, all very dark-skinned Nubians in period dress that included ballooned pantaloons and puffy shirts in shades of white, red, and yellow. There were feathers involved as well.

"Welcome back sir," chimed one of the Nubians as they stepped out of the car. "And ladies," to Libby and Gussie.

"Thank you," replied Jake. "Please take the bags to our room."

"Yes sir. They will be there in fifteen minutes. Have a good day sir."

Another costumed man with a white towel draped over his arm offered them cold towels and small glasses of hibiscus juice from a silver tray. They sipped their drinks as they walked across the lobby, a breeze sweeping through as it was open to the outside this time of year. The whole place had the feel of the British heyday in Egypt.

#

They dressed for dinner in the main dining room, an overly formal-looking area modeled after the great Moghul Empire of India in the eighteenth century. White tablecloths, napkins, and starched white uniformed waiters contrasted with the rich and colorful décor. Jake ordered for the table, a mix of grilled meats, curry dishes, and pickled things. Gussie had grown up eating exotic foods and did not bat an eye at the food. Libby on the other hand was more American and felt the need to ask about most of the offerings on the table. She liked almost everything, commenting on how different the spices tasted.

Tonight a man was playing traditional Hindustani classical music on a sitar in the middle of a small, raised stage. Jake asked the maître d' to come over and tell them about the man, who evidently was quite famous across the Middle East. He told them about the instrument which became popular in northern India, near present day Pakistan, in the sixteenth century, and had a brief period of popularity in the west during the sixties with bands like the Beatles, Fleetwood Mac, and Led Zeppelin. After dinner, the three continued listening to the music until it stopped, then retired to their rooms. Jake left Gussie alone in their room for a few minutes to get ice, stopping at Libby's room to give her a goodnight kiss.

"Sorry we can't share a room," he said.

"You don't have to explain Jake. You're a good dad. There's nothing else we can do with Gussie along. I wish it didn't have to be like this but it's OK. It's one thing for you and me to share a bedroom at the ranch. The house is so big it doesn't seem weird. Gussie has her own room there. When it's just the three of us in a hotel that's different. I suppose if we got a big suite with multiple rooms it might work. But I know you try to respect your daughter and her memories of Paula." Libby sighed, "It's just so romantic here you know. Gives me the quivers."

"Quivers? I don't think that's a real thing. Maybe tomorrow I can get a sitter. We could have that romantic dinner. Maybe play around in your room? What do you think?"

"I'd like that, but I love Gussie too much to stick her with a sitter. She's fun to have around, so let's all do something special tomorrow for our last night in Cairo."

"Yeah, OK. Goodnight my love," giving her one more kiss.

#

The next morning Gussie was in the pool where Jake could keep an eye on her from a café table. Just beyond her, towering over them, were the pyramids of Khafre and Menkaure, the former being the second tallest pyramid and still retaining some of its original limestone cladding near the top. Jake and a friend once climbed up Menkaure, although it was illegal to do so. It took several bribes and a couple hours of careful climbing to get to the top, where there was a flat spot from which each of them hit two golf balls into the ether. That was a very expat thing to do.

Jake looked at his watch. He was waiting for Salah el Gindi, who had never before been late. Libby had also not shown up at the appointed time. But his *ahwa mas boot* was delicious and he did not mind watching the people milling about. When he worked in Cairo for a half dozen years, he developed quite a liking for these small coffees, very strong, very sweet, with a thick layer of sludge on the bottom. Now that he was an intermittent visitor to Egypt, he had to limit himself to two per day or he would get jittery.

In the hotel lobby, Libby intercepted Salah en route to the meeting. He was hard to miss, dressed in his usual tweed jacket regardless of the time of year or level of heat, and standing more than six feet tall, thus towering over the general population. Salah had been a friend of Jake's for years before they became partners four years ago on Jake's Sinai gas prospect. Salah had been well positioned in Egypt's oil industry before moving to the Emirates to work offshore Abu Dhabi. He made enough money there in seven years to retire at age fifty. Now in his sixties, he continued to make deals and consult. Jake chose to partner with Salah because he was plugged into the local oil and gas community, and because they got along so well. Salah knew everyone, especially at the ministerial level and in EGPC, the Egyptian General Petroleum Corporation that oversaw all developments and production for the government. What Jake had not appreciated was how multi-dimensional Salah was, active in the Cairo symphony, the visual arts, and in fact spending most of his time buying and selling real estate. He appreciated good Bourbon, a result of his years at the University of Tulsa. In spite of this heretical practice, the local people in power loved him, and he had been indispensable in helping Jake navigate the system to consummate his gas deal. Salah was light-skinned and more European than Egyptian in facial features. His eyes were dark and piercing, and his straight Roman nose anchored his face. Libby thought him as handsome as Mohammed, in a less weathered way.

"*Salaam al aleikum*, Salah," Libby said. She was learning Arabic little by little, finding it a very frustrating experience.

"*Aleikum al salaam, madame. Izayak?*" replied Salah.

"I'm well Salah. Good to see you."

"I am on my way to meet Jake by the pool. I am late. Shall we go together please?"

"Sure, but first I must ask you something privately."

"Normally I would object because I'm late, but I always have time for a beautiful woman."

"You flatter me Salah. Be aware my needs are purely professional."

"Not a surprise to a man so advanced in years. Although disappointed, I'm at your disposal nonetheless. May I assume this does not involve our mutual friend Jake?"

"It does involve him, and we'll talk about it with him shortly. But I want to tell you something first. Let's have a seat for a few minutes, shall we?"

Libby quickly summarized their recent four-day horse trip in the southern Sinai. She skipped over the leisure aspects and focused on the mineral drill cores.

"Sometime in the past, a company used a small drilling rig to cut borehole cores looking for mineral deposits. They were probably looking for gold, silver, copper, zinc, that sort of thing. You don't know me well Salah, but like Jake I'm a geologist. Unlike Jake I've spent much of my career searching for those metals, and can recognize the rocks they like to hide in. I think some of the cores showed prospectivity for an economic deposit of either copper or gold."

"Jake told me you own mines in America. Do you think you might find something similar in our desert?"

"Well Jake and I would like to find out. I'm a little more excited than him at this point. That's why I wanted to ask you something privately."

"What is that?"

"Do you know how to file a mining claim out there?"

"I do not. I understand the oil business in Egypt very well, but have no experience in mining. Of course I have friends who can help."

"Great. Jake thinks it's premature to work on this yet, but I disagree. If you could get me information on starting a mineral claim it would be helpful. I need to understand what the process would look like just in case we decide to pursue it. Here's my business card with the address and phone number. Please contact me directly with this. While you're at this task you might focus some of your time on making necessary contacts."

"Your wish is my command, madame. I always welcome a new adventure."

They shook hands and walked down a long hall to the courtyard, Salah already considering who he would approach to learn about the mining business. When they met Jake, he felt the need to explain his tardiness.

"Good morning my friend. Excuse my lateness. There was unbelievable traffic on the road from downtown."

"At this hour?" asked Jake.

"Yes. Cairo is getting worse every year, every day in fact. But today, there were protestors blocking the road at the Qasr al-Nil bridge. It's a relatively new group who've taken the name NOFORTH, which means 'No Foreign Thieves'. It's interesting they chose a Western name, the Western alphabet, and that acronym. Clearly they're targeting foreign audiences for their message."

"And what is their message?" asked Jake.

"It's quite simple really," answered Salah. "They wish to keep the foreign devils out of our country. People like you. People who want to develop Egypt's resources and steal the profits from the Egyptian people. They've been schooled in how the British and others profited at Egypt's expense. They think we can develop our own resources."

"Maybe that's not a bad thing Salah."

"But it's not realistic Jake. We can't do it ourselves. We need foreign technology. Foreign expertise. Foreign money. If we don't get all that we will not develop at all."

"Clearly you're at odds with NOFORTH, my friend. How much of a threat do you think they are to our plans?"

"Who knows," said Salah. "Groups like this come and go. As long as they don't get violent, they are manageable. We will see."

"Salah, there's something I need you to do. Our friend Mohammed took us to a pile of drill cores in the desert near Saint Catherine's. Libby and I separated some, and Mohammed is keeping them safe for us; maybe two or three hundred pounds worth. Can you retrieve these from him and ship them to me in the US?"

"Of course I can," answered Salah. "It will be a bit tricky. Normally the government frowns on people shipping Egyptian property out of the country, and our rocks qualify as our property. But there are ways around that problem. It'll take some paperwork and probably some money under the table, but this can be done."

"If it's OK with you Jake, Salah can send the cores directly to my office. We've got people who know where to get them assayed. My people are also better equipped to describe the geology of the cores properly"

"Sure, that's fine," replied Jake.

Gussie came over to the table, dripping wet from the pool. She gave Salah el Gindi a hug, took a drink, and jumped back into the water.

"Ah to be so carefree," said Salah.

"Yes, to be a kid. I can watch her forever," said Jake.

"What a great daddy," said Libby, drinking her own *ahwa mas boot*.

"Since the mess a few years back, I've told myself it's all about Gussie," said Jake. "Whatever she needs she gets. My time, my love, my resources. "

Libby loved his dedication to his daughter. That was one reason she was going slow with him on the mining idea, and had asked Salah to investigate the filing process herself. She suspected Jake would beg off at this point, saying he had no time, and saying he needed to spend all his free time with Gussie. Libby needed more concrete data to tempt him before getting him on board.

#

Their flight to the US the next day did not leave until late evening, so Jake arranged a horse excursion for the morning. He planned this weeks ago, a mirror trip of one he took years ago with Paula and Gussie, a four-hour jaunt between the Giza pyramids south to three lesser pyramids at Saqqara. Most of the ride was through desert, where they rode up and down dunes, watching others riding horses or camels.

Although heat radiated from the desert floor, Jake was bathed by a breeze from his horse's forward momentum. Sand puffed up around them like plumes of desert smoke. Halfway through the ride, they stopped for tea and mezza. Their guide, Youssef, jumped off his horse first and laid down a large blanket woven in colors that looked unnatural against the sand. They sat down, feeling a bit unbalanced, a land-based version of sea legs. The guide, dressed in an off-white galabeya, unpacked the food and drinks and took out a *ney*, or Egyptian flute. While his guests drank tea and ate baladi bread with hummus, baba ghanoush, tabbouleh, and olives, he played traditional *Sufi dhikr* rituals, which are basically sung prayers, close in rhythm to ancient Egyptian music.

Jake lay on his side, his head propped up by his right arm. He had drifted away, transported to the past by the music, the food, and the setting. Transported to times when he and Paula kept rented horses at a stable near Giza. They tried to ride every week but sometimes missed days. Jake felt warm and cozy, comfortable in his daydream. Comfortable enough that Libby had to repeat what she said, aware that he was not hearing her.

"Wow," said Libby. "This is quite unreal." She cocked her long neck and looked up at the pinnacle of a pyramid.

"What do you mean Libby?" asked Gussie.

"I mean here we are, sitting on the sand looking at pyramids, listening to a galabeya-clad man playing music. Eating wonderfully exotic food and drinking incredibly sweet tea. It's a once in a lifetime thing. A thing I've never even thought about."

"But we used to do this all the time," Gussie said, shrugging in a dismissive way. "What's the big deal?"

Libby looked at her and laughed. She felt like she was finally getting to know this complicated ten-year-old. Unusually mature, yet still a child.

"I guess 'normal' is a state of mind Gussie. This may be normal to you, but not to me."

Jake took in the conversation, knowing that most Americans could not identify with many of the experiences Gussie looked at as mundane. He knew from experience that most of his friends and relatives back home had a short attention span to even listen to stories about life overseas. He was happy he could introduce Libby to a bit of the world he loved, and of which Gussie was a product.

"Let's get going," he said, finally rising and helping to pack up the meal. "We have another hour of riding before we reach Saqqara. There are pyramids and tombs there, including the famous Step Pyramid of Djoser. It's the oldest intact stone building in the whole world, supposedly built in the 27th Century BC. That's hard to imagine and I can't wait till you see it."

When they approached Saqqara, Jake watched Libby's long mane of chestnut hair blowing around her shoulders. He tried to see her eyes as they focused on the horizon. As they got closer and the Step Pyramid rose from the sandy floor, Libby became visibly excited. She rode faster until she was right below it, her eyes pointed upward.

"Incredible," she said.

"Very old," said Youssef. "Want to climb?"

"Thank you Youssef but I don't think so. We'll just look."

Libby grinned at their guide. It was illegal of course to climb the monuments, all designated a World Heritage site. But it was clearly something Youssef looked at as a possibility. The Step Pyramid was actually more dangerous than the Giza pyramids to climb, but some people still did it. They spent a couple hours exploring the area before Jake finally corralled his dusty crew into a waiting van, which took them back to the hotel, where they showered, changed, and grabbed a quick bite before heading to the airport.

"Thank you Jake," Libby said resting her head on his shoulder in the van. "It was another day I'll never forget." She closed her eyes and felt the warmth of Jake's body.

"You're welcome," he replied, taking in the subtle scent of still slightly damp hair.

"Next time we come, I want to ride a camel out behind the pyramids. Can we do that?"

"Anything you want," he whispered in her ear.

Jake smiled and gently kissed Libby's head. It was a long flight home to Denver, and he was afraid that sleep would likely elude him once again.

CHAPTER 3

AL-GAMA'A AL ISLAMIYYA, Egypt's largest militant group, started in the 1970's and became ever more violent in the nineties. They targeted Egyptian police, civilians, and foreign tourists alike. A Sunni Islamist movement, their goal was to topple the current government and replace it with Islamic rule. Some credit its popularity to Sayyid Qutb, an Egyptian educator, poet, revolutionary, and leader of the Egyptian Muslim Brotherhood in the fifties and sixties. Qutb was convicted of planning President Nassar's assassination and was hung in 1966. Like similar groups, al-Gama'a al Islamiyah first flourished in universities. In recent years however, some students found the increasing violence unappealing. They thought that toppling the government was not necessary, and that keeping foreigners out of Egypt should be the main objective. Thus the birth and development over the past few years of NOFORTH.

Omar Foda was the de facto head of the group, which had not yet evolved to have formal officers and a tight structure. It remained composed of dedicated members who operated in a confused and nebulous atmosphere, pursuing their goals through generally uncoordinated movements mostly in the same direction, like salmon swimming upstream towards an unknown yet undeniable target. Omar and a dozen organizers were in Alexandria discussing plans for the coming year.

"We all agreed to our principles, one of which is that we will not kill," said Omar. His face could not disguise frustration. Crazy eyes dominated his face, reflecting a fanatical attitude. He was not attractive.

"That's true," said Abdel from the Faiyum, "but sometimes it cannot be avoided. We tried to throw wrenches down the drill hole without getting caught, but a man came up behind us with a piece of pipe. If I did not shoot him, he would have crushed Ayman's head and then one of ours would be dead instead of one of them."

"I still don't like it. We have to be more careful. This can't happen again."

The Faiyum, southwest of Cairo, was a hotspot for revolutionaries and home to the Muslim Brotherhood. Abdel was a man of the desert, rough and accustomed to fending for himself. He grew up with violence and did not think twice when he shot the derrick worker. The man's innocence did not factor in Abdel's mind. He only wanted to accomplish his task of throwing junk down the oil rig's drill hole to thwart its progress. The worker merely got in the way. To Abdel, the ends justified the means. The rig had been drilling in the Abu Gharadig oil field a hundred miles southwest of where they were meeting. The Western Desert producing area was one of NOFORTH's targets, even though the area, discovered in 1966, had been developed years ago by foreign companies that still ran the production operations.

"Let's talk about new targets for next year," said Omar, clearly exasperated by Abdel and his simplistic view of the situation.

The group discussed various options spanning the breadth of the country, but focused on petroleum, mining, and banking. Telecommunications were not targeted out of a selfish need to keep those avenues working for the group. Similarly, import and retail were not highlighted as members of the group enjoyed increasing access to foreign consumer goods.

Near the end of the meeting, the group listed oil and gas as their primary target, with mining second. Both could be attacked in isolated areas at random times. Banks tended to be centralized in populated areas, too well guarded, and too diffused. An attack on a large oil field or facility would garner more publicity with less empathy from the general population.

"There are new gas discoveries in the Mediterranean, off the shore from Damietta," said Omar. "We should try to damage the boats they use in the port. Maybe sink some of them or at least disable them."

"I like that," said Abdel. "I have a cousin who can help. He has a boat we can use."

"We saw what oil platforms did to the Gulf of Suez," continued Omar, who was pacing and getting ever more disturbed. "I grew up near the beach in Alexandria and don't want platforms and oil leaks to ruin it. The foreign companies have made three or four discoveries so far and yet they keep drilling. I saw on television the big gas flame last month on one of those offshore rigs. A lot of gas was coming out and it burned for days with a big black smoke. You could see the glow at night from Damietta. We must do what we can to stop them."

The other men nodded in agreement, some of them thrusting their fists to the sky.

"I heard there is also new oil drilling in Sinai," said Omar. "I have a relative in Nekhel who has seen big equipment moving in the desert there."

The group had never operated in the Sinai before but agreed to explore new options there. At the same time they would continue their more general protests across Cairo which had attracted good press coverage over the past year.

"And remember," reiterated Omar, "we don't want to hurt anyone. We want to make very visible statements that will be picked up by world news outfits. But we don't want our targets to excite sympathies from our own people or from other countries. We are on the side of our people who want jobs, profits, and development to stay in Egypt."

CHAPTER 4

ALMOST a foot of snow fell overnight in the Mile High City, with eighteen inches in Genesee, in the foothills twenty miles west of downtown Denver. This is where Libby had a house that was much too big for one person. She built the house when her second oilfield in North Dakota started producing. Her accountant convinced her it was a good thing to do with some of her newfound money. It was a timber frame, made of large solid beams of white pine with mortice and tenon connections secured with wood pegs. She loved lying on the couch in the evenings staring up at the wood, reflecting on how all the perfectly cut timbers clasped each other in a way that could be defined as art. The beams were cut and put together in Pennsylvania before being disassembled and shipped to Colorado. When they erected it on-site, she thought of the Lincoln Log creations she made as a child. The off-white walls between the timbers lent themselves to her collection of Native American art, Navajo blankets, saddles, and geological specimens. She bought a number of western rugs, pots, and baskets over the past decade, but her real treasures were two items from her dad, who started collecting Native American pieces in Michigan decades ago. A large glass case harbored an Ojibwe 19th century beaded bandolier, a very colorful item with green, red, and blue leaves and flowers. Below that was a pair of Odawa moccasins, made of hide with wool cloth, and finished with white glass beads and diamond-shaped pieces of blue and black silk.

Libby built the house in Genesee because of the neighborhood's secluded nature. There were tall Blue Spruce and Engelmann Spruce, Bristlecone Pine and Boxelder, Cottonwoods and Aspens. Deer regularly congregated in her yard, along with the occasional porcupine and coyote. Next to the pond down the hill was a bald eagle nest, housing the neighborhood's most famous couple.

Today, snow had forced Libby to drive her SUV instead of the Porsche. Traffic was slow coming down the mountain as she passed several cars and trucks that had slid off both sides of the interstate. She felt her snow tires grip the road but occasionally slip over icy spots. She crept eastward along Sixth Avenue and finally reached Downtown, where the roads were worse. Straining to see the black ice patches, she gripped the steering wheel firmly to guide the car to her office on Arapahoe Street and Eighteenth. By the time she entered the office, her hands were cramped and she was ready for another coffee. Libby wondered why she had not spent last night in her condo a few blocks away and made a mental note to pay more attention to weather forecasts.

"Good morning Ms. Joyce," said the guard in the lobby. "Welcome back."

"Mornin' Floyd, nice to be here. Crazy roads this morning, huh?"

"Not crazy roads ma'am. Crazy drivers."

She walked cautiously across the tiles of the lobby, slick with wet spots, concentrating to remain upright on the four-inch heels she changed into at the car. She rode the elevator to the eighteenth floor, at the top of an older, historic brick building Libby purchased a decade ago. Pimple Creek Enterprise accommodated her business holdings, which included mines in Nevada, Wyoming, and California, numerous oil and gas interests, several buildings in Denver, and other sundry investments. She chose the name early in her career after the stream in Taylor County, Florida where her favorite aunt had a cabin and where Libby used to spend summers. The name was hard to forget and Libby kept it as she continued to acquire business interests through the years. She knew many people found the name distasteful while others found it funny or asked about the unusual logo that reflected the company. No one, however, forgot it. Libby's niece had drawn the basic version of the pimple logo when she was around nine years old. It reminded Libby of her roots.

"Did you have a good trip?" her secretary asked as she walked into her office.

The corner office had expansive windows offering panoramic mountain views. Libby looked at this indulgence as a token of her success. Besides, she loved looking over west Denver at the Rocky Mountains beyond. Libby had not been to the office since Egypt, stopping to see her father in Michigan before touring some of her properties out west. Over the past few years, as she hired more competent people, she felt comfortable letting them operate more autonomously for longer periods of time.

"Yeah, I did Flo. Not my favorite time of year in Wyoming, but our mine there is doing well. It was good to visit."

She conversed with her assistant while quickly going through the mail and extraneous pieces of correspondence stacked on her chrome and glass desk. The office was refined but functional, with Persian carpets mixed with the clean lines of contemporary leather furniture.

"How's your dad doing?" asked Flo.

"You know, as well as can be expected after cancer treatments. His attitude is great. And he's got a circle of friends that's been good for him since mom died last year. Just wish I was closer. It was nice spending time with him. We had snow but not too much that we couldn't do some hunting. Dad loves the pheasants, and we did OK. He wanted to do some ice fishing but I drew the line there. Sitting in a hut on the ice with a fire going never appealed to me. It was near zero for God's sakes."

"We all wish we could be closer to family. Can I get you a coffee?"

"That'd be great, thanks. I'm still frazzled after the drive in. And Flo, please ask Janet to come by in a half hour."

"Yes ma'am. You have lunch at noon with Mr. Goodard from Cross Creek Oil. It's at the Brown, so you'll have to trudge through some snow."

"OK," Libby replied, already dreading the walk in the high-heeled boots she would need to change into.

#

Janet Robinson walked into Libby's office a half hour later. The Chief Geologist had worked for Pimple Creek more than fifteen years and was largely responsible for the acquisition of the Wyoming mine. She spent most of her time now keeping track of all the operational parts within the company. Libby often thought of appointing her Chief Operating Officer, but Janet kept saying 'I'm a geologist, dammit, and don't dare call me anything else.' So Janet kept the Chief Geologist title, got the COO salary, and did not put up with shit from anyone inside or outside the company.

Libby first met Janet at a club in Denver, back when she was starting her career and Janet worked for an independent oil producer in the Denver Basin. Libby heard her present a technical talk at the Rocky Mountain Association of Geologists and was impressed, first because the material presented was so unique and her delivery so smooth, and second because Robinson was black. Libby had never met a female black geologist before and wondered how she got into the field. Libby asked around and got good reviews from people she trusted. Janet had a reputation in Denver as a top-notch geologist with a highly creative approach and a good work ethic. When things began to fall into place for Pimple Creek, Janet signed on and neither Libby nor Janet ever looked back.

"Morning Libby," she said, plopping down on the couch.

Libby got up from her desk and moved to a nearby chair.

"Those Egypt samples here yet?"

Robinson had seen her excited about opportunities in the past, but sensed this one was different. Libby seemed more obsessed, passionate, and impatient than normal, if that was possible. A casual colleague might think her interest reflected a second chance to expand overseas, after she passed on Jake's offer to participate in the Sinai gas venture. Janet thought differently, having met Jake Tillard and seen Libby's demeanor change when he was around. Libby seldom discussed her personal life, but Janet put the pieces together. Visits to Montana, trips to Egypt, more time than ever out of the office. She knew Libby was becoming close to the Tillard family, and thought it a matter of time until she and Jake formalized a relationship. Libby would be a challenging catch for any man, and maybe an even more challenging partner, but Janet thought she met her match in Tillard.

"They arrived at the warehouse yesterday. Tommy says everything's there, in good shape, and there's no problems left with customs. The paperwork was all screwed up but we were able to fix it."

"Janet, I want you to personally handle them. Get them slabbed, photographed, thin-sectioned, and sent for assay. I want your view of what geologic environments they represent, a paragenesis of which rocks and minerals formed when, age dates, mineral suites, the whole nine yards. And how's that Sinai report coming?"

"No problem on the cores, I'll get all that done. As for the report, it should be ready end of the month. On the phone you said you wanted a fairly quick job so it'll be based on available literature. No original work. No real digging. But I think you'll like it. The Sinai's been mined for thousands of years. All pretty small scale. But the geology is really cool. Complicated and varied. No reason to think you can't find something worth goin' after. If we get the assays fast enough I can work them into a preliminary picture of your specific area."

"Great. I'm anxious but not desperate. If you need more time that's fine. My goal is to decide whether or not to do any more work out there. So if it's a big negative that'll be final. If you get somethin' we'll figure out what to do next."

"You got it. How was Wyoming and California?"

"The South Pass operation is going really well. It'll always be small, but this quarter should see above expected gold come out. Randy's doing a good job, safety's been ramped up, and morale's high. I didn't think they could surpass our production goal but it's happening. We need to figure a year-end bonus to reward that group."

Libby sighed and continued, "The rare earths venture is behind physically and fiscally. We knew going into that thing that we'd face two issues. As bad luck would have it, both are playing out at the same time. The Chinese continue to dump product, depressing prices. Washington is no help with that, and the international market is getting worse. Prices will continue to fall. And California started that supplemental tax on extractive businesses last quarter. Fact is they just don't want anyone there tearing things apart. They don't want drilling. They don't want clear cutting. They don't want mining. They want the products as long as they're not from their own backyard."

Libby stood and moved to the window. She stared at the mountains.

"You can build a concrete highway a hundred yards across and hundreds of miles long that cuts off wildlife migration in a big way, and no one squawks. Everyone needs those for their cars and their commutes. But try to clear out six hundred acres to produce tantalum or some mineral that everyone needs in their cell phones and they're all over you. There's always some bug or critter that will perish if you dig up a square mile of nothing. Where do they think all the metal comes from that goes into their cars, phones, and the rest? It's just plain weird Janet. That being as it is, the demand for non-Chinese rare earths is strong. We need to figure out how to increase production now. If we can lock in some higher volume, longer term contracts at this price we'll be OK. Get Fred working on options for boosting production. I want that to be the main topic in our monthly meeting next week."

Janet nodded as she took in everything Libby said, making a few notes on her tablet. Finally she responded to her boss.

"OK. Everything is good on the oil and gas front. Got that drill pipe unstuck up in South Dakota, and the Williston fracking is going well. Hard working bunch in both places. I hope you're working on year-end bonuses for everyone."

"You talking about you?" said Libby smiling. "I've never heard you complain before. Now get back to work."

"Yes ma'am."

CHAPTER 5

"**MA** *hdha?*" what's that, asked the younger Bedouin in a colloquial dialogue specific to the Gebeliya tribe. While most of the ten tribes in the southern Sinai are considered ancestrally Arab and likely originated from Saudi Arabia, the Gebeliya show a strong non-Arab influence. Most likely they derived from eastern European stonemasons brought to the area by Roman Emperor Justinian in the sixth century to build a basilica and fortress near Mt. Sinai, known as Gebel Musa in Arabic. This is where many scholars believe that Moses received the Ten Commandments. The tribal name Gebeliya literally means 'people of the mountains'. Throughout their history, they were less nomadic than other tribes, staying more or less around the St. Catherine monastery.

Looking at the core pile, his elder answered in the same dialect, "It's been here half my lifetime. Since the Jews were here. I saw them making these things with big machines, and much noise and smoke. They put a hole in the ground and pulled up these rocks. This is where they had their camp, but the rocks came from three areas out there." He pointed to the east and north.

"What are they?" a third man, perhaps the youngest, asked again.

"They are rocks," the older man answered. "Who knows why they took them out of the ground. Who knows why they left them here? Crazy people. There are rocks everywhere. No one needs to dig into the ground to find more."

They sat next to the core pile and started a fire to brew tea. While drinking, the youngest man pointed towards the horizon where a cloud of dust indicated a moving vehicle. Soon, they could distinguish two Niva's, old Russian Jeep-like vehicles, heading straight at them across featureless desert. Thinking it odd that the cars were coming directly towards them, the elder Bedouin picked up his rifle.

"Put the girls together and sit with them over there," he said, pointing to the other side of the core pile. "Keep the hashish with you and do not let them see it."

The half dozen Bedouin were making a smuggling run from southwest Sinai to Israel. Bedouin have been transporting hashish for decades, maybe centuries, although that stopped for about fifteen years when Israel occupied the peninsula, beginning in 1967. In the mid-eighties, smuggling started again, but this time they moved people in addition to drugs. The four people they were smuggling on this trip were all young Romanian girls hoping for a new life in Israel.

When the cars got close, they stopped; two men got out of each and walked towards the local men. It is customary in the Sinai to offer visitors tea, but the Bedouin did not do that. They stood up and looked at the visitors.

"*Salam al aleikum,*" said one of the visitors, with a heavy Russian accent.

"*Aleikum al salaam,*" they replied.

The visitors spoke only a few words of Arabic, a little more English, and even better French, which the eldest Bedouin could understand. Although the conversation moved along in various languages, French was the most productive.

As the Bedouin put down his rifle, tea was offered to the four Russians, and the group sat around the cores looking at each other. Finally one of the Russians broke the silence.

"We take rocks," the Russian said in broken French, pointing to the cores.

"*Pourquoi,*" replied the Bedouin.

"Business," came the reply in English. Then in French again, "*Vous aidez? Chargez? Prenez a Sharm el Sheikh*"? He pulled out some currency and offered it to the men.

The old man looked at the money and shook his head 'no' while waving his hand. The Russian pulled out more bills. It was now a significant amount, in US dollars. The Bedouin intuitively understood that loading the rocks into the vehicle was not why the Russians needed their help. Guiding the cars and rocks to the port was the real job. It would have been suspicious for the men to drive on main roads to Sharm el Sheikh with these rocks. The Bedouin did not know what the rocks were for, but knew they were Egyptian rocks. There were two permanent checkpoints between here and Sharm el Sheikh, and another temporary one that moved around. One of the stations was manned by Egyptian soldiers, the other by MFO, a multinational peacekeeping force established in 1981 following the Camp David accords and the Egyptian-Israeli peace treaty. Soldiers at both checkpoints would want to see official papers for the rocks before they let them through. Soldiers at the MFO roadblock would be inquisitive but professional. They were not the real problem. Soldiers at the Egyptian checkpoint would be jumpy if they suspected trouble. Their training was sub-par, but their guns shot real bullets. Anything could happen, most of it not good.

The Bedouin were on no real schedule and could take on this 'side job' if they wanted. The men quickly reached an agreement and started loading core pieces into the two Russian jeeps, which seemed too small and lightweight for the task. When about half the pile was moved, one of the Russians decided it was unsafe to load any more.

"*Ckopee! Y'alla!*" he said to the group, "Hurry, let's get going."

He waved at the Bedouin, two of whom got in the cars to guide them through the desert and around the checkpoints. Four other Bedouin and two of the Russians stayed behind, guarding the remaining cores as well as the Romanian girls and the hashish. While they were sitting with the cores, one of the Russians tried to 'rent' one of the Romanian girls. The Bedouin were not a stupid bunch. They knew what the girls might end up doing in Tel Aviv. But they were a proud people who respected women, and they did not agree to the offer. Things got a bit tense, but soon the Russians gave up the idea and took naps.

The Nivas returned, but before the Bedouin would help load the second batch, the Russians needed to cough up another wad of US dollars. By the end of the next day, all the cores were in the port of Sharm el Sheikh, loaded onto a Yemeni fishing vessel. After the boat sailed from Sharm, the Russians spent the next few days on the beach of the Movenpick, drinking Stella beer and eating fried calamari and grouper.

A Plan Emerges

1994

CHAPTER 6

JAKE was excited, but seemed calm compared to Gussie. It had been four months since they were with Libby in Egypt, and more than a year since Libby had been to the ranch. Even Jake's dad was eager for her arrival. Marv was lonely. His wife died years before and Marv's ranch manager and best friend Lester was shot and killed three years ago while protecting Gussie and Libby in the ranch house. That was when Middle Eastern terrorists kidnapped the two women along with Gussie's nanny Layla. Fortunately, that experience had a good ending for the women, but not for the kidnappers. The authorities conducted post-action reviews of the whole operation and found some issues in how the rescue was handled by Joe Faraday, a Montana State Trooper with a history of getting the bad guy mostly dead. In the end, no charges were filed, but neither was there a kidnapper captured alive who could shed any light on the rescue.

The Bar-J Ranch sat fifty miles south of Missoula, near the town of Hamilton. To the west it abutted National Forest leading up into the Bitterroot Mountains. The nearest neighbors were miles away, separated by groves of aspen, spruce forest, and grazing fields. Two perennial streams which had never been dammed meandered through the ranch on their way to the Bitterroot River, providing perfect habitat for rainbow, brown, and cutthroat trout. Jake grew up here hunting, fishing, and riding horses when not helping with ranch duties. As a kid growing up, he never really appreciated his good fortune in being able to call this home. His father Marv was a stereotypical western rancher. Independent, skeptical of the government, willing to fend for himself and take what nature and God threw at him.

Jake acquired his parents' love of the outdoors and their preference for privacy and individualism. Growing up surrounded by billion-year-old granite of the Bitterroots guided him towards a career in geology. He still loved poking around old mine diggings, looking for crystals, and still wore a ring inset with a sapphire he had found while panning a stream with his mom in the mountains to the east. Jake was not as private as his dad but did enjoy his alone time.

"I hear the car," shouted Gussie, bolting up from the dining room table and running to the front door. Jake and Marv followed, leaving their half-eaten lunch on the table.

One of the Bar-J's pickups crept up the driveway, crunching snow as it came. It had been a snowy winter with over ten feet falling so far. Although the intense sun melted it quickly after it fell, and compaction took a toll, the white stuff was still three feet deep in most places, more where it had drifted. Daytime temperatures hovered just under freezing, and the sun was a bright, sparkling, yellow disk in a big blue sky.

"She's here," yelled Gussie, running down the steps to meet the truck, without a jacket, hat, or gloves.

"Gussie, you're looking more like a teenager every time I see you," greeted Libby as she climbed out of the pickup and hugged the young girl. Gussie was clearly pleased and just beamed as they embraced and spun around a couple times. Libby finally threw her arms around Jake and kissed him.

"Hello stranger," she said before turning to Marv and hugging him. "How are you Marv?"

"Better now that you're here Libby. This ranch needs a woman."

Marv grinned, pleased to see her. Libby looked at Marv and thought he had aged over the last year. He always had that weathered rancher look, but his face was more wrinkled, and his hair grayer. It was long enough for a ponytail, although he did not bother tying it up, but rather kept it beneath a cowboy hat from which it poked out all around his head. Maybe most telling, it seemed he had put on weight. She hoped this was just a sign of contentment and not depression.

Marv liked Libby the first time they met, three summers ago. The tall, slim, attractive woman had gone to graduate school with his son, but Marv had not met her until she visited the Bar-J years later. Jake and Libby were friendly in school, but had not fallen for each other until that first visit to the ranch, after Paula had died. Libby subsequently traveled to Egypt with Jake as he worked on his gas venture, and took a quick trip to New York City with him on business. Jake had asked Libby to join the Sinai venture as a partner, but Libby declined, saying she was all full up with her own business endeavors and had little interest in international risk. Marv learned later that Libby had built a small conglomerate of mining, oil, and commercial properties and was worth a lot of money. Looks, brains, money, and a nice personality. Marv wondered how his son had been lucky enough to find another amazing woman. After Paula passed, he thought Jake would never find love again, but maybe it was possible. Maybe Libby could be the one. Marv loved it when she visited the ranch and wished it were more often.

"Let's get you inside and settled young lady," said Marv, reaching for one of her bags. "I assume you'll stay in Jake's room."

Libby winked at him, and threw her arms around Jake again, hugging him as they strolled towards the house. "I'm so glad to be here. Can we ride, or is the snow too deep?"

"We can as long as we stay in the valley," replied Jake. "There's too much snow high up. We were in the middle of lunch, so let's get you a plate and finish eating first. I'll get Ralph to saddle horses."

"Pack a bottle of wine. I've got news," she teased.

#

There was a natural stone bench along the stream, just upstream from the ranch house, that the hands kept relatively free of snow. Jake brushed off a few inches of fresh powder with his gloved hand and laid down a blanket. They sat and watched the water slip by, swirling around ice formations clinging to rocks and boulders in the stream. Jake pointed out a rainbow trout lounging in a pool just below. He opened the Chardonnay and poured while Libby held two glasses.

"I had visions of riding up to the hot springs where we first made love," said Libby. "I wanted to make this special."

"It's always special with you," Jake said, kissing her.

"What a romantic. Salut." They clinked glasses.

"You know my brother and I used to camp here when we were little. We imagined ourselves cowboys, looking out for Indians, protecting the ranch. We'd spend a couple days here, pull some fish out of the creek, maybe shoot a rabbit, cook 'em over a wood fire. We didn't think about it at the time, but mom could watch us from the ranch house and keep tabs on us. We thought we were in the wilderness."

Jake felt a rush of emotions thinking of his mother and his youth. They were close and though she died years ago, he still missed her greatly.

"You were in the wilderness though, weren't you? A bear could've come and pounced on you at any time."

"I suppose. We never worried about that. We were invincible."

"What about your chores?"

"That's why we never stayed more than a couple days. Mom made sure we got back to do our work." Jake laughed. "When we got back we always noticed mom had piled up a few more things for us to do. Kinda' like payment for the time away. But we didn't mind."

She sat next to him in silence, taking in the magnificent scenery. Trying to imagine a young Jake, with the younger brother she never met, confronting the wilderness, living the ranch lifestyle, growing up, evolving towards an empathetic man. Jake sat reflective as well until he finally broke the silence.

"So what's up Libby? I know you're dying to tell me something."

"I am. It's been tough to not blurt it out." She had that broad smile again, her eyes lasering in on Jake's as she cocked her head. "You remember those drill cores? We got the assay results back."

"Really," replied Jake. "I mostly forgot about them. What do you know?"

"I didn't think they would lead to anything Jake. I knew you were busy. I knew you wanted to spend more time with Gussie. So we received them, did the whole description exercise, and sent bits off for assay."

"And what did you find out.?"

"OK. There's two things really. First, my geologist Janet Robinson finished a geological report on the southern Sinai, and fit the core descriptions into that report. And second, there's the results from the core assays. What do you want first?"

"You choose."

"OK, I'll start with the report. Keep in mind it's based only on published data, much of which is old and done by various expeditions of French, British, and others. As you might imagine, Egypt's been a popular place to do field work for a long time. Turns out that the Sinai's a fascinating place geologically. Very diverse, with Precambrian rocks older than a billion years in the south, and younger rocks further north. Everything from metamorphics to volcanics, limestones, and sandstones. Plate tectonics stuck a three-thousand-foot-deep crack to the east filled by the Gulf of Aqaba, and another crack to the west where the Gulf of Suez heads south to the Red Sea. These rifts are really young but significant. Coral reefs ring much of the Sinai coast, and the elevation onshore gets up over eight thousand feet at Mount Catherine."

"Libby, I lived in Egypt for six years and worked the Sinai for half that. I discovered a big gas field there. I've got over a hundred dives in the water. I know a lot about the area. Give me the bottom line here please."

"OK. Sorry. Janet focused on mineral exploration. I'll give you the report, but bottom line is the cores cut Precambrian shield which might hold a greenstone belt. Remember from school days that those are packages of volcanic and sedimentary rocks, sea floor basically, that were tectonically heated and squeezed into metamorphic rocks. The degree of metamorphism created a lot of the green mineral chlorite, thus the green color and the name of the rock package. One of the most well-known greenstone belts is the Barberton, where gold was first discovered in South Africa. A less famous one is the South Pass belt in Wyoming, with rocks around 2.8 billion years old, site of the first gold discovery in that state in 1842. Not far from that discovery is where I have my Bessie T gold mine. So Janet and I know something about greenstone belts."

"Cool. I'm going to guess that nobody is producing anything from greenstone belts in the Sinai?"

"Not yet," Libby smiled even wider. "In fact Janet couldn't find any mention in the literature of greenstone belts there. She doesn't think anyone knows they exist there."

"But you think we've found one?"

"Maybe. Now for the second part, the cores. Janet unraveled the puzzle and identified three major rock suites. First is a standard granitic type, with continental rocks that were metamorphosed over a billion years ago. Boring stuff but what most of the Sinai Massif is made of. Second is a mafic suite, another boring group of metamorphosed old oceanic crust. Third is a suite that resembles a greenstone belt, with several different rock types. Janet has worked the Bessie T for a long time and has visited other mining districts. She knows what to look for. It's subtle but she believes a greenstone belt is definitely there."

"OK, so what about the assays?"

Libby smiled even wider. Jake thought she was absolutely beaming.

"No mineralization in the first two rock suites, which you'd expect. In the third, we've got promising numbers for copper and gold."

Libby finished and just kept smiling. Jake looked at her and could not help smiling as well. She looked like a kid in a candy store. He expected there would be no stopping her, and anticipated what would come next. She would want him to go in on the prospect with her. He did not think he was ready, being very much committed to raising Gussie the best he could. That required all his time not spent on his gas field.

"You're excited, aren't you?" he said.

"You betcha. You know I love mining more than oil. It's just so sexy."

"I think you're sexy. You're crazy to be doing this. I thought you didn't want to get involved in business overseas? You know what happened when I was doing the gas thing. All sorts of bad players came out of the woods."

"Yeah, well. When you asked me to fund your project, that was oil. Or gas actually. Anyway it just didn't do it for me. This is different. They say diamonds are a girl's best friend. I love them of course but I'm rather partial to gold. And I can't imagine we'd be so unlucky to run into bad business competitors again. Kind of like lightning never striking the same place twice, right?"

Jake looked away, across the valley at the Sapphire Mountains. He was enjoying life now, at a more leisurely pace. He worked hard on the gas project and was gone from the ranch all too often, but got to spend more time than most dads with his daughter, and was really reconnecting with his dad. He looked back at Libby, who was still smiling and looking hopefully into his eyes.

"It's getting dark Libby. I know you're excited and all, but we need to ride back. I guess I know what we'll be talking about tomorrow."

They stood up, hugged, and got on their horses. On the ride back, Jake thought about a possible mining venture in the Sinai and imagined nothing but obstacles in the way. He did not want to spend more time on business. Before they reached the ranch house, they agreed to not discuss this with Marv, Gussie, or anyone else. They would explore the option tomorrow and figure out a forward plan. Jake was not really interested. Even if was, he thought, it was early days; nothing might come of the idea.

#

Breakfast at the ranch was always eggs, bacon, hash browns, toast, and beans. No one ever complained, though Libby was glad she was not a permanent resident.

"What about doing some ice skating after school today," said Jake.

"Yeah," said Gussie. "We can take Libby. She's never skated at the ranch."

"I've hardly skated at all Gussie. It's been ten years at least since I've been on skates. Maybe twenty. And it wasn't pretty then. Besides I don't have any skates."

"What's your size?" asked Marv.

"No you don't Marv. I didn't agree to make a fool of myself."

"We'll help you Libby," Gussie gushed. "Please. It's easy. Like riding a bike. Pretty please."

"Your size ma'am?" asked Marv again.

"Eight."

Libby did not look at all happy, but Marv grinned at her. "We've got a pile of skates in the closet. I'm sure we can come close to an eight."

They finished breakfast, then Jake walked Gussie down the drive to the main road to catch the school bus, as he did every day when he was there. When he had a business trip, Grandpa usually filled in, with several ranch hands competing to help out. They all loved her.

Marv and Jake did chores while Libby took a soak in the hot tub and lounged around for the rest of the morning. In mid-afternoon, Libby volunteered to wait at the bus stop for Gussie while Marv got the skates ready. While light was waning, they all walked down to the little pond next to the stream. The weather had been well below zero at night for over a week and never above freezing, so the ice was almost a foot thick. Marv had flooded it a few days ago to put on a smooth surface, and Gussie had her first skate the day before Libby arrived.

"You're gonna have to hang on to me," Libby said to Jake.

"I thought you'd say that. I'll hold your hands and skate backwards with you for a bit. But I brought hockey sticks for everyone. After you make a few circles you can lean on a stick for a while. Might be better for getting your balance back."

"That implies I had balance to begin with and it went somewhere," Libby said sarcastically.

It did not take long for Libby to become somewhat stable. She marveled at how proficient the other three were, even Marv. She never imagined the old rancher as an ice skater. Jake glided over to the bench and got a few hockey pucks, which the four of them began passing around. Most of the pucks coming towards Libby kept going past her, which elicited a whoop or laugh from Gussie every time.

#

Breakfast the next day was a repeat performance. It was another pretty day, slightly warmer, with the same intense sun they got at this elevation. While Libby cleared the plates to the kitchen and Gussie went off to play something, Marv turned to Jake.

"How 'bout we all ride up the hill to the overlook?" said Marv.

"Dad, I'm not sure that's altogether wise," answered Jake. "The snow's pretty deep and there are some tricky spots."

"You worried you can't make it, son?"

"I'm thinking more of Libby and Gussie dad."

"Those girls of yours are better riders than you've ever been."

Jake knew that was not true but let it go. He said he would ask Libby what she thought. Gussie of course would not hesitate. Libby expressed some concern about Gussie making the ride, but agreed with Marv that the girl was good on a horse. Marv pushed through any hesitancy, saying any granddaughter of his could outride the best of the men. In the end Marv won and the group saddled up.

An hour later, they were plowing their way across the lower meadow, the horses walking through three feet of snow. Libby maneuvered herself to take pictures of the other three and Marv asked for her camera to take a photo of Jake and Libby. Before long, they started ascending the couple hundred feet up to a wonderful overlook. They got to a large rock which was exposed to the wind and sun enough to be largely snow-free. They dismounted and Marv poured hot chocolate for everyone.

The view from the cliff was spectacular. Forty miles to the east rose the Sapphire Mountains, where Jake had panned the gemstone in his ring. Behind them to the west was the Bitterroot range, running north-south for over three hundred miles and reaching over eleven thousand feet in elevation. The real view however was the Bar-J Ranch. Nearly the entire spread could be seen from this spot. Black angus foraged in the northern pasture, standing out against the white snow. Also known as Aberdeen Angus, the breed originated in Scotland and did well in the western Montana climate. After a good period of time, Marv pointed out smoke coming from the chimney of the ranch house and suggested they head back for lunch.

Picking their way down the trail was tougher than coming up. The horses slowly found their way, following the tracks they made going up. Jake was behind Gussie when suddenly her horse went down, slipping on some unseen rock or patch of ice. Jake watched in seemingly slow-motion as both horse and girl careened to the right and rolled over, in the snow, sliding down the slope to a landing. Jake watched as Gussie was crushed beneath the big animal. She now lay next to the horse, which whinnied before shaking it off and standing up.

Jake and Libby jumped off their horses, agony on their faces, and slid down to where Gussie lay still. They reached her at the same moment, assessing the situation. She was unconscious but breathing, they saw no bleeding, but one leg was bent at an unnatural angle. Libby moved the horse away from her while Jake bent over his daughter, fighting back tears. They hesitated to move her, afraid of neck or back injuries. Blood had started to spread out in the snow around her leg, however, so they got a knife from the saddle bags and cut away Gussie's left pant leg. Libby looked at Jake and saw the tears on his cheeks, and pain in his face like she had never seen. A bone stuck out of her skin above the knee, and blood was oozing out.

"It's not her artery," said Jake.

"Doesn't look like it," Libby added. "Too slow a bleed. But might be worth a tourniquet. What do you think?"

By this time, Marv reached them as well, with his cell phone out. Fortunately, they had cell connection here, a relative oddity for the ranch overall. He was connected to the 911 operator, explaining what happened, where they were, and was now answering questions.

"She's breathing, yeah.... Unresponsive.....Compound fracture to an upper leg.....Yeah it's bleeding but not squirting out......No we won't move her...tell the pilot to land just west of us....Yeah, Bar-J Ranch five miles south of Hamilton, west of the river...... We're one mile southwest of the big house......I'll lay out a red horse blanket where he should land."

"They said to put a tourniquet on it," Marv said. "The paramedics can assess it when they get here."

They got the first aid kit from Marv's saddle bag and rigged up a tourniquet, then had nothing else to do except cover Gussie with blankets and jackets, and wait. Jake felt helpless and time slowed to a crawl, the helicopter not coming for what seemed an eternity. Libby tried to hug him, but he would not leave Gussie's side, his face just inches from hers, keeping track of her breathing. Ten minutes after ending the 911 call, they heard the *whoop-whoop* of an incoming helicopter, announcing the arrival of the paramedics. The high-pitched whine of the engine got louder as the chopper landed where Marv had laid down a red blanket, some forty yards away, and a woman came running to where Gussie lay. She gently pushed Jake out of the way and triaged Gussie. Using a walkie-talkie, she gave instructions to her colleague, who was still pulling things out of the helicopter.

A few minutes later her colleague and the pilot brought over a stretcher and other equipment. They put a neck brace on Gussie, checked the tourniquet, put a brace on her leg, and worked to stabilize her on the stretcher. Before long, she was bundled up and strapped in with only her face showing. Jake and Libby helped the two paramedics carry the stretcher to the helicopter. Not more than fifteen minutes after landing, it took off with Jake inside.

Libby could not reach Jake by phone as she and Marv drove to the hospital in Missoula. They talked the entire way, running through the possibilities and hoping for the best. Had her neck been broken and blood flow to the brain obstructed? Was she dead, or would a head injury render her disabled for the rest of her life? How bad was the break in her leg? Would she ever ice skate again? Marv pushed the truck way past the speed limit, slowing down only when they rolled into the city.

They were directed to a waiting room on the surgical floor, where Jake could not give them much information, other than Gussie was alive and in surgery. A nurse came in shortly after to tell them she was stable and the doctors were working on her. She said it would be at least another hour before they could tell much more.

"We never should have taken that ride," said Jake.

"No one could have foreseen this accident Jake," Libby patted Jake on the shoulder.

"It was too snowy," said Jake. "We should have realized that going up the hill."

Marv was silent, reflecting on the fact that he was the one to push them into the ride. He felt devastated and guilty. It was another ninety minutes before a doctor in green scrubs entered the waiting room.

"She's out of surgery," said Doctor Singh. "We've treated two major issues. She had a compound fracture of the femur, which we've fixed with a rod. I'll give you more detail later. That wound caused a good amount of blood loss before she got here, but we transfused her and don't think the blood loss caused any major problem. You may have saved her life with that tourniquet. The second issue is a head injury, which might have been fatal were it not for the riding helmet she was wearing. An MRI showed swelling in her brain, so we've put her into an induced coma to let her brain rest. We'll do another MRI tonight and again tomorrow to check the swelling. She's a very strong young girl, and very lucky. There appears to be no damage to her neck or any internal organs."

"Will she be fine?" asked Jake.

"With head injuries, it's notoriously difficult to predict long term effects. From the data we have, I'd rate her concussion as severe. When we bring her out of the coma, she might show no symptoms or could have some impairment. We have to wait to see."

"What kind of impairment?" Jake asked. "Could it be permanent?"

"I'd rather not speculate Mr. Tillard. There's really no way to predict."

Jake found this answer troublesome.

"When will you bring her out of it?"

"That depends on MRI pictures. Not for three days at least."

The doctor said it was likely she suffered no pain during the accident. He continued refusing to speculate on the head injury and whether or not there would be lasting damage, but said several months of physical therapy would be required for the femur. With proper rehab she should be able to regain full leg and hip motion.

"Can we see her?" asked Libby.

"She's in post-op now but should be in an ICU bed in a couple hours. You can see her then for a short visit, then I'd like you to go home. She needs to rest and I think it best she have a quiet room at least today. You can come back tomorrow although she'll still be out."

After the doctor left, the three sat in silence. Marv was finally able to get them to the cafeteria where they got coffee. Finally, a nurse came to bring them to Gussie. Their first look at her was shocking. Tubes and wires seemed to run everywhere. She was intubated, with the *whoosh whoosh* of the breathing machine interrupted by various other periodic beeps and sounds. Jake walked to her bed and took her hand, careful not to disturb the IV needle or the oxygen monitor.

He talked softly into her ear, hoping his words might reach her and provide comfort.

#

That evening was agony for them in the ranch house. Marv could not utter a word, Jake could not stop crying, and Libby felt powerless to give either of them any comfort. The hands at the ranch all loved the little girl and moped around, not knowing what to do. Dinner was put on the table, but little was eaten. Finally, Marv said a few words of loving praise about his granddaughter, said she was a strong girl and would be fine, and everyone found the way to their rooms. Their thoughts were centered on her regaining full consciousness and not suffering any lasting mental deficiencies. Libby fought to stay awake until she knew Jake was asleep, then allowed herself to drift off.

The next day was not much different, with the three of them in Gussie's room most of the day. They returned to the ranch in early evening, after being asked to leave the hospital when visiting hours ended. Jake walked in the house and straight out the back door, with Marv and Libby watching him.

"Where's he going?" asked Libby.

"I think I know," answered Marv. "Let him go."

Libby stared at the door and asked Marv to explain.

"He never got over his brother and mother dying, although time did help him return to normal. Losing Paula was almost worse, but I think you've helped that healing come along. Almost losing Gussie has hit him hard. You may not see it but Jake is a sensitive man."

Jake walked through the snow towards the creek, past some aspens and then a large Black Cottonwood tree. He opened a gate in the white picket fence that formed a perfect fifty-foot square, and walked to where Paula was buried, next to his mother, brother and other family members.

"I almost lost Gussie today sweetheart. I'm so sorry. She's in the hospital and I don't know if she'll be the same girl when she comes out. It seems I keep making bad decisions, Paula. Can you forgive me?"

He knelt down in the snow and lowered his head. Libby could see him from the bedroom window. She hoped whatever he was saying would help him move on.

#

All three were in the room again when the doctor brought Gussie out of the coma two days later. The last two MRI's showed the swelling reducing, and the medical staff was glad to have avoided a lobectomy. They still could not predict how her brain might have been affected.

"Gussie, can you hear me?" said Doctor Singh. "You have a tube in your throat, so nod or blink your eyes if you understand."

Gussie opened her eyes and blinked. They carefully removed the intubation tube and worked with her a bit before letting Jake talk to her.

"I love you Gussie. It's nice to have you back," he patted her on the head.

Gussie struggled to talk but Jake heard her whisper.

"Where've I been?" she asked.

Tears welled up in Jake's eyes as he laughed and hugged his daughter.

"Your horse fell a few days ago and you've been sleeping ever since. You're going to be fine."

Gussie looked up at her father, glanced over at her grandpa and Libby, and realized that this must be a big deal.

"So can I get my ears pierced please?" she asked, loud enough for everyone to hear.

Jake turned to see smiles on Marv and Libby. He had fought his daughter for the past year about ear piercing, which Libby thought was ridiculous. Seeing Gussie survive and having the wherewithal to ask this question made him tear up again.

"Of course you can peanut," he said to her.

Gussie glanced over again and saw Libby wink at her. She was released later that day, after it was clear she had no serious mental problems. Dinner at the ranch broke with tradition, substituting pureed chicken soup and ice cream for steak and potatoes.

CHAPTER 7

BORIS Oblonsky looked out his office window at the Moskva River, clogged with ice, just past the Kremlin complex. His building at 1 Arbat Street had a very prestigious address; his office was the best in the building. For one of Russia's top Oligarchs, nothing was out of reach. As a poor boy in the Ukraine, Boris learned to fend for himself and to trust no one. He never diverged from that *modus operandi* as he progressed towards billionaire status. Like his fellow Oligarchs in Moscow, Boris was suspicious of everyone, convinced he was a constant target for assassination, and always kept two bodyguards by his side. Even those he changed out regularly, except for Victor Popov, who was right now sitting outside Boris' office door.

Like most Russian Oligarchs, Boris liked to flaunt his wealth, owning several luxury properties around the world, a yacht, Lamborghinis, an extensive wardrobe, and a brothel in Moscow from which he could source women for personal pleasure whenever needed. Unlike most of his peers, Boris drank alcohol sparingly, watched what he ate, exercised regularly, and kept in shape. He was a handsome and attractive man. A few years back, he made Moscow's Most Eligible Bachelor list after he dumped his third wife Natalya. Dumped as in divorced, not dumped as in what was widely believed he did to wife number two, who suddenly disappeared from the Moscow social scene in which she actively participated. Her body was found months later in a lake north of the city, identified through dental records. Through the nineties, marrying a Russian Oligarch had progressively become a high risk, high reward endeavor.

A knock on the door was followed by the entrance of Roman Novikov, one of Oblonsky's most trusted managers. Originally from Azerbaijan, Novikov resembled the stereotypical Russian. Medium height, medium to slightly overweight build, round pudgy face, pale complexion, dark hair, surly demeanor. If a witness described Novikov to a sketch artist, the result would resemble half the males in Russia. Novikov did, however, stand out in intelligence. He held a PhD in Geological Engineering and oversaw the mining and oil segment of Oblonsky's empire. Indeed, his education, training, and ability to get results were the reasons Oblonsky brought him into the organization.

"The claim is done," Novikov said in Russian.

"No problem to keep it secret?" asked Oblonsky.

"No problem. The owning company is listed as BFC Co, incorporated in Latvia. We were going to put it under Bofrid, your company that exports flowers from Colombia and Kenya, but thought they could trace that to you easily. We created BFC as a stand-alone, new entity, with so many shell companies behind it that no one will even trace it back to Russia. We included all the land we discussed without filing too many claims to arouse suspicion. It took three claims. The filing mentions turquoise, but no one is looking for turquoise in Egypt as far as we can tell, so I doubt anyone will bother us. There are no other active mining claims for a hundred miles in any direction. The nearest mining ventures are building sand, gypsum, and limestone for cement. The nearest claims for metal mining are in the Eastern Desert on the west side of the Gulf of Suez."

"Excellent. What progress have we made on the geology?"

"Some bad news boss. The fishing boat with those cores disappeared after it left Sharm el Sheikh. As far as we know there was no bad weather. The head of the fishing company that owned the boat says it never reached Djibouti, where the cores would have changed boats for Yemen. He suspects pirates but no one knows. He wants us to reimburse him for the lost boat. He has no insurance. I told him that is not our problem and maybe we will sue him for the loss of the rocks."

"Do you think the boat sank or could it be captured?"

"Who knows. The Red Sea is crawling with pirates. Mostly Somalis, but also thieves from Ethiopia and Sudan. They typically board a boat, offload anything of value, and sink the rest. They try to get rid of all evidence, including the crew. They probably had no idea what the cores were. I suspect they are at the bottom of the sea."

"*Der'mo. Pridurki.* What about the field work?"

"We did not do much. We have ideas on geologic work we could do, but we were waiting for information from the cores. Now that we won't get that information, I'd like to take a couple of geologists down there. See if they can find surface evidence for the turquoise. Our claims were based only on where we found the cores, so we don't know if they are in the right place or not."

"Do it. Get me something to believe in soon, or I'll shut this down."

Novikov sensed frustration in Oblonsky and knew to leave quickly. He backed out of the office, nodded at Popov, and walked out onto Old Arbat, the artists and vendors starting to set up their stands and booths. He strolled the pedestrian-only ancient street paved with Belgian cobbles, walking past stacks of matryoshka dolls, men painting caricatures, and the smell of fresh baked pastries. As he passed a small crowd watching a woman juggling, he reflected that in a week he would be out of this icebox, laying on a beach in Egypt. Life was good for Roman but he knew that Boris could change that in an instant.

CHAPTER 8

LIBBY was drinking her morning coffee while wading through mail after returning to the office from a quick trip to her rare earths mine in California. Although very small, she loved that open pit mine that extracted exotic elements from an equally exotic rock. Rare earths metals only recently became a hot commodity, driven by their necessity in evolving technologies, starting in the sixties with mass production of color television sets, and expanding to growing consumer electronics, critical defense uses like night vision goggles, and GPS systems. These minerals, including yttrium, cerium, and neodymium, are found exclusively in rocks called carbonatites, which are composed dominantly of calcite instead of quartz. In fact, rare earths metals are not really rare, with all of them being more abundant in the earth's crust than gold for example. They are, however, almost never found in concentrations high enough to mine. Therefore, only a few rare earths mines exist around the world. The Mountain Pass Mine, just over the hill from hers, had supplied most of the world's demand over the past three decades, but recently China began to dominate the world market, driving prices down. That is why Libby was able to buy her mine.

She picked up a memo from Flo conveying what Salah had said by phone the day before. Someone had staked a mining claim near their area of interest in the Sinai. All he could find out was the name of the company filing the claim, BFC Co, registered in Latvia.

'That's not good,' Libby said to herself.

#

Jake thought the sixteenth street mall deteriorated every time he came to Denver. When it was built in the early eighties, it was a glistening modern marvel. Cars were banned, pedestrians ruled, and electric buses whisked passengers up and down more than a dozen blocks through the central business district. The ground was paved with five different types of rock pavers, workers kept the litter picked up, and Colorado's blue sky shone down through leafy trees and occasional small skyscrapers. Little by little, taller buildings obscured more of the natural light, the grime of age increased, growing litter eluded the workers, and the homeless problem mushroomed. Parts of the business district were becoming seedy, particularly when you veered off the mall in either direction. Which is what Jake did, navigating one block over to The Broker restaurant on seventeenth.

The Broker had been renowned for expense account dinners since opening in 1972 in the basement of a former bank. Huge steel vault doors were the centerpiece of the dining room, where free peel-and-eat shrimp brought regulars back time after time. Libby had reserved a table in the vault and was waiting for Jake. She stood as he approached, greeting him with a hug and a kiss on the cheek.

"Hi sexy," she said a little too loudly, looking at the next table where an older couple had turned towards them.

"Hi yourself," he answered, giving her a pat on the rear. "You're working on a bottle of Rombauer Chardonnay, I see."

"Nothing better with shrimp."

They casually conversed while perusing the menu, ordered dinner, and then ordered another bottle of wine while working on the second bowl of shrimp. Jake was never a chatty guy, but since Gussie's accident had been alternately morose or talkative. He was not verbose tonight.

"How are you?" Libby frowned slightly, uncomfortable when he trended toward this inward focus.

Libby worried about Jake. Gussie's accident had really impacted him. She was not sure the ranch was the best environment for him, with all the memories. One month after Gussie got out of the hospital, Jake had to leave her at the ranch, hiring a live-in nurse/nanny to help ensure she got the best rehab. Marv of course was in charge, but Jake would not trust him alone with her. Libby felt that Jake needed time away from Montana to heal. She hoped he felt close enough to her by now to share and open up, but that was happening slowly. Jake blamed himself for Gussie's accident, but even more he blamed his dad. Libby knew from experience that nothing was gained by assigning guilt. Although Jake could not stay at the ranch full-time, she was not forward enough to suggest he move in with her.

When Libby had been hurting in the past, she buried herself in something, focusing to the point of obsession. When Libby's mother died of cancer while she was in college, she laser focused on her studies, allowing her to graduate at the top of her class, Summa Cum Laude. Two of her best business properties were acquired after similar traumas. She thought Jake needed a diversion now, something to concentrate on besides Gussie.

Jake was not a guy typically in touch with his feelings, much less the feelings of those around him, but he did sense Libby's concern. He sighed and slowly shook his head, offering a glimpse of his internal struggle. He reached out and took her hand in his.

"Listen, I know I haven't been myself lately. I just need to get through this and right now I'm not sure how to manage that."

Jake's eyes glistened from the tears he was fighting to contain. He gripped her hand a little too tightly. Libby reached across the table and rested her other hand on top.

"Get through what exactly, Jake. Gussie is fine. She'll make a full recovery. Life has its challenges."

"I know, I know. I'm not sure what's wrong exactly."

"I'm here for you, you know."

"I know," Jake replied. "I know I can't keep camping out in hotels and apartments. I need a place to call home. The ranch just isn't home now, not with all the memories."

"I get that. I'm sure it's hard," Libby offered.

They held hands for several minutes, silent. Libby waited for Jake to continue.

"I bought a condo in Cherry Creek," he said. "Denver seemed a good place. Mostly since you're here. And I've checked out a few boarding schools for Gussie. I don't want her growing up a cowgirl, can't see her staying on the ranch, and I can't dedicate myself to raising her alone. I don't want a nanny to do it. I think she might really like a boarding school environment."

Libby was surprised. First because he bought a place without her knowing and did not even ask for her help. Second because he bought it in Denver, a place she thought he did not really like. Third because he bought a condo in Cherry Creek, a spot more popular with yuppies, and as far as one could get from the great outdoors. But mostly because he had never talked about boarding schools before.

"Well that's something," she said. "I never thought about boarding schools. How did you come up with that?"

"Lots of families I worked with overseas went that route, because there was no good local option, for example in Nigeria. Or because they thought their kids would get a better education and experience with the rigors and continuity of elite schools. Lots of Brits thought that was the way to go. It wasn't as popular with Americans."

Libby was careful to not inject too much opinion into the conversation. She was not inherently the boarding school type.

"Gussie might like it, I guess. I don't doubt the educational advantage. I would think the social aspect might be more of an issue for her."

"Well, her social life would be better there than at the ranch. There are some good schools near Denver, so if I have the place here I'd see a lot of her and she'd have a room she could call home close-by. I see her spending the summer at the ranch then starting in school down here end of August. She should be pretty much back to normal by then. Physically at least."

"Jake, I know you're not flush yet, waiting for the Sinai field to kick in. You actually bought a condo?"

"Yeah. It's a small place but I don't need much. A bedroom for me; another for Gussie. It's in a good location, within walking distance of cafes and restaurants. I close next week then I can get stuff out of storage and stick it in. You wanna lend a hand decorating?"

"Sure, let me know," she said as the Caesar salad cart was rolled up next to them. "I'll expect something in return though. You need to get out more and stop isolating yourself. Can you agree to that?"

"I can try."

Jake knew she was right and hinted at a smile for the first time since he sat down.

"While you're waiting to close on the condo, think about something," Libby leaned closer. "I want you as a partner."

"I hope you're not talking about the Egypt thing again."

"I absolutely am. Salah told me some Latvians filed a claim for turquoise near that core pile. I can't say I see any indication of turquoise, but I do see potential for gold or copper. Anyway, I doubt our claims would be exactly where they filed, but we don't know yet. I do know that we need to speed up our evaluation."

"I'm not up for it Libby. I've got enough on my plate."

Jake was exasperated that she could not take no for an answer. Her tenacity was one of the things he liked in her, but focused on him it got annoying.

"No, really you don't, Jake. You're filled with sorrow, self-pity, and anger. You blame Marv for Gussie's accident and you avoid going back to the ranch. You blame yourself and I think you blame me too. You've pulled away from me."

Libby took a deep breath and closed her eyes. She paused and then continued.

"You've been reluctant to help me with this deal all along. You need something new to concentrate on, and I need your knowledge and connections in Egypt. I can't do this alone."

Her face flushed with emotion, anger and tears just beneath the surface. She continued, "I hate seeing you like this Jake."

They sat in silence for a long time, then sat in silence even longer as they ate their steaks. Libby's feelings were bruised, and she did not trust herself to say more, afraid it would come out wrong, colored by hurt and anger. Finally Jake broke the silence.

"Equal partners?"

She wondered if she heard him correctly, and looked at him in disbelieve.

"What?" she sputtered.

"Would we be equal partners?

"Yes" she paused before adding, "Well almost. You know the devil's in the details. As CEO I'll provide all the funds we need through Phase One, whatever I decide that means. As COO you'll do all the work at least through start-up, if that ever happens."

"So you've really thought about this. What if we do find something worth mining?"

"Well, we'll cross that bridge if it comes. Oh and one more thing."

"OK, what?" Jake rolled his eyes and sighed.

"The company name. I've thought about this a long time. It's non-negotiable. I've already started the incorporation paperwork."

"I'm not sure you can beat Pimple Creek."

"It's in a different vein, no pun intended," said Libby.

"If it's non-negotiable, then why bother asking me. What's the name?"

"I want to call it GusCo."

Jake finally smiled, tearing up again, and replied, "Yeah, that's perfect."

GENERAL Mohammed Latif sat behind a large wooden desk in his office on the fourth floor of the Mogamma, the large government building built in 1940's modernist style to house most Egyptian government functions. It was south of Tahrir Square, in the spot where King Farouk ordered the demolition of British barracks when those colonialists were forced out of the country. The General was an imposing figure, tall in stature, large in girth, thick black mustache, always wearing his highly decorated uniform. He was second in command at the Egyptian State Department but reported directly to the Foreign Minister. Salah thought that Latif was one of the good guys, unencumbered by corruption, driven by service to his country, and not afraid to confront criminals. His contacts extended beyond Egypt to other Arab countries and Israel. Salah had never seen him without a Cleopatra cigarette hanging from his mouth, and today was no different. Tendrils of smoke rose from the glowing tip, keeping the air in Latif's office hazy and smelly.

"Welcome Salah el Gindi," Latif said standing up and coming around to greet his visitor. Salah thought he must be a very dominant commanding officer, most likely breeding fear in his subordinates.

"It's been too long Mohammed," replied el Gindi, kissing him on both cheeks, as they did in this part of the world.

The two became friends relatively recently, during the mess surrounding Jake's gas deal. Latif worked with his counterparts in Israel and the CIA to unravel the mystery behind Jake's troubles. These days, he focused on the increasingly violent terrorism blossoming across Egypt. The previous year was the most devastating ever for terrorist attacks in the country, with over a thousand people killed or wounded. Just last month, gunmen attacked two trains, a bus, and a Nile cruise ship. The group called Gama'a had taken responsibility for most of these attacks, but there were a dozen active groups to keep track of. The general was a busy man.

Latif ordered tea from an impossibly feeble-looking elderly gentleman, who scurried off to fill the order. After catching up on personal happenings, he asked el Gindi why he had come.

"Besides the chance to visit my old friend," said el Gindi, "I want to tell you that Jake Tillard and I are working together again in the Sinai."

This caught Latif's attention and he perked up immediately.

"And is the woman with you as well?"

"If you mean Libby Joyce, yes she is."

"Please give them both my regards."

"I'll do that."

"Now tell me why you are here, really. I know you started developing the gas field. What else are you up to. And how can I help?"

"We are exploring for gold near St. Catherine's. There is no mining anywhere nearby and it's actually a very remote location, but we have indications there might be something worth pursuing. We haven't gotten far but already have problems with local Bedouin, some Russians, and a group called NOFORTH. I wanted to see if you knew anything about any of them."

Latif stretched back in his chair and lit another cigarette, blowing smoke rings towards the ceiling. The acrid smell of Egyptian tobacco assaulted Salah's nostrils.

"It's my job to know about them all my friend. The Bedouin there are like Bedouin everywhere. They do what they want and are impossible to control. The government has a good relationship with most of them in the south. But these days some are back to smuggling. Mostly taking drugs and women into Israel. This is not a priority for me. I wouldn't think they would be a problem for you either. As for the Russians, you'll have to tell me who you're concerned with. I might be able to help. And NOFORTH is a small group of disorganized young people. Mostly students. They are annoying but not dangerous like the Gama'a. At least so far. We don't spend a lot of time on them because they mostly want to be seen, to protest, and to get out their message. They have done little damage but that will change as they grow. Each new group starts with idealistic intentions and peaceful messaging, then things escalate to violence. What problems have you had?"

"From NOFORTH, as you said, mostly passive interference. People with signs blocking the roads, graffiti, that sort of thing. But we've had a couple serious incidents at the Seth Field, from who knows who. We've had things stolen, and we've had someone throw metal tools down our hole to cause problems. Do NOFORTH people usually claim responsibility? Because no one has come out and done that."

"Normally, they do because they're all about publicity. But who knows. Sometimes if things go wrong people will hide and not speak up. Sometimes the Ministry covers up things to manipulate the attitudes of people. We want our people calm and society going in a happy way. We have not done that yet with NOFORTH, as far as I know."

"Our biggest problem from them is protestors at the field," said el Gindi.

Latif laughed and shook his head.

"I wouldn't worry if they walk around carrying signs. You need to worry when they put the signs away and start carrying weapons. If that happens, I can help you."

They talked more about the government and its attempts to reign in violence. NOFORTH staged a large protest two weeks ago at the Egyptian Museum, which Latif watched from his office. He showed Salah photographs of that event, and even commended the protestors for holding a fairly organized event. Latif stood up, held out his hand, and invited Salah to return with any issues.

"When you come next time, please bring Mr. Tillard and Ms. Joyce. Maybe set up a small meeting in my office during their next trip to Egypt. And tell me who is this Russian that is giving you trouble. Then I can really help."

CHAPTER 10

MISSOULA looked soggy, grey, and mostly dead, after a tough winter. Jake remembered mud season as the worst part of the year as he trudged across The Oval, heading for the Charles A. Clapp building and the Geology Department. He looked up at the 'M', a large concrete white letter situated six hundred feet up in elevation, on the side of Mount Sentinel. Jake used to hike to the 'M' at least twice a week, always trying to better his time ascending the eleven switchbacks and nearly a mile to the letter. As he traversed campus, he recalled his first summer here as a student, when he tried to grow tomatoes. He never succeeded in getting any of them to turn red or even yellow. He found out later that the growing season between frosts was just over a hundred days. He entered the building, climbed the steps, and found the office of Professor Don Hynde exactly where it had been two decades before.

"Jake Tillard," Hynde smiled as he rose from a cluttered, overflowing desk. "It's been a while stranger."

"I know Don. I always intend to stop by when I'm back to see my dad down near Hamilton, but never made the time. I've been overseas the last couple decades but that's no excuse."

"Well you're here now. Have a seat and let's catch up."

Hynde had been one of Jake's professors, but not a thesis advisor. Therefore, they knew each other, but not well. Don was a professor of structural geology when Jake was a student, but was now the department head as well, which is why Jake sought him out. After quick synopses of their activities over the last couple of decades, Jake launched into his agenda.

"Don, do you have any graduate students looking for a thesis topic? I've got an economic geology project in Egypt looking at greenstone belts, and I need some field mapping. It's original field-based research and would make a great little project."

Hynde sat up straight and blew out a long breath. He put his hands behind his head and stretched before answering.

"It's really late in the year Jake. Most Master's candidates pick their topic and field areas in the fall and are already well researched into them by now. But one student had his topic blow up last month. He's not mine, but I hear he lost access to some private land he needs for mapping. He's a really good kid and I'll have to check if he's still looking for a new topic. He's actually a student of Rocky's and interested in hard rock stuff so your project might be a good fit. Why don't we chat with Rocky. He's in a class now but it's about to end so we might be able to catch him."

"OK great," replied Jake.

Don left a message with the department secretary and twenty minutes later Rocky Winston walked into the chairman's office.

"I can't believe you're back," said Winston, holding out an enormous hand. Jake remembered that giant hand, which was connected to a giant body. The aging professor stood well over six feet tall, with flowing red hair now turning gray and bundled in a ponytail. Jake recalled he came from a Nordic family of giants, his grandfather emigrating to Canada just before the turn of the century. Rocky's father moved his family to North Dakota and then to Montana. Rocky grew up around Helena, loved Montana, did his undergraduate at the University of Montana, and his graduate work in Washington. He landed a teaching job at the University of Montana and never left. Rocky had been one of Jake's two thesis advisors and the one who accompanied Jake to the field on more than a few occasions.

"It's been too long Rocky," answered Jake, happy to see his old mentor. "I was hoping I could take you out for a beer when you're finished here. We could do some catching up."

"Sure. I've got no plans tonight. Since you're buying, would you mind if I dragged a few students along? It's always good for them to meet with alums, especially those gainfully employed in industry. And especially those who will pay for beer."

"I don't mind at all," Jake said laughing. He knew the department secretary Gracie was already putting out the word for free drinks at the Missoula Club later.

"Don's note said you were interested in David Li?"

"If that's the Master's guy in need of a project, then yes. I need someone to do field mapping in Egypt. I'm trying to find a greenstone belt. You might remember Libby Joyce? We're in this together."

"Libby Joyce, there's another name from the past. She's stopped by the department more often than you, but is still a stranger. How's she doing?"

"She's great," said Jake. "Tearing it up with a company holding oil wells, mines, and commercial properties. And she's as foxy as ever."

Jake fleshed out the project, summarizing what they knew already, the scope of the field work, the risks involved, and the timing requirements. None of the faculty in the department had ever worked in Egypt, so Jake added some cultural aspects, at least as they might impact a graduate student doing fieldwork there.

"That sounds like a great opportunity Jake. I think David would be interested and I think he'd be well suited. He's on our top handful list of grad students this year. Very bright, inquisitive, detail-oriented, hard-working, ambitious. He needs to find another project right away or he's looking at another year here, which I don't think he wants. Some kids don't mind spending as long as they can in Missoula but David is more driven. He'll be at the bar tonight so you can meet him. Maybe take a read on his demeanor before you foist the project on him. How's that sound?"

"Yeah, good. Can I get a resume, transcript, or whatever else you can muster on him now?"

"I'll have Gracie pull what she can. But you won't be disappointed in his technical side."

#

Jake sprawled on the hotel bed, perusing Li's material. Born in Hong Kong, he moved with his family to California when he was six. Suburban upbringing, Stanford undergrad, involved with the geology club, chess club, head of the outdoors club. Chose Montana because of its emphasis on mining and because of Professor Rocky Winston, who also graduated from Stanford. Universities could be nepotistic, especially when capturing students who could actually pay for their education. Jake wondered if Li would have any interest in working overseas, particularly in the Middle East. He assumed the boy looked Asian and knew he would stand out in a region that harbored large amounts of prejudice.

He finished reading the material, concluding that Li fit the bill from a resume point of view. The big question would be his interest in mapping in a third world environment, and Jake's assessment of his personality and fit with himself and Libby. Dropping the papers on the bed, he took a quick shower and threw on jeans and a shirt. The Missoula Club was not a club at all, but a downtown dive that had cheap beer by the pitcher and the best hamburgers in town. It had a huge student following bolstered by the fact it did not close the bar or food service until three o'clock in the morning.

#

As their group drifted in, Rocky and Jake sat by themselves for an hour, reliving some of their joint fieldwork and recapping what had happened in their lives since. Rocky always liked Jake and had wondered through the years what he was up to. He remembered that Jake's mom and brother were killed by a drunk driver while he was at the University, and heard he later divorced his first wife, who Rocky knew from University. He was astonished at Jake's continued misfortune losing his second wife and almost losing his daughter, empathizing and thinking about the strength of a guy who kept his momentum through all of that. Rocky felt it best to not dwell on these things, instead talking about geology and oil exploration around the world.

Rocky's specialty was mining so he asked a lot of questions about the oil business and what Jake had done. He was fascinated by the Egypt experiences, asking many questions about Jake's time there. For his part, Rocky's research had drifted into paleomagnetics, trying to age-date rocks by taking oriented cores from outcrops and using the directionality of iron minerals in those cores to determine when the earth's magnetic reversals happened in a rock section. He could compare these reversals to published data and date the rocks. It was a fairly new technology and had pushed Rocky to field work in Pakistan. Jake found Rocky's descriptions of Pakistan familiar and understood why Egypt was of interest to the professor. Finally, Rocky called David Li to their table, pouring beers for the three of them.

"David let me introduce you to Jake Tillard, an old student of mine. He's been successful in the oil business but why anyone as bright as Jake would go into oil is beyond me," Rocky joked. "The gods have blessed him and he's now seen the light, focusing on hard rocks and mining. He's got something that might be a project for you. Listen to what he has to say and I'll catch you both later."

With that, the giant of a man rose and maneuvered his large frame to the other side of the bar. Jake and David shook hands and fell into easy conversation. Jake liked David more and more as they chatted, seeing in the student a bit of himself at that age. Understated and shy, but tenacious and ambitious, overall curious about geology. After they covered the softer side of things, Jake motioned Rocky back to the table to join them and Jake proceeded to explain the project.

"The southern Sinai Massif is Precambrian, with rocks in the one to two-billion-year-old range. It's the northern portion of the Arabian-Nubian Shield that extends southward into Sudan, Ethiopia, Saudi Arabia, and Yemen. In the Sinai, it's composed mostly of unexciting granitic rocks and meta-basalts originally from the sea floor. What we're interested in is a greenstone belt, a sliver of ancient sea floor that was buried, heated, and squished up to the surface. As you know, those are sweet spots for mineralization. We found old diamond bit cores cut a couple decades ago that contain some gold and copper, with traces of silver and zinc. We're not exactly sure where they came from, but probably not far from where they now lay. There's some history of gold and copper being mined in the Sinai but really small stuff. Nobody is actively pursuing it there, but we're seeing companies exploring to the south and west, largely in Sudan."

Jake paused and both David and Rocky nodded, taking in the information. They ordered wings and another pitcher of beer and Jake continued.

"What we'd need you to do is map every outcrop you can find, exhaustively analyze and investigate the cores, prove the existence of a greenstone belt, maybe run another coring program, and tell us where to stake mining claims. It's really remote out there, hot as hell in the summer, miles from help, and dangerous due to old landmines and unexploded ordinance. In addition, drug smugglers go through the area. If you work for our company, you'll have to sign your life away, waiving any legal recourse if you get hurt or killed. But all in all, it's pretty standard stuff."

Jake again paused to gauge David's interest. The young man looked interested but anxious. Jake liked that he was not too cocky and showed a bit of fear. This meant he would be cautious and cognizant of his surroundings. Their conversation continued for a while, and before they left the Missoula Club, Jake told Rocky he wanted Li, Rocky asked Li if he was game, and Li voiced his overall excitement. The three of them agreed to meet the next day to outline his new thesis project, make plans for the summer field season, and agree on funding and other logistics.

Jake left the Missoula Club well before its closing time but not before consuming way too much beer. Fortunately, his walk to the hotel was short and he reached his room just in time to use the bathroom. Sleep came quickly.

#

"I'll be here for the rest of the month," Jake told Gussie several days later.

They were sitting in rockers on the porch at the Bar-J, sipping lemonades and watching the sun go down. The temperature was above normal but they still wore down vests.

"I miss school daddy," said Gussie.

"I know you do peanut. There's only a month left before summer break. You're doing schoolwork here at home so you won't have to repeat the grade. But you're still working on your leg, doing rehab, and we can't have you running around with your friends. Once you get those leg muscles squared away, you'll be good as new. I want you to be a hundred percent fixed when you start St. Cecilia's in Denver the end of August."

"Do you really think I'll like it?" she asked. "I'm scared to start another school."

"You're going to love it. If you want we can make a trip down there so you can check it out. But I'm sure you'll love everything about it. The school is great. Seems like the kids are really cool, and from all over the place, even Europe. It's in Denver so you've got a lot of city stuff to do, like museums and parks."

"OK," she put her finger to her chin. "I want to take a look. When can we go?"

"How about the end of the month, when I need to leave anyway for business? We can take grandpa with us, then he can fly back here with you afterwards. Maybe the three of us can even go to a baseball game while we're in Denver."

"Yeah, let's do that. I like grandpa and he never gets to go anywhere."

"That's the problem with a ranch Gussie. It's tough to leave it for any length of time."

CHAPTER 11

'BESSIE T' was the name on the mining claim when Libby bought it more than fifteen years ago, taking it off the hands of a very small company in Cody that was about to go through bankruptcy proceedings. The company was owned by an old man going through a bitter divorce, and he was motivated to unload the claim quickly. It was an old claim, originally filed in 1924. Rumor had it the original prospector named it after the sweetheart he left behind in Pennsylvania. Rumor also had it that the prospector never got to test the claim, having met his maker the next year in the form of a moose that trampled him to death. Various people since had scratched around, drilled a few holes, and did work required to maintain the claim, yet no one had been encouraged enough to dig down into the earth. The prior owner, a friend of a friend, accepted pennies on the dollar, paid in cash to an offshore account. It was Libby's first foray into mining and frankly she barely knew what she was getting into.

"I never get tired of visiting the Bessie T, David."

Libby was enjoying showing the personable young man around her property.

"Yes ma'am. It's gorgeous out here."

Libby had not been thinking of the landscape when she said made her comment, and looked up to take in the scenery which she normally did not notice. To her it was all about the mining. South Pass was a term attributed to a couple actual passes, low points on the Continental Divide that ran from Canada to Mexico. The whole area near South Pass was a broad open saddle filled with prairie and sagebrush, with not a lot of elevation change. Not what one thought of when discussing the Continental Divide. The Wind River Range sat to the north and the Great Divide Basin to the south. The first recorded passing of the area was by representatives of John

Jacob Astor's Pacific Fur Company in 1812. After that, it became incorporated into the Oregon Trail, along which hordes of fortune seekers traveled back and forth from St. Louis to the Oregon coast.

"You need to stop calling me that if you want to stay on this project, David. How did a Chinese guy ever begin saying 'ma'am' anyway?"

"Well, my mom grew up in Houston, crazy as that is. I'm fourth generation American on her side. Of course her Chinese ancestry goes way back, and my dad is from China. I was born over there and moved here when I was young. My mom taught me to say 'ma'am' and she was a stickler for politeness."

"Old habits are hard to break," Libby said laughing. "Well at least it's a good habit. I had a niece who learned to say 'fuck' when she was two, and that was hard to stop."

Libby brought David Li here to learn about the geology. He would be looking for similar rocks in Egypt and needed to learn to recognize each type instantly. Greenstone belts could have many different rock types, only a few of which were conducive to mineralization.

"When I bought this claim, I really didn't know what I was doing," Libby confessed. "I'd gotten my geology degrees then spent most of my time working the oilfields. Mining was not a strength. An acquaintance pointed me to the Bessie T, trying to help out a friend of his. They say luck is better than brains, and in this case that's true. I bought the property on a lark, taught myself the business, hired good people, and learned to love mining more than oil. The Bessie T makes a profit most years. I guess I'm attached to this mine and we now share a history."

They stood still for a few minutes and looked out over the grassland.

"We brought you up here to look at the rocks. But just a bit of history first 'cause it's pretty cool. This place was on the old Oregon Trail linking the Missouri River to Oregon towns in the early 1800's. Gold was discovered in 1842 about thirty miles east of here, kicking off the Lewiston District mining boom. Just ten miles west of us, high grade gold came out of the Carissa mine beginning in 1867, and a few years later someone found a thirty-four-ounce gold nugget that's now in the Los Angeles Museum of Natural History."

"This is the rock that produces here at the Bessie T," Libby said as she bent down and picked up a fist-sized piece of medium green tinted rock. They were standing next to the mine office, which had a small garden ringed by pieces of ore. "It was named the 'Miner's Delight Formation' because it housed many of the early deposits found. What you need to take away is how diverse the rock types are here. You can tell just from looking at the rocks we've placed surrounding this garden. In the Sinai you'll find square miles of granitic rocks. They're of no use to us. We're interested in this darker, varied, exotic looking stuff. Only rarely can you see any gold with your naked eye, so you need to know what associated minerals to look for. Spend the afternoon with Janet and learn. We'll take the plane back to Denver around five."

"We're gonna pick around the dump pile," said Janet. "We can find every rock type there and then we'll head into the shack to look at some maps and put everything into perspective."

Libby drifted off, leaving Li with Robinson.

"Where's Libby going?"

"She's gonna head underground and check on safety, techniques, and staff. She always goes down when she visits. Says it's to show the miners she's interested. Honestly I think she just loves being at the face, loading a couple holes, and being part of the action before they blast. The Bessie T is fairly small, so there's still a lot of hand work done; bigger mines are mostly mechanized now. It may be small but the Bessie T pays a lot of Pimple Creek bills."

Robinson and Li stumbled around the dump pile, which was in front of the opening to the main drift. A railroad track coming out of the tunnel was perpetually made longer as worthless host rock from the mine was dumped at the end of the track. The ore itself was redirected to the crusher off to one side, where pieces as large as your head coming out of the mine were crushed first into pea-sized pieces and then into a dust. This product was sent on a conveyer across the field to the processing building where it was made into a slurry, sent through leaching, adsorption, and electrolysis processes, then processed into bullion. Many small mines did not do the whole sequence of processing, but Libby had become fascinated with pouring liquid, molten gold, and wanted to do it herself. It was a big event every month to watch molten gold being poured and bars of bullion cooling. Finally, Janet bent over and picked up a couple rocks.

"This is the specific rock that contains the gold here," said Robinson. "It's a conglomerate within the Miners Delight formation, where fluids were able to flow around as metamorphism wound down. Most of the time you can't see the gold and the concentration is low. That's why most mines around the world in these rocks are open pits. It usually doesn't pay to sink a shaft or go underground. The Bessie T is different for two reasons. First, because our gold concentrations are higher. Second, the layers are tilted vertical. They named these rock packages 'greenstone belts' because of this green rock, which contains the green minerals chlorite and actinolite. This stuff makes up most of the belt, but it's the conglomerate where gold hides out."

Robinson went through the other dozen or so rock types common in the area, explaining each one for Li and hammering off a golf ball sized piece of each that he could take home with him to refer to. They moved to the office where Robinson laid out a series of geologic maps, showing where each of the rock types outcropped and how they were distributed in three dimensions below the surface. She also showed him a map of the whole mining district and where some of the richer, more historic mines were located.

"All you need to do in Egypt is find one of these suckers," said Robinson smiling. "We would really appreciate that."

Though it sounded as if she was teasing her young student, she could not have been more serious. After they exhausted the geology, Li and Robinson kicked back, sitting and drinking Cokes on some rocks with a view out over the prairie, waiting for Libby to reappear. It was the first time they had interacted much.

"So how did you get into geology David? I haven't run across many Chinese Americans in the field."

"I'll tell you if you tell me. I've run across a few black geologists but never a black female one."

"OK, sure," said Janet laughing. David began.

"At Stanford I started out as a math major with a minor in Chinese, planning to work for my dad and one day take over his business. But calculus did me in. Oh, I could do it, but I didn't see the point. My roommate talked me into a geology class sophomore year, and I fell in love with working in the field. We took trips to look at turbidite deposits along the beaches, volcanoes in the Cascades, and old mines along the Sierras. I switched majors and the rest is history. I can't say my dad was very happy. What about you?"

"I never knew a geologist growing up in Jamaica, but we kids climbed around on a lot of rocks. My father was a dentist, but his hobby was collecting minerals. He'd take us all over the island looking for specimens, then at night read to us about the geology of where we had been that day. Jamaica is very interesting geologically. We've got mountains that have shallow water limestones and rift basin clastics along with island arc sequences, all of which have been uplifted and twisted by two major strike-slip faults associated with the nearby subduction zone. We lived in the highlands and went to visit many of the island's geologic sites. After we moved to New York when I was in my teens, my dad and I kept collecting. When I went to college I took geology the first semester and never looked back."

"So we're both in it for the science," said Li.

"And not for the money," Janet laughed. "Although the money's not been half bad."

That night on the plane to Denver, Libby satisfied herself that David Li had absorbed as much as possible from a day at the mine, that he knew how to identify the different rock types, and that he knew how to prepare for a field season in Egypt. He was both competent and ambitious. When their plane landed at DIA, she bade him farewell as he walked off to the public terminal to catch a flight back to Montana. Libby herself climbed into a limo waiting to take her back to her office.

EGYPTIAN Drilling Company rig EDC-1 was 'turning to the right', drilling the second development well in Jake's natural gas field, which he named 'Seth' after the Pharaonic god of violence, chaos, desert, and storms. He thought this about summed up the trials and tribulations of bringing that prospect to fruition. Phase one called for six wells completed and hooked up before gas could be compressed and sent down the pipeline, across the Israeli border near Be'er Milka and on to Be'er Shiva and Jerusalem. If all went well, the phase one infrastructure and the export pipeline would both be finished within two years, and revenue would start flowing in 1997. He was getting pressure from his funding partners in St. Louis to replace the outflow of cash with an inflow.

"The views are amazing," said David Li, looking out over the desert. "You can see for miles in any direction. It's like we're sitting on a high spot."

David was enjoying being in Egypt so far. He loved how exotic it felt and that there were continually new things to stimulate all his senses. It was different than anything he had experienced in North America or Asia.

The Seth Field was north and east of Nekhel, a small town in a relatively flat part of the northern Sinai. Jake and Mohammed had conducted much fieldwork north of this area where it was mountainous and rock outcrops were abundant, but the area around the field was largely featureless, arid desert, paved with sand and pebbles. Small undulations in the topography lent an expansive and almost impressionistic look to the terrane.

"You're right, we are on a high," replied Jake. "The topographic dome we're on reflects an anticline in the rocks beneath us. I mapped all the topographic highs early in my exploration work, paying attention to where streambeds bent around features you could barely see. Once I finished a couple years of field work and ran a few seismic surveys, I was able to high-grade some of those domes and narrowed our prospects to three locations. Luckily, we hit gas on the first attempt."

"So what's the geology like?"

"The geologic basin here is really shallow, with Precambrian basement rocks around ten thousand feet down. The productive formation is a Jurassic limestone layer eight thousand feet deep. It's thicker than I predicted, with four hundred feet of pay. Porosity in the rock averages twenty percent with great permeabilities. Methane flows out easily, and we have to do minimal processing before we put it in the pipeline. Underneath the limestone is more than a hundred feet of Jurassic Maghara Group shale with total organic carbon well over three percent. There was a lot of stuff dying back then. Before we drilled the discovery well, my main concern was source rock; I wasn't sure there was enough and wasn't sure if it had been buried deep enough to generate gas. The basin is not very deep now but in the past, before the Sinai was uplifted, and before several thousand feet of sediments were eroded off, it was deep enough to cook the organics into methane. Our modeling was a gamble but fortunately it paid off. I was right."

"That's pretty cool," said Li. "I don't have any oil and gas experience, so this is fun to see. You said you mapped a bunch of topographic highs so do you have other prospects?"

"I do. But I don't have enough money to drill them yet. We've got them under license, but we'll be sure this field makes a profit before we drill the other prospects."

"I'm glad you brought me here to see this Jake but it's a bit far from my work area. You could have come here alone. What does this have to do with my work?"

Jake smiled, pleased that Li was confident enough to question why he was brought all the way out here. They were developing a very healthy relationship.

"It has absolutely nothing to do with your work, David. I wanted to check on what's going on and I thought it'd be educational for you to see it. But honestly, the main reason we drove over here was to pick up Mohammed."

Jake pointed to the west. Walking towards them was a tall man in a flowing tan robe and a headdress waving in the breeze. He was coming from an area that contained nothing but desert. David strained to see a car or camel or anything else past Mohammed but nothing was there. He looked at the approaching bearded man as one might look at Moses walking out of the Dead Sea.

"*Salama al aleikum,*" said Jake, extending his hand

"*Aleikum al salaam,*" Mohammed took his hand and threw his other arm around his friend. "Your trip was good?"

Jake had not seen Mohammed in a year, and had since been to three continents, a handful of countries, and several homes. He knew Mohammed had been almost nowhere and that the Bedouin had a strange concept of time.

"*Colou tamam.* All good. Mohammed, this is Mr. David Li."

Salah el Gindi had hired Mohammed to watch over Li for the next three months as he mapped in the southern Sinai. Mohammed had been happy to accept with the proviso he brought his cousin, another Bedouin who had spent much of his life in the army, serving during the war of 1973 as desert guide and sharpshooter. Abu had saved Mohammed's life a few years ago when Israeli thugs followed Jake to gain information on the gas prospect. Abu shot one of them in the shoulder in Mohammed's trailer with his old military sniper rifle before he could bash in his cousin's head. They had tied the man up and tried to extract information from him, but he died before they learned much.

"*Marhaba* David. That is a Jewish name?"

"*Ahlan*, Mohammed," David replied, using one of the ten words he had learned on the plane. "Maybe it's Jewish, but not in my case. I was born in Hong Kong and fled with my parents from the communists in China. We moved to the States when I was six."

Never one for verbosity, Mohammed nodded and walked to the manager's trailer to get a drink of water.

"You'll learn to love him," said Jake. "Time to head south."

"SON-OF-A-BITCH, Mohammed," said Jake, perplexed. "Are you sure this is the right place? Absolutely sure? I don't see any cores. There was a big pile of them. They didn't just stand up and walk out of here. Maybe you've got the spot wrong."

"Right spot," Mohammed replied simply.

He bent down and picked up something, handing it to David Li.

"Looks like a core chip to me," said Li, holding it out for Jake.

Jake came over, looked at the chip, then began finding other small pieces on the ground. He knew Mohammed was not wrong but could not believe the cores were gone. Whoever took them did a good job of removing it all. Only the smallest pieces remained. Without Mohammed's skills they would never have been able to find this spot again.

"Who the hell would take all those cores? Why? And why would they be so careful to try and pick up every last piece? The last five percent must have taken half the effort."

Mohammed answered, "Last night I talked with local men. They said smugglers come through this area on their way from the southern coast to Israel. They said we need to be careful because it's the route for hashish. Maybe when these smugglers come next time I will ask if they saw anyone. I am sure they did not want the rocks, but they probably know something."

Jake researched the area before leaving Denver. He knew a lot about the northern Sinai but not as much about the southern part. Bedouin in the south have been transporting goods for centuries. Originally, it had been consumables like spices, grain, wine, and that sort of thing. But in the 1950's some tribes got into drug smuggling, with those activities providing as much as thirty percent of the Bedouin population's income. The Bedouin never considered moving any goods as criminal; they had been traders for centuries with only the products changing with shifting demand. Smuggling had largely stopped during the Israeli occupation from 1967 to 1982 but had rebounded since. Over the past decade, they added human cargo which had increased exponentially. It started with women from Eastern Europe lured to Israel with promises of jobs and subsequently forced into becoming sex workers. More recently, an increasing number of Africans traveled this route looking for a better life. The Bedouin served a role similar to the coyotes that bring Mexicans to the United States. Jake knew these were people to stay away from, and discussed this with Li and Mohammed.

The next day the men used surveying equipment to locate the corners of the three mining claims staked by BFC, walking out the boundaries. Nowhere did they come across a post or cairn to mark the claims, which was a legal requirement. Jake stayed another couple of days to help David start his field mapping, then left the graduate student with Mohammed and Abu. Jake had misgivings leaving the young man here but thought back to things he had done at a similar age. He knew Mohammed and Abu would keep him safe.

A week later, as the sun was heading for the horizon, David and Mohammed heard gunshots. Being alarmed they immediately drove the Niva back to camp. Nothing was out-of-place, but Abu was not there. They waited hours before they saw him walking back, gun over his shoulder, and the carcass of a Nubian Ibex around his neck.

"What happened?" Mohammed asked his cousin in Arabic.

"Yemeni hunting Ibex," he answered.

"Why didn't you stop him?"

"It was too late. He already killed this one."

"What did you tell him?"

"I told him nothing. I shot him."

The Nubian Ibex was a goat species listed as 'vulnerable' by international agencies; a mere three hundred were thought to remain in the Sinai, their numbers being decimated during the Israeli occupation. In prior days the Bedouin themselves hunted the goats but these days they were highly protective of the Ibex, along with the environment in general. Most modern Bedouin would never think of killing one of the majestic light sandy colored animals with backswept ridged horns flattened like sword blades, but most would not consider killing a poacher either. Abu was not like most of his countrymen, having learned during three wars to shoot first and not worry later. He also had no fondness for Yemenis.

David Li was still confused, thinking he had not understood the two Bedouin's conversation.

"What happened?"

"A Yemeni poacher was hunting Ibex," said Mohammed. "The goat was dead, so Abu thought we should eat it. He's never eaten Ibex and felt it should not go to waste."

"And what about the Yemeni," asked David, wondering what he did with him.

"I kill him. But I not eat him," said Abu with a straight face. "I left him for the animals."

#

Two months later, Li had almost finished mapping, visiting virtually every piece of exposed rock within a hundred square mile area. As always, he spent the day with Mohammed. Their typical day was to eat breakfast over a camp stove, load the Niva, and drive to their mapping area. If it was too rugged for the Niva, they walked around looking for rock outcrops. Mohammed would stay with the car and keep track of Li using walkie-talkies. Li would make marks on his aerial photographs showing where he took rock samples and other geologic information. Most days they would bag a dozen samples weighing approximately a pound or two each. In the course of his project they covered a five by ten-mile area in detail and another couple hundred square miles in a more cursory fashion.

This particular day, they returned to find their camp in disarray. While Abu was gone to get supplies from the nearest village, someone had ransacked their tents, scattering the contents. A quick assessment indicated nothing was missing. Li had his notebooks and maps with him, and the only work items at the camp were the numerous rock samples in white cloth bags closed with drawstrings. The pile of those looked like it had not been disturbed. Neither had the provisions, food, water, or medical kit.

"Bedouin?" asked David Li.

"No," replied Mohammed. "We have no locks in the desert because they are not needed. We have rules, and they prohibit this. It is our code. It is why there are seldom skirmishes between our people."

"Then who?" David queried. At this point he had spent enough time with the Bedouin to show he was not happy and wanted answers.

"I must go find people to ask. Someone will know. I take the Niva for a day or two?"

"Sure, go ahead. I can catch up on paperwork. Or should I come with you?"

"Better you stay here. Abu will stay with you. Wait for him."

With no more explanation than that and even though it was dusk, Mohammed took a small bag from his tent, climbed into the Niva, and drove off to the northeast, which was not the direction of the nearest village. As far as David knew, there was nothing in that direction except empty desert.

Abu returned before midnight and expressed little concern over the mess or Mohammed's sudden departure. David tried to explain to him what had happened, but he was not sure he got the message across. Abu did however begin cleaning his guns.

#

It took three days for Mohammed to return.

"Russians did this," he said over tea.

"Are you sure?" asked Li.

David had missed his companion and felt apprehensive while he was gone. In addition, Abu had not been much company.

"I found a caravan of smugglers moving hashish. They know about our camp and moved their normal path to avoid us. It took a while for me to find them. Russians have been here for maybe a year they think, moving around the desert like us. They could be the ones looking for turquoise. Why else would they be out here?"

"I can't imagine why anyone would be out here," said David. "They clearly know what we are up to. Maybe they were looking for results of my mapping. Why haven't we seen them?"

"We saw them last year. Maybe it got too hot and they left. Maybe they finished their work. Who knows? But it looks like they are back."

A week later David finished. They loaded the samples and camp equipment into the Niva and left for Sharm el Sheikh. None of them noticed the man lying prone on a small rise to the north, peering through binoculars. He had been there on and off for several days.

They spent the next couple days in Sharm, where they regrouped, relaxed, and shed unwanted materials before making the seven-hour drive to Cairo. There were people at the Movenpick hotel from across the world, but Li saw no Russians. According to the bartender, Russians were scarce in Sharm, but he thought there might be a couple of them at the resort for diving. When Li left for Cairo two days later, he had still not seen them.

#

Roman Novikov was in his room at the Sinai Star during Li's stay at the Movenpick. The Sinai Star was a dump and Novikov knew that Li would never come near the place. He and his aging assistant Gregori looked like typical Russian men, and they had been very careful to avoid Li and his Bedouin. The Star had been his base for the past couple of weeks as they did reconnaissance in the desert, kept an eye on Li, and tossed Li's camp, looking for geologic reports or other information on what he was finding. The only thing they learned was that he seemed to be mapping a very large area. They picked up no evidence as to anything he found. His bagged rock samples seemed to be of every rock around the area. Gregori had just returned from the desert.

"I saw them pack up everything boss. Then I waited until they drove off and went down to the campsite. There was nothing left. What do we do next?"

Gregori poured himself a vodka and collapsed into a nearby chair, listening to Novikov's reply.

"Now that Li has packed up his stuff, we wait until he leaves Sharm and then go back out to the field. Look again for anything we might have missed. Maybe something they left behind. Do a bit more geology and see if we can determine where to put the drill rig."

"Do you think we have enough information to drill?"

Gregori was a geologist as well, was older than Novikov, and had spent more than twenty-five years exploring for precious metals, albeit entirely in Siberia. He was amazed at how visible the rocks were in the desert and was fairly certain they had not yet encountered enough evidence of turquoise to merit spending money on a drilling program."

"We'll put a report together and present it to Boris. He'll make the decision," said Novikov.

The two men packed their Montero with the equipment needed for several days, including tents, food, water, maps, and geologic tools. In the afternoon prior to their departure, they walked to the Sinai Star's beach, which was nowhere near as nice as the Movenpick's. They drank the Stella beers they had brought, but had no chairs, no towels, and worst of all no women in bikinis to watch. The next day they drove to the field and set up camp on the spot David Li had just vacated.

The first day they spent within the area of their mining claims, revisiting sites where they had originally found cupriferous sandstone in the Cambrian-aged Serabit el Khadim Formation. Those rocks had been mined in ancient times for copper and malachite, but Novikov had not done much research on the extent of mining. The next three days, they wandered outside of their claims and found no evidence of turquoise, copper, or anything else. On the fourth and final day, as they were having lunch and deciding where to expend their remaining energy, a Niva approached them. When it stopped next to their own vehicle, two men got out and walked to them, waving and greeting them in Arabic.

"*Salaam aleikum,*" said the pale, Western-looking, jolly man, while the darker skinned Arabic man clothed in robes stood silent.

"Hello," replied Novikov. "Join us for lunch?"

"You speak English," replied the studious looking, slightly built Dr. Harold Jones.

"I do," answered Novikov.

Dr. Jones declined lunch, but did sit for drinks. Novikov learned that Jones was an Egyptologist from the University of Chicago doing field research in the southern Sinai. His area of expertise was Pharaonic three-dimensional art, which basically meant masks, jewelry, sarcophagi, and the like. He was the scholar sought out to describe and explain a recent find in the Valley of the Kings, and was one of the experts called on to help organize, describe, and put together a show of King Tut artifacts for the Egyptian Museum. Novikov looked at Jones with humor, dressed as he was in khaki shorts and shirt, pith helmet, fly whisk hanging from his belt, leather satchel around his neck, and leather notebook by his side. Even his accent fit the stereotypical cartoon of an archeologist. Jones was an extrovert and felt the need to impress his new Russian friends, going into great depth on his background.

"We're from the Oriental Institute at the University of Chicago," said Jones, using the royal 'we'. "The Institute began in 1919 with funds from John D. Rockefeller, Jr. Its mission is to document human development in the Near Middle East, and our collection of Egyptian artifacts in Chicago is second in renown only to that of the British Museum. Well, of course the Egyptian Museum has the largest collection, but they can't find anything and really don't know what they have. In any case, I've been with the Institute fifteen years and have chosen two desert regions as my focus. Most materials used in artifact construction came from either the far Western Desert or the Sinai. Up till now, I've been working largely near the border with Libya. Last year I turned my focus to the Sinai. You have to be careful in both places because of all the lingering land mines and unexploded arms. That's why I always have a local guide, like Mahmoud here."

Novikov had still not told Dr. Jones what he was doing here but the man seemed more interested in his own story than the Russians'.

"What materials are you talking about?" asked Novikov.

"Well, all the metals of course, like gold and silver. Along with semi-precious stones like amethyst, topaz, malachite, and turquoise. Even pigments and dyes for coloring. Most of what they used was sourced within Egypt. There was trade of course but not so much for these materials."

"So you're out here looking for old mines?"

"That's a small part of what we do, yes. I first visit all the known Pharaonic sites, photograph what has not yet been documented, and put together a picture of internal sourcing and trade of materials. With many artifacts you can identify what area the raw materials came from, sometimes even the specific mine or location."

"Do you know of any turquoise mining in this area?"

"Ah, is that what you're doing here Mr. Novikov?"

"It is. We are geologists and we are looking for turquoise."

"I think you might be on to something, sir. I remember in my initial literature work on this area there were turquoise sources. I can't recall exactly where, but I could do some work for you."

"You mean as a consultant? Do you hire out your services?"

"I can, in a limited scope. We're always looking for funding of course. If your goal fits into ours, then we can provide a fee-based service to you as long as it doesn't impact or hinder our own research goals."

They discussed the issue further, or rather Novikov largely listened to Dr. Jones. The result was they agreed that Jones would put together a report on the area within a hundred miles of where they were sitting, summarizing what was known about turquoise. Jones thought he could finish the work in four months or so. He promised it would have essentially everything that could be found in the literature, together with anything he turned up during his field work over the next two months. His graduate students in Chicago would do most of the literature searching and Dr. Jones himself would edit and approve the final report.

Novikov and Grigori drove back to the Sinai Star that night. The next day, knowing that Li had left the country, they moved to the Movenpick and spent a few days enjoying the beach, the pool, the food, the cocktails, and the women, before flying back to Moscow.

CHAPTER 14

CICI'S, as everyone called it, had a stunning setting between the hogbacks southwest of Denver. It's full name was St. Cecilia's College for Girls, founded in 1933 and offering grades K through twelve. Jake drove up the long drive that focused one's eyes on a particularly spectacular spire of red rock which he knew was part of the Fountain Formation, formed three hundred million years ago as the ancestral Rocky Mountains were uplifted. Cecilia's had an entire class for eighth graders on the Fountain, for which Mother Catherine had convinced Jake to be a guest lecturer and field trip leader. He parked in the visitor's lot and walked to the central courtyard.

"Daddy," shouted Gussie as she left her group and ran to him.

"Hi peanut. How's it going?"

"Great. Come meet my friends," she took his hand and dragged him to her pod.

They spent the afternoon together, talking with her teachers, meeting with Mother Catherine, and mainly walking the grounds chatting. School had been in session almost a month, and it seemed Gussie loved everything about it. Her rehab was complete, allowing her to join the lacrosse team. She had no lasting issues from the head injury. Because of that event however, Jake had forbidden her from playing soccer. 'No more head impacts,' he had said.

"It looked like some of your friends might be from outside the US," Jake said.

"Yeah, there's kids here from all over, daddy. Shahira is from Egypt. Her dad works in an oil field somewhere. And Andy is from Australia. His father works in Africa. They think it's cool I lived in Egypt. They're all nice."

"I'm glad you're making friends Gussie. It's important to be nice to everyone you know."

She rolled her eyes, "I know that. I'm not stupid."

Mother Catherine had suggested Jake stay for dinner in the dining hall. He almost made an excuse, but once he sat down with Gussie, was glad he accepted the offer. Seeing her interacting with her peers was rewarding, and he realized again that he had made the right decision.

#

"You've done something to your office," Jake said to Libby.

"You noticed. That's good. I wasn't sure you would. Can you put your finger on what I did?"

Jake looked around in desperation, trying to identify what was different. He was a geologist, supposedly trained in observation.

"No, I can't."

Libby laughed,

"There's yet to be one male able to say what I did to the place. Almost every woman has come out with it immediately. At least you knew something was different. I'll give you that. Say uncle?"

Jake took one last look, and gave up.

"I switched the paint on the ceilings and walls. It used to be white ceiling and light blue walls. It's now white walls and light blue ceiling. 'Non-traditional and modern', said my decorator. I think it seems to open the room up and brighten it. Oh, and the floors are new. Light oak that used to be dark. They did that just by sanding and staining – the floors themselves are the same boards. Do you like it? Think it was worth it?"

"I do like it. It looks more contemporary. You should probably get some new furniture while you're at it."

"It's on order. Next month you really won't recognize the place."

"I got some news last night from the Seth Field," said Jake. "They think someone contaminated the water tanks. Half the crew is sick with e-coli of some sort, two of them hospitalized. The government's got involved, trying to pinpoint the specific bug and trace its origin. They seem fairly certain it was intentional and not just a food or sanitation issue."

"That's awful Jake. Are they still operating?"

"Drilling has stopped until we get those guys back or find replacements."

"Did Salah call you with this?"

"He did. He's headed out to the field as we speak. When he swung by Latif's office on his way out of town, the General was aware of it already and sent guys to investigate. They don't know who's responsible yet but hopefully they'll figure it out. Meanwhile, the water systems are being cleaned and should be operational in a couple days."

"Seems this business is tough enough without having this kind of shit happening," Libby said. "What say you come up to my place tonight?"

"I was thinking of asking you over to mine."

"You're closer. Gussie in school?"

"Yep."

"Let's grab dinner on the way. I've a craving for Thai."

SEVEN faculty members showed up for David Li's interim thesis review. All faculty had an open invitation to every review, but few interim reviews attracted anyone besides the main thesis advisers. The other faculty attending Li's session came largely because this was the first time the department had worked in Egypt. They hoped it might start a trend to get more students involved in that country. There was also an interest in the topic of greenstone belts, given no one in the department was actively researching these rock packages.

The agenda called for Li to review his data, his interpretations to-date, and to get agreement on a forward plan. He had a dozen or more maps stuck on the walls, a couple dozen or more tables and graphs on celluloid sheets which he showed using an overhead projector, and a table full of rocks, each with their own label. After three hours of intense presentation and back-and-forth discussions and challenges, Li summarized the session.

"I believe there is strong evidence for a NW-SE trending greenstone belt, possibly fifteen miles long and a couple miles wide. Most of it lies unexposed beneath the desert pavement but there are enough outcrops to substantiate the formation and some evidence it will contain gold and copper. The only other deposit of interest in the mapped area is turquoise. Interestingly, it's at the far north side of the study area, well away from the existing claims posted by a Latvian company last year. By far the bulk of the mapped area is underlain by fairly homogenous granitic rocks which are of no economic consequence."

Jake knew all this before the meeting but wanted to see if the expertise in the room could add anything. Dr Hynde had the only useful input based on his work more than a decade ago on the Abitibi greenstone belt near the Quebec-Ontario border. Since much of that belt lay beneath glacial sediments, remote geophysical and geochemical techniques were useful in mapping its location and extent. Similar methods might prove useful in the Sinai. They would need to use remote methods to determine where potential mineralization might be found.

When the thesis review ended, several professors came to shake David Li's hand, tell him he was doing a good job, and urge him to keep it up. After everyone cleared out, Li joined Jake and Janet Robinson for a private follow-on session in another meeting room in the department. Robinson again summarized the report she had completed on Sinai mineral potential.

"By far the most important economic extraction will be building materials, manganese, iron, some coal, and gypsum-kaolin. There are hints of cupriferous sandstones with associated malachite, silver, and uranium. And some precious and base metals, the most famous found so far being at the ancient Regetia mine which had copper contents up to 8.85%. There are also accounts of turquoise being mined. The pharaohs did like their turquoise."

"But no hints in the literature of greenstone belt rocks?" asked Jake.

"Not a mention anywhere."

"Hynde talked about using remote geophysics to see through the alluvium on the surface. What do you think Janet?"

"I would definitely run aerial gravity and magnetics, maybe ground-based gamma ray, and possibly a geochemical survey. David's got the belt roughly hemmed in. What we're looking for now is where to expect mineralization. Before you start spending money on drilling, I think you could narrow the area down a bit more. Right now it's thirty to forty square miles. It would be nice to get that down to five or so."

"OK, I'll ask Libby to cough up some dough. Janet, give me a list of work you see with an estimate of what each survey might cost. David, once I give you the go-ahead, work with Janet to contract the work this winter. I'm gonna assume you can find somebody to get in there that quick, but you'll have to hurry. This work should feed into your final report due next May. I want you to tell us then whether to pack up and go home, or where to put a coring program."

"Will do Jake. I can't spend much time in Egypt but that shouldn't be a problem. Any contractor should be able to do the work mostly on their own. I've got a lot to do here just analyzing the samples I brought back."

"You sure you're not just spooked by the Russians?"

"In reality I am a bit scared by them but that's not the reason for staying. I really do have a ton to do here."

"OK, then, get after it."

Pieces Fall Into Place

1995-1997

ROMAN Novikov was unsure how Boris Oblonsky would react when he learned that their Sinai drilling gave little hope for turquoise. Before he could mention the only remaining glimmer of hope, his boss interrupted him.

"How could this happen after the initial reports we got," asked Oblonsky, clearly irritated at the news.

"I'm not sure Boris. We never knew where those cores were drilled. A lot of what we pursued was based on what we saw in those cores, but because we lost the damn things we don't have any hard data. Maybe we were overly optimistic. Maybe they were cut somewhere else and brought to that location."

"That's a poor explanation," the Oligarch said, thumping his fist on the desk and rising. "I have spent more than I wanted, done a lot of work, and we are nowhere."

"Well there is some positive news," said Novikov, rattled by the powerful man's reaction.

"What?" barked Oblonsky.

"I got the report from that archaeologist. The one from the University of Chicago I told you about, that we hired last summer. He was supposed to finish a report for us a couple months ago, but I got it just last week. All the literature and museum research is done, and he's incorporated his first field season. Basically, two months last fall of wandering around."

"And what does the report say?" Oblonsky asked after Novikov paused.

"When I first met him last summer, Dr. Jones remembered something about turquoise deposits from his initial work, but he was not specific. The report says that the main turquoise mining area for the New Kingdom Period of Pharaonic time was a place called

Serabit al-Khadim, maybe fifty miles north of us, near Abu Zenima. The New Kingdom lasted from 1550 to 1070 BCE. Archaeological work by Sir Flinders Petrie revealed ancient mining camps and a long-lived Temple of Hathor, the Egyptian goddess who was a protector of desert regions. Apparently, most Sinai turquoise came out during this period. The mines played out way back then."

"While doing fieldwork, Dr. Jones came across a stele with readable hieroglyphics five miles north of our claims. He cannot be sure, but the stele seems to be a road sign of sorts that says there were turquoise workings within a mile or two of where it stands. He thinks that is why the thing was put there. He did not spend any time looking for the turquoise diggings but feels sure they exist based on reading the tablet. If he's right, then our claims are in the wrong area. We located them based on those cores, but the things may have come from anywhere."

Oblonsky quizzed Novikov further, then poured vodka for both of them and sat down to think. He was obsessed with precious and semi-precious gems, and did not have any mines in Egypt. He dearly wanted to supplement his import/export business to Egypt with a mining venture, if for no other reason than the tax write-offs and money laundering opportunities it could provide. It was never good policy to throw good money after bad, but the Oligarch had a weakness for pretty gems.

"I will approve one last field venture. Meet your professor in the Sinai. Find that stele and see if you can locate any sign of turquoise. If you find anything, go ahead and cut some cores. But you have a cap on spending."

Oblonsky called Marat Bragin to join them and poured another round of vodka while waiting for his Chief Accountant to show up. While waiting, Oblonsky walked across his office and picked up a necklace that was displayed on a mannequin.

"Have I ever shown you this necklace," he asked Novikov.

"No Boris. It's very beautiful."

"Yes it is. It has over a hundred carats of diamonds from the Mirny mine along with rubies and sapphires from Burma. The gold is from our Vishnuvo Mine, which also produces silver. I want to be able to create jewelry using that silver. I want it to be silver and turquoise. So Roman, you see what the missing link is here. Turquoise."

Marat Bragin joined them and Oblonsky immediately gave the man a glass of vodka, holding his own up for a toast.

"To my turquoise mine," he said knocking back the drink.

"I'm at a loss Boris," said Bragin, confused. "You don't have a turquoise mine."

The accountant looked like an accountant. Small in stature, old, bent over, reading glasses hanging from his neck by a silver chain. He had a habit of tilting his head when listening that bothered Oblonsky but he was a genius at hiding money around the world and whittling away tax liabilities in more than a dozen jurisdictions. For the last few years, Oblonsky paid him more than anyone else in his organization.

"Not yet anyway," answered his boss. "I want you to give Roman another hundred thousand US dollars and no more. Roman, use this money wisely and find me my mine. The next time we discuss this venture I want better news."

Bragin looked at Novikov, glad he was charged only with releasing the money. It seemed that delivering on that money might be difficult and he knew Oblonsky did not like to see his money used in non-productive ways. They toasted again, this time the Oligarch saying it was to their joint continued good health. He stared at Novikov while saying this, and Novikov recognized the warning. He was beginning to hate the whole idea of turquoise.

CHAPTER 17

HASSAN Barakat reentered his office with a very large binder of printed materials. He was an old man, reduced in height, stooped, with a long gray beard that did not in his case indicate a fundamentalist leaning. In fact, he had not shaved in three decades, more out of laziness than ideology or fashion. His wife died that long ago and there was no woman to keep him looking good. His clothes hung loose on his frame as if he had recently lost weight, but he had not.

"This contains what you need to file a claim," he said in Arabic.

Salah el Gindi took the binder and bowed slightly. He remembered Dr. Barakat from his days at Cairo University, where the older man was a professor when Salah did his studies. He never took a class from him but remembered students talking about his classes, which were usually easy to pass. 'The man must be in his eighties,' thought Salah.

"*Shukran, habibi,*" said Salah. "I must ask you about some of your mementos."

While he was waiting for Dr. Barakat to return, El Gindi had perused the trinkets, photos, and memorabilia in his office. There were many trophy-like objects and knickknacks, but he pointed first to a photograph prominently displayed above the credenza.

"Ah," said Barakat. "Gamal Abdel Nassar was a good friend of mine. When I graduated from Alexandria University in 1941, the army got me and sent me to Sudan. You know that the University then was called Farouk University. Anyway, Gamal was my lieutenant in Khartoum. We overlapped only a short time but became friends; he was a few years older than me and served as a mentor of sorts. After Sudan, he got involved with politics and some ten years later played a role in the revolution. In 1956, he gave a rousing speech on nationalizing the Suez Canal and rode a wave of popularity to become Egypt's president. This photo of us was taken the day after he assumed that role. I have to say he did not seek the presidency, it just happened. Soon after, I got a job in the Mineral Resources Authority thanks to Gamal. Friends are important to one's progress in life, are they not? In any case, I enjoyed my new job and I have never left the department."

"I bet you've seen a lot, my friend. You have things here from everywhere. Many countries. Many companies. Including this," Salah pointed to a matryoshka doll.

"A recent addition," Barakat said eyeing Salah inquisitively. "What attracts you to this trinket out of all the others?"

Salah looked at the old man and smiled, letting a small amount of time pass for emphasis. Barakat did not say anything but waited for el Gindi to answer.

"We plan to file mining claims in the Sinai, Dr. Barakat. I understand that Russians have recently done the same. We have not seen a lot of Russian involvement in the oil or mineral industries in Egypt so this doll stood out to me."

"You know I can't divulge details on ongoing matters. If this was something I acquired a long time ago it would be different. It would be unethical for me to link this gift to anything we've been discussing, for example your Sinai area. Or to tell you that the Oligarch involved is a frequent visitor to our country and has numerous business ventures already in our country. I could not say that, legally or ethically."

"What can you tell me about the claims just filed?"

"I can tell you that the claims mention turquoise, which is publicly available information. It says that right on the claim which is available for anyone to see. As to the matter of the matryoshka, I believe this particular doll is nothing special. It is something one might buy cheaply at a market, to give to one's niece. In matters of state visits, one should always give gifts of value if one is going to play that game at all."

"Do you think we need to file our claims with urgency, or can we do our work first without worrying about competition?"

"We don't know each other well Mr. el Gindi, but we have mutual friends who have known us both a long time. I took the opportunity before you came to seek counsel from some of these friends. You are a respected member of our community and I think we will have a fruitful relationship going forward, for the betterment of Egypt. If I learn of any more activity in that area, I will call you for tea. My job is to help Egypt best develop its resources. Experience tells me it is not with Russians."

Barakat shifted topics and talked about the position of the government and the people towards foreign development. It was his opinion that the average Cairene wanted development of Egypt's natural resources. They might be uneducated, but generally thought that foreign companies made things happen that would not happen if only Egyptians were involved. A different, more naïve view, led to the growth of NOFORTH, a group which Barakat knew worked in opposition to his department's goals. He said for now the government was ignoring NOFORTH, but the time was coming when they would need to be more proactive in reigning in the group. At the end of his hour-long appointment, Salah stood and offered his hand to the head of the Geologic Survey.

"Thank you so much for meeting me Dr. Barakat. It is reassuring to know the future of our great nation is in the hands of men like yourself. I look forward to our next meeting. By the grace of God I hope my company can be successful and open a gold mine in the Sinai. It would provide many jobs and much foreign capital to Egypt."

"I hope you are right. Please let me know what you need next."

Salah el Gindi left the building with a smile on his face.

GEOPHYSICAL Surveys Inc. (GSI) had spent the past three months conducting programs over the GusCo claims. They had no problems acquiring the airborne surveys, which included a gravity study and a magnetic study. The former was acquired by mounting a gravity gradiometer on a fixed wing single-engine plane and flying a grid pattern at an altitude of five hundred feet above ground. When processed, the data revealed the density in the subsurface, allowing geologists to infer rock types. In the case of this particular survey, Jake hoped it could indicate areas where mineralization was present. The aeromagnetic data was acquired at the same time by dragging a magnetometer behind the airplane and recording data in the same grid pattern. Once the data was corrected by subtracting the effects of solar, regional, and aircraft interference from the total magnetic signature, a geologist could map the relative abundance of magnetic minerals, largely magnetite, in the subsurface. Aerial magnetic surveys were most useful in finding and mapping iron deposits, but were also used for other purposes. Magnetite was present in many rocks and the concentration of this mineral varied from formation to formation. In the case of the Sinai area, magnetite was more prevalent in the greenstone belt facies.

More problematic for GSI had been the acquisition of the land-based survey. The initial problem had to do with ordinance clearance. While not as prevalent here as in the Western Desert, unexploded bombs and land mines were not unknown. Before they laid out equipment on the ground, they needed to clear safe paths, a manpower-intensive process using handheld metal detectors. This activity accounted for two-thirds of the time and half of the money for any ground survey.

In the planning phase, Janet Robinson had decided not to run any geochemical surveys, believing that the alluvium at the surface shifted

around too often with water and wind to accurately predict where
they would find anything in the subsurface. She did recommend an
induced polarization (IP) survey to paint a picture of the electrical
properties of the rocks beneath the surface. To implement this, an
electrical pulse is sent into the ground via electrodes and instruments
measure the slow decay of this voltage in the ground after the current
is switched off. It is one of the most common geophysical techniques
used to delineate buried ore bodies. During the acquisition of the
Sinai survey, GSI had equipment problems along with staffing
issues. As a result the survey took twice as long as planned.

David Li had visited the Sinai operations only once in those three
months, flying into Egypt at the end of the acquisition phase to
meet the GSI representative responsible for the surveys. Li had a
choice of meeting either in Egypt or in Norway, where GSI was
based. He chose Egypt so he could meet Salah and do anything else
he needed to do. They met at the Semiramis Hotel in Cairo with
Salah el Gindi present.

"We are done," began Arvid Eriksen, the tall, slender, blond,
Norwegian operations manager with GSI.

"Did you get all your equipment out of the country?" asked el
Gindi.

"Yah, the plane is off to its next assignment in Tunisia. I fly to
Norway today to supervise the processing of your data. We had no
unexpected problems except with the IP. We had equipment failures
and getting replacement parts into Egypt was a nightmare, but we
did it. We also had problems with the local staff. It was Ramadan
and some of them just left in the middle. No warning, they just
didn't show up one morning. I guess the daily fasting and nightly
partying took a toll. We had to get people from a survey we were
doing in India. But it's done now. I'm satisfied. The data is good and
you'll have your reports within a month."

"Can you tell anything at this point?" asked Li.

Arvid appeared irritated. He was a no-nonsense Scandinavian. If
there was anything else he would have told Li.

"Not really, no. You can't tell much from the raw data. It's all over
the place, being acquired one line at a time in a somewhat random

order. It needs to be processed. I did notice that the values are not all the same, so it looks like you have variability in the rocks. This might mean you will see what you want. We just need to put all the data where it belongs in three dimensions and see what comes out."

They finished lunch and bid Arvid farewell, as he started to the airport.

"What else is happening Salah?" asked David.

"My friend in our Egyptian State Department tells me Russians have been in Sharm el Sheikh again. It is likely our friends with the claim. Do you think I should get Mohammed and head there in case something is happening?"

"I can't answer that Salah. You should check with Jake."

"Ok. I'll do that. *Insha'Allah* everything will be fine."

"*Insha'Allah,*" replied Li.

CHAPTER 19

EGYPTOLOGIST Dr. Harold Jones landed in Cairo on the British Airways night arrival from London, having started his journey in Chicago a day before. He went straight to his downtown hotel and crashed. The next morning, he met Roman Novikov for breakfast before they loaded the Montero for a six-hour drive to the field area. Jones would be in the field for four weeks so had several bags and foot lockers with him. The road down the western side of the Sinai was paved but treacherous. It was two lanes wide, with no markings, no shoulder, and seemed to transition seamlessly into the desert. In fact, in some places after a flash flood, desert covered the pavement which could not be discerned. The road was generally straight, sometimes for tens of miles, inviting drivers to lose track and underestimate their speed.

The intense, sullen Russian drove the SUV a hundred miles per hour as his passenger looked on helplessly, grasping his arm rest. Every five or ten miles was a large pothole or series of them, eager to snag a tire. Less frequently, there were rock cairns, small pyramids of bread loaf-sized boulders that drivers built behind broken-down vehicles so cars would not plow into them. Many times the drivers were lazy or careless and left the cairns on the road when the truck was fixed and drove away. It was easy to run into these cairns, which could be fatal when driving a hundred miles per hour.

In spite of the danger they reached their destination in late afternoon. Novikov had started their field program the week before so they had tents to stay in and supplies to sustain them. They spent the rest of the day drinking vodka and reviewing Jones' report and information he had since gained. Before retiring, they laid out plans for the next day, beginning with a visit to the stele that mentioned turquoise.

#

Novikov watched as Dr. Jones traced his finger down the columns of hieroglyphics etched into the stone tablet jutting four feet out of the ground. Some of the detail had been eradicated by sand and wind, and it appeared some of the writing might be underground, as sand had piled up around the base of the stele. Most of what Jones read was tedious detail about important people but he finally came to the part which interested Novikov.

"Queen Hatshepsut, fifth pharaoh of the Eighteenth Dynasty of Egypt, daughter of King Thutmose 1, favored turquoise from near Wadi Sidri and other wadis near this stele, within ten thousand cubits. The color of this gem is bright and the quality is good."

"You can really read all that from the stone?" the suspicious Russian asked, obviously skeptical.

"It's what I do Mr. Novikov. It's like any language, I imagine not much different than learning Chinese which is also character-based. No one could understand hieroglyphics until Napoleon's army found the Rosetta Stone in 1799. That tablet has an inscribed decree, which is not very unusual. What is unique is that the decree was repeated three times, in hieroglyphics, in Demotic or ancient Egyptian script, and in ancient Greek. Since people could read those other two languages, it was possible to decipher the hieroglyphics. I studied for years to be able to do what you've just seen me do. I won't say I'm giving you a precise translation but for your needs it's a good one."

"So what's a cubit?" asked Novikov.

"Ancient Egypt measured distance in anthropomorphic terms. The cubit, from your fingertip to elbow, was the most common. Of course people differ, but better standardization was apparently unachievable. How they built the pyramids with measures like the cubit astonishes me. Ten thousand cubits, mentioned on this stele, is just over five kilometers. I assume they put this stele in the middle of their area, so you might find your turquoise three or so miles in any direction from here."

"There is no more detail on the stone?" asked Novikov.

"I'm afraid not. That's it. But it's unusual to find such writing on a stele. Normally they are basically gravestones. You are very lucky we found this and it's so legible.'"

Novikov and his assistant Grigori took photographs of the stele before they all returned to camp. Grigori drove Dr. Jones to Sharm from where he would return to Cairo while Novikov put together a reconnaissance plan for the next couple days.

In the course of two days, they found small pieces of turquoise-bearing rock on the surface in their area of interest, but it was 'float' which had been moved around by water. They could not tell from where it originated.

"Clearly," said Novikov to Grigori, "our claims are not in the right area. The turquoise must be somewhere near that damn tablet. We'll put together a drilling program around that area and see what we find."

"That seems like shooting in the dark," replied Grigori. "How are you going to explain it to the boss?"

"I'll tell him about the tablet, what Jones read, and show him the pieces we found. Tell him the only way to confirm a valuable deposit is to drill. We'll drill shallow core holes, maybe fifty feet each, and hope we intersect something good."

Novikov had contracted a rig and crew already, due to show up and start drilling within the week. He and Grigori would wait in Sharm for their arrival. The program would be short and would be completed before the end of April. Meanwhile several days on the beach were not a burden.

"CONGRATULATIONS David," said Dr. Hynde, patting David Li on the back after the grueling four-hour thesis defense. "That was very well done. The committee will meet tomorrow to discuss the review and render our verdict. I'm fairly sure you have the support of all members but sometimes there are unresolved issues in someone's mind. In the event you pass, I'll host a gathering at the Missoula Club tomorrow night. I'll let you know before noon tomorrow. Invite whoever you want. Of course it'll be an open invite to the whole department."

Li was happy the defense was over and wished he could celebrate for real tonight. Waiting a day would be stressful. Fortunately, Jake arranged for them to have dinner tonight to take his mind off the waiting. Jake had said nothing during the defense but stayed for the whole thing.

"Thanks Dr. Hynde," said Li. "And thanks again for your help with the project."

"I wanted to ask you more about the geophysical work," said Hynde. "I think you did a good job in the defense summarizing the results, but one thing bothered me. I'm sorry I had to leave at that point, but when I returned you'd moved on. I need more detail on those surveys."

"Sure. On what aspect?"

"The airborne gravity documented a good solid body where you think the belt is. The aeromag supported that. But the Induced Polarization survey was offset. What do you make of that?"

"The IP data broke out into five different response signatures, as I said earlier. The signature that coincided with the conglomerate has high resistivity and high chargeability. Greenstones schists that make up the bigger part of the belt have only moderate resistivities and chargeability. Both of these facies look similar on the airborne surveys. So the IP is what really differentiates the ore body from the bulk of the host rock. At least that's how I interpret it."

"Did you find any analogies to support that?"

"Yeah, the Gwanda greenstone belt in Zimbabwe has a lot of published exploration work. There's one deposit in particular that looks similar. It's a whopper of a mine. I dream we find something half as rich as that one."

Dr. Hynde was satisfied with the way Li answered his questions, and David was happy he could provide the answers. He hoped this additional information might help him pass his defense.

"Do you know what you'll do after graduation?" asked Hynde.

"Not yet but I want to get on with a mining company," replied Li. "Either production or exploration work, I don't care. I'd considered going for a PhD and doing research or teaching, but truthfully I've enjoyed having an expense account and being involved with real life work."

"Well I can understand that. Good luck David. You'll do well at anything you pursue. I hope you find the kind of position you want. Stop by my office tomorrow just before noon. I should have the results."

#

Murray's Steakhouse was the nicest restaurant in Missoula; David had never eaten there. Jake ordered an expensive Zinfandel from Paso Robles and toasted Li before they even looked at the menu.

"That was a smooth defense David. You answered everyone's concerns and put forth your case for a greenstone belt expertly."

Jake appeared relaxed, enjoying his wine as he conveyed the compliment.

"But I'm still not positive it's there," said David. "I'm not sure I've got the dimensions right and am not sure about the mineralization. It's a bit nerve wracking to think that your company will spend that much money when I feel this uncertain."

"Yeah well that's exploration. The remote sensing worked out well. You got lots of encouraging information and I think the deposit is better defined than you think. You identified the most likely spot and that's where we'll drill."

Jake and Libby had kept up with Li's work and were sufficiently satisfied with the results that they agreed the week before to go forward with a drilling project.

"You really feel comfortable doing that," asked Li, still amazed at the confidence they placed in him. It was quite a transition to go from student to professional.

"Yes. Especially with you doing the oversight. Libby and I would like you to work for GusCo. Full time, starting next month, running our Egypt operation."

Jake slid several papers across the table towards Li.

"Here is the official offer letter with employment terms and conditions. Take them home tonight and if you have questions call me. Or tomorrow morning you can call our HR person Judy Winland. Her number's in there. If you want the job sign the paperwork and give it back to me tomorrow."

The young man was speechless. He had hoped for this but didn't think it would happen so soon.

"We want the coring program to start in the third quarter," said Jake. "It will be a challenge to make it happen that fast, but I want results by the end of the year. If you come on board you'll start immediately and be very busy. I guarantee at times you'll be frustrated and might dread my calls."

Jake smiled at the stunned kid, saying "Now let's order."

The salad bar was extensive, the steaks excellent, and the conversation good. Jake was good at pulling information out of people and most of the conversation during dinner revolved around Li's upbringing and family. His father, who was involved in high level Chinese politics, had to flee China during the political shift but kept many contacts both on the mainland and in Taiwan.

David had traveled to Asia several times since leaving as a boy, and had met many of his dad's business partners. He retained fluency in Mandarin, bolstered by a minor in Chinese during his undergraduate days at Stanford. Li's father built several successful businesses in California with links to Asia but had never been back to mainland China, concerned that he might not be allowed to leave. David wondered if his father's fear grew out of some involvement with espionage. Not that he thought his father was a spy but rather he had something to do with intellectual property issues. David knew his father had been visited by the FBI and other US officials. Partly because of this, David had chosen not to work for his father but to set off on his own.

Jake tried to imagine how Li's connections might help GusCo in the future. He came up short, given their current business focus had nothing to do with Asia. But he thought you never knew, maybe GusCo would be involved in Asia one day.

OCTOBER was Jake's favorite time in the Sinai. Temperatures were reasonable and mornings could be crisp. The surrounding sea was splendid, warm, and inviting, and the sun generally had the sky to itself. This year was even better for those willing to visit. Since the recent terror attack in Cairo, tourists shunned the entire country. Jake remembered loving life in Cairo during these months-long periods when expats would tour the country, taking advantage of discounts and exploring fantastic places all to themselves. A terrorist incident was a virtual invitation to travel in-country. His group of friends increased their visits to Sharm el Sheikh during post-terrorism periods, when dive boats were rented for less than half the normal rate, hotel rooms for a third. The best part was the lack of crowds, be it on the coral-rimmed coasts of the Sinai, the white sand beaches of the Mediterranean, the archaeological sites of Upper Egypt, or cruise ships on the Nile. Another advantage was the appreciation locals showed for having your business. Normally cheerful and laughing Egyptians were even more anxious to interact with travelers.

Jake looked down as his plane made its final approach into Sharm el Sheikh. He had chosen the window seat on the starboard side just for this last two minutes of the flight. Below him slightly off to the right was the beach at Ras Nasrani. When Jake lived in Egypt, one of his favorite dive locations was right there, in the Gulf of Aqaba next to the airport. The Gulf was a sliver of water a hundred miles long, fifteen miles wide at its widest point, and reaching a depth of over six thousand feet. He remembered expat friends packing picnics and laying out blankets on the sand, some of the moms staying with younger children, while most of the group donned their gear, walked thirty yards over reef terrace, and plunged off the edge of the living reef. Most would blow their buoyancy compensating vests and sink down to eighty or so feet, while others were satisfied snorkeling on the surface. Once, just as they all got in the water, three hammerhead sharks cruised past thirty feet below. Even the snorkelers felt up close and personal with these menacing-looking creatures and talked about it for years. As he saw the runway appear beneath him, he could still see shallow reef table to the east, and the deep blue beyond.

From the airport they drove into Na'ama Bay for lunch at Jake's favorite food shack. It was not fancy, was not on the beach, and was randomly closed whenever the owner did not feel like opening. It featured a dirt floor, battered old mismatched wooden chairs and tables, and the best fried calamari and shrimp on the planet. It had been Gussie's favorite place to eat.

David Li wondered about Jake's pick when they pulled up to the food shack. It did not look like anywhere he would eat in a third world country. He was generally careful to avoid all risks of parasites and stomach issues when eating, nevertheless he followed Jake to a table and sat down. Pigeons walked on the dirt near his feet and the young boy who brought glasses of water did not wear shoes.

"Did you get the drill pipe unstuck?" asked Jake sipping on a lemon mint drink; no alcoholic beverages were served here.

As expected from the beginning, the Egyptian drilling crew had been less than perfect in carrying out operations. The drilling campaign had suffered one setback after another, this latest being a two-hundred-foot-long pipe getting stuck in the hole. The pipe itself was expendable, but the diamond-studded bit on the end was expensive. If they could not pull it out in a couple days, they would have to leave it there and suffer the financial loss. The worst part of this incident was that the hole needed to go another hundred feet to fully evaluate the formation. If they could not get the pipe out and continue drilling, they would have to redrill another hole through the same rock before they cut new rock. Time and materials meant money lost.

"We recovered it all this morning," Li answered. "We got a company man from the bit outfit and he sorted it. That was really fascinating to watch. He called it 'fishing' and he just Gerry-rigged a tool to get it out. Built the thing on-site. I've never seen that in any textbook."

Their food arrived, and David paused for a bit before continuing, a bit uncomfortable with what he was about to say.

"Jake, I know this local crew was cheap, but they've really been a screw-up. I don't think they're competent. I can't imagine how much money they've cost you because of all the problems they themselves caused."

"Yeah, well. There's other reasons to use locals. You have to consider the politics and the optics. We are guests in a strange land here and need to give back when we can. It's about goodwill. So what's the timing of the operation?"

"We should wrap up the acquisition program mid-month. It'll end up being just over two months, a couple weeks over schedule. We'll shut down the rig, pack up camp, clean everything out, box the cores, vacate the site, and be out by the first."

"You've seen all the cores so far. What do you think?"

Jake got weekly reports of course, but Li was under strict orders to not include anything interpretive. The reports contained stuff like feet cut, percent core recovered, and other fairly dry operational information. After Jake's experience years before with faxes being intercepted, he did not want anyone hearing about what they were finding. At least the drill site was remote, and the drilling crew did not go to bars every night. In Jake's experience, that was how most leaks occurred during exploration efforts.

"We've got our greenschist facies," Li said, looking around to make sure there were no westerners within earshot. In fact there were no westerners around at all. "It looks great, with loads of mineralization. Better than what I remember seeing at the Bessie T."

Jake smiled and pulled on his mustache, experiencing a feeling of déjà vu. In his quest for gas several years earlier, he had the same moment when coloring a mud log with his daughter. That 'aha' moment when you know you found something worthwhile. It was not about the money and profit at that point, it was about the discovery. Finding an oil or gas well was rewarding but your average geologist could find dozens or even hundreds of productive wells in a career. Finding an economic mine was much rarer; only one out of ten economic geologists find something worth developing in their whole lifetime. It was one reason Jake did not pursue mining exploration. He smiled and thought of Libby, without whom he would not have gone down this path. Then he thought of Gussie, and what this could mean for her.

"I can't wait to see the cores tomorrow," Jake said. "Let's check into the hotel and enjoy an afternoon dive."

David Li had taken only a few days off work during his time in Egypt, but did treat himself to one weekend in Sharm, when he hired an instructor to teach him to dive. It was another bonus of this opportunity that he never imagined.

#

The Galabeya II dive boat hovered over the two men as they neared the end of their dive. Captain Abdou had insisted they see the reef within Ras Mohammed National Park, a marine preserve off the southern tip of the Peninsula, where over a thousand species of fish had been catalogued. The name literally meant 'Mohammed's Head', a reference to the headland which looked like a bearded man. Abdou had also insisted that Jake take a spear gun down with him, even though such guns were illegal in Egypt, and even though they were in a National Park that strictly prohibited fishing of any kind. Abdou's rationale was that he had been coming to this area with his boat since before the National Park was created. Jake considered his explanation before taking the spear gun down, concluding that Abdou's rationale was not bad. As the pair ascended to the boat, careful to not rise faster than the smallest bubbles, Jake trailed a stringer with several snapper and a big grouper.

Abdou was happy as he helped the men on board, after first taking the spear gun and then the stringer aboard.

"Nice grouper," he said before going below deck to put the gun back in its hiding spot. He was willing to break the law but he was not stupid. After coming back out of the cabin, he tended to the fish, gutting them and putting them in the ice box.

"Abdou, I think the Movenpick can fix the grouper for us tonight," said Jake. "Do you want the snappers?"

"Oh yes. *Shukran.* My wife is an excellent cook. Maybe instead of the hotel you can come over my house and eat with us?"

"Thanks Abdou. That's kind of you. But we plan to leave early in the morning. I fear if we come to your place we'll stay too late. Besides I would not burden your wife with unexpected guests."

"But you are always welcome, *habibi.* Never unexpected. It is never a problem."

"Next time I promise. Maybe we can catch a tuna. Then your wife can cook it for us."

"*Insha'Allah,*" Abdou said. "We will get calamari as well."

#

Their drive out to the field camp in the morning was easy. Another sunny day. Almost no one on the road. A quick pass through both checkpoints. After greeting Mohammed and Abu, Jake immediately went to look at the core. David Li watched as Jake took his hand lens, similar to what jewelers used, and went down core after core. He smiled when he was done, obviously pleased with the cores. All the rocks he expected in a greenstone facies were represented, and as Li said, there was a lot of mineralization. He could not see any gold with his naked eye or even with his loop, but saw other minerals that occurred with gold. Mohammed watched Jake, and after a while offered him tea.

"Is it good?" Mohammed asked.

Another bout of déjà vu hit Jake. Years ago when Mohammed gave Jake a box of old mud logs from an abandoned trailer, he did not want to take them, and actually planned to throw them away. Mohammed insisted he take them home. When Gussie started coloring them, he let her keep several that he had not yet thrown away. When her coloring highlighted gas shows in an old well, he got excited. Jake told Mohammed about the logs, and predicted big changes to his tribal area. A major gas field would bring intrusive development to that timeless land, potentially displacing natives, infusing money that altered local values and lifestyles, and heaping impacts on a fragile desert environment. As the Seth Field now underwent development, all this had started, yet Mohammed never complained. Jake thought he himself was more troubled by the changes than Mohammed. When the Bedouin first showed the core pile to Jake and said, 'I thought you might know what these mean', he likely knew the risk. Mohammed was a very wise man.

"It is Mohammed. It's good. Very good. I think we'll have a gold mine here my friend. I owe you once again."

"It is nothing habibi. *Insha'Allah* it will be easier than last time."

With that Mohammed lifted the tea pot off the fire and filled their cups.

"**WELL** smack my ass and call me Sally," said Libby.

"OK, that's an odd expression," said Jake, laughing out loud.

"Got it from my aunt down in Florida. Pimple Creek area. Seemed to fit the moment."

She had met Jake at El Chapultepec, a dive jazz bar in a somewhat shady part of downtown. Libby loved the place, which had served green chile and jazz since 1933. It was a Denver institution. Libby insisted on ordering green chili and Pabst Blue Ribbons for both of them. This was the only place she would drink a PBR. It was that kind of place. It was also the kind of place where no one would listen while they talked about their core analysis results.

Those results came back the week before and they were stellar. Since Jake was running the project as COO, he got them first, immediately got excited, and faxed them to Libby. She had more experience with mining; when she looked at the numbers, she immediately called her Chief Geologist. Robinson took a quick look, smiled, stood up in Libby's office, walked to the credenza, and poured them both a bourbon. She had said 'congratulations' as she held up her glass to toast.

"So Janet thinks the numbers are good, huh?"

"She thinks they're really good. She spent some time putting together a plan for the next phase. We need ten million bucks, give or take. It's time to find funding."

"You have anyone in mind Libby?"

"I'll try my normal sources. A couple investors, a couple banks. Folks that made plenty of money from my other ventures. I'll get with them this week and see who's interested. Maybe we can generate a bidding war. In the meantime, why don't you do the same. Go see if your St. Louis guys are up for it. If we go through phase two and it still looks good, we'll need closer to a hundred million to start-up."

They talked through dinner while listening to light jazz emanating from a sax player who appeared to be a hundred years old. Libby ordered more beer, jalapeno poppers, and another green chile for each of them. Jake did not understand how she ate like this and managed to stay in such good shape. His mind drifted off, thinking about her shape, her body, and what they might be doing two hours from now.

That night Jake did not go to his condo, instead heading up the mountain to Genesee with Libby. Gussie had spent Christmas with Jake on the ranch in Montana, and then New Year's with him and Libby at his condo in Denver. For that week in Denver, the three of them did lots of things together, like, skiing, ice skating, and some museums. Just yesterday Jake had dropped Gussie off at Cici's for the start of winter term.

When they got to Genesee, they barely made it through the front door before Jake grasped Libby and passionately kissed her. Libby met his intensity with her own pent-up emotion, assisting Jake as he began removing her clothes. She was adept in guiding his hand to where she wanted it. They moved through the house, aimlessly guided only by the intensity of their desire for one another. Somehow their random path led to her bed where they made love, expressing their growing level of intimacy. Their hands were the instruments they employed to map not the earth, but one another's bodies, searching out erogenous zones rather than oil or gold.

After cooling down, they migrated to the hot tub with a bottle of wine. It was a clear night and the Quadrantid meteor shower was peaking. They saw a half dozen shooting stars, and maybe a satellite or two.

"What do you want out of life Jake," asked Libby.

"That's a large question," he replied. "Since you're asking, you must have been thinking about it. You go first."

"Health and happiness," Libby said.

"Health is always good," said Jake. "But what does happiness mean? For you?"

"I suppose living a life of purpose. Having friends, a job that contributes to society, a loving partner, kids. The normal stuff that everyone wants."

"That's a good list Libby. I've had all that and it made me happy. I have most of that now. It's when one of those key elements is missing that life goes unbalanced."

"Life throws curve balls Jake. You have to stay in the game."

"Easy to say."

"So what do you contribute to society?" she asked.

"Energy. I think our business is much maligned, and unfairly so. Virtually everyone uses our products without much thought to how it all happens. I'm including heat / light / cooling to plastics to fertilizer. Hell they even make vodka out of ethanol cracked from petroleum. Modern society hates us but can't do much of anything without our products. I feel proud to have participated in raising the standard of living of the world. Does that sound corny?"

"Not to me. I'm in exactly the same place. Except I can say I supply metals and minerals as well. Nobody's cell phone could work without tellurium, lithium, cobalt, and a host of rare earths metals. I've got a rare earths mine. Not many people can say that. We make the world a better place my man."

"And get heaps of shit for doing it," said Jake.

They talked into the night, sharing childhood experiences, reliving harrowing geologic adventures, and remembering friends from the past.

#

Two weeks later, they met in Libby's office. Peter Owens, Chief Negotiator for Pimple Creek, was present as was Janet Robinson. Owens had been with Libby for two-thirds of Pimple Creek's existence, cutting his teeth on the Bessie T acquisition. A product of California, he earned a history degree from the University of California at Berkeley before spending three years in Mali with the Peace Corps, then getting an MBA from the Wharton Business School in Pennsylvania. He was opposite sides of the same coin, exhibiting characteristics of a flower child from the sixties while also being an ardent capitalist. While he looked professional when he was on the road, in the office he wore Reyn Spooner Aloha shirts every day, even in January. Today's shirt featured large leaves in blue and aquamarine. Somehow, he always managed to sport a deep tan.

"None of my prior sources want in," said Libby. "Too risky, too third world, too immature, you name it. I heard every excuse. I can't believe it, but I can't seem to hitch up any of them."

"Same here," said Jake. "I thought the Wintham group in St. Louis would bite, but they're happy with their interest in the Seth Field. They're not willing to increase exposure in the Middle East. Charles Lister gave me the name of another Dartmouth classmate who's funding stuff, so I flew to Florida to chat. He's Jewish and apparently deathly afraid of the Middle East and Arabs in general. He didn't know anyone else to approach."

"So we've exhausted everyone we know?" asked Owens.

"Pretty much yeah," replied Libby.

"What do we do next?" asked Jake. He knew that Libby and her negotiator had more experience raising money than he did.

"As for funding, we sleep on it," said Libby, exasperated. "It's gonna be more challenging, but we'll get there. As for something more concrete, I think you should go ahead and file claims. Get with David and figure out where we put them. Expedite this. I'll foot the bill. Shouldn't be much. I'll come up with someone for the next tranche of funding."

#

It was a week later, and still Libby did not sleep well, tossing and turning as she worried about funding. Perhaps she dreamt it, perhaps not, but she woke up excited by an idea. It was unorthodox but they had exhausted normal channels with no results. After her second coffee in the office, she called el Gindi in Cairo.

"Salah, you need to talk with Jake and expedite filing our claims. Let me know if you don't hear from him within a couple days. I want you to file this month. Meanwhile, I really need the name of the principal person behind the turquoise claim."

"Certainly madame. I'll do my best. The claims should be no problem. Finding the name of the other guy remains doubtful. He's still trying to remain anonymous. Is there any particular reason you want it," replied el Gindi.

"Well it's obvious that Russians are interested in the area. The Latvian thing is likely a ruse and I can't understand why they are going after turquoise out there. There are plenty of other areas in the world to find turquoise. So maybe it's not really turquoise, but something else. They have no problem spending money. Maybe I can help them spend it more wisely. I want to meet the man in charge."

"OK Libby. I'll see what I can find out. But I think you need to be careful dealing with these people."

HASSAN Barakat kept Salah el Gindi waiting for over an hour, his secretary refilling his teacup regularly. A younger woman, Amina was nice enough, but not chatty like some women he knew better at the Egyptian General Petroleum Company. El Gindi noticed that more of the women in the Egyptian Mineral Resources Authority were veiled, reflecting a growing trend in the country. It seemed the trend was more popular in younger women; most of the older ones resisted the change. Salah wondered if it was because the women themselves wanted this change or was it their husbands? Worse yet did they perceive taking the veil made it easier to find a man? In the case of Amina, Salah thought taking the veil might make her more appealing; she was short, overweight, and suffered from a permanent scowl and a prominent mole on the side of her forehead. 'She might be better off with a whole burka', he thought to himself.

Finally, a western businessman came out of Dr. Barakat's office, shutting the door behind him. Salah thought he recognized the man but could not place him. He was ushered into Barakat's office minutes later with another offer of tea.

"Salah, sorry to make you wait," said the head of Geologic Surveys.

"No problem, my friend. You seem very busy."

"It's that time of the year. New calendar. New budgets. New activities. At least this is good for Egypt if not for me. Most activity is relating to the construction industry. Incredible as it may seem, Saudi Arabia is running out of sand. At least the kind of sand they can use in construction. Their sand grains are too round. One needs angular grains for cement and they don't have any. They are importing more and more of it, and they see Egypt as a good source."

"Sand," replied el Gindi. "Who would have predicted we could export sand to Saudi Arabia."

Both men chuckled at the thought. They then politely chatted about the weather, their families, the football team, and other small-talk subjects before delving into business.

"So Salah, what can I do for you?"

"I wanted to tell you we expect to file claims in the next week or so. Will you be able to receive them and process them in a timely manner?"

"Of course. We are busy, but that will take priority as always. You didn't make the trip here to tell me that."

"No I did not. I also need a favor from you," said Salah.

"What is this favor?"

"A small thing really."

Salah picked up his teacup again before proceeding. The two men had no history, and he was taking a risk in asking, but thought it might be a way to progress their relationship. They shared a university experience and were both nationalists at heart. From their last meeting he thought Barakat might be pliable if he thought it could benefit his country. Besides, if Barakat did something for Salah el Gindi, he would own a chit, to be called in sometime in the future. At his age, getting closer to retirement, Barakat might be interested in accumulating chits.

"My company would like to contact the man who filed the Sinai claim for turquoise. I know you cannot divulge information like that, but I believe it would help both causes if we could communicate."

"You want to cooperate with this man in business?"

"Let's say we wish to accelerate development opportunities there."

Dr. Hassan Barakat studied el Gindi's face then reached for a pen and paper. He flipped through a Rolodex and copied something onto the paper.

"I'm unable to give you any person's name by law. I'm sorry but I am sworn to secrecy in this matter. In fact the company that filed the claims is from Latvia as you know. I assume you tried to track down the owner's name without luck. He does not want to be known. So there is little I can do."

Barakat pushed the piece of paper across the table towards el Gindi. It had two words on it, 'Exerco Limited'. Salah looked at the older man, who had a smile on his face, his hands folded under his chin like a teepee.

"On a different topic, you might find it interesting to look into this company. They have moved cereal and rubber from the Soviet Union to Egypt for years. Apparently the Russian owner is a personal friend of Mubarak. I have heard that not even our great leader likes the man. Nasty in business and nasty in person, according to the rumors."

"*Shukran habibi*," el Gindi picked up the paper. "Have you met the man?"

"Never. He has never before been involved in petroleum or mining. But he visits our country several times each year. He stays at the Oberoi in Cairo and the Movenpick in Sharm el Sheikh. Usually rents out blocks of rooms. Drops a lot of money."

"Any idea when he will visit again?"

"No, but I think the State Department has records of his personal jet coming and going."

Barakat glanced at his watch and stood.

"I need to prepare for my next visitor Salah. It was very good that you came by."

"You are like gold Hassan. I'll see you later this week perhaps, with our claims."

Salah knew he was now obligated to bring an envelope with the claims. A small payment to Barakat for his help. He was sure Jake would understand. The amount would be small enough to be placed somewhere in the GusCo books without raising suspicion.

Salah looked at the piece of paper again after he left the building. Exerco Ltd. Salah had never heard of it.

#

A few days later, Salah el Gindi arrived at the Mogamma, where he was shown to Mohammed Latif's office. The General was standing by the window watching a small protest below, in Tahrir Square, in favor of women's rights in Egypt. A hundred or so people, mostly young women, all of them in black, circled the square holding signs.

"Hello again Salah," Latif said as he turned around to face his visitor. As always, he wore his uniform, looking almost regal, and certainly imposing.

"Hello General," replied Salah. "How are you?"

The normal back and forth of social niceties lasted shorter with Latif than most colleagues. He was a busy man who liked getting things done. Time was a limited commodity for him.

"Does this visit relate to the American partners, and why did you not bring them?"

"I will do that when they are here next," answered Salah.

"I assume then that you have a specific request?" Latif teased.

"I do. I need to discuss my work with Jake Tillard and Libby Joyce."

"I like the gas guy and his beautiful woman."

Salah smiled while Latif remembered Libby from the desert ceremony celebrating the gas discovery. After months of working on Libby's kidnapping, he finally met her the next year, surprised to see how lovely she was, both physically and in the manner with which she dealt with people. Latif was a happily married man but felt tempted by Libby at that celebration.

"So tell me what you want?"

"A Russian named Boris Oblonsky is making a play for turquoise in the Sinai, close to where we are pursuing a gold mine. Ms. Joyce would like to contact him to make things happen more smoothly. We know Mr. Oblonsky visits Egypt from time to time in his private jet. If we knew when he was coming next it could facilitate a meeting."

Latif lit another Cleopatra from the one almost burned down in his mouth and blew out smoke rings. He knew the reputation of Boris Oblonsky and felt no allegiance to him.

"Why does Ms. Joyce not contact Oblonsky for a meeting?" he asked.

"Mr. Oblonsky does not want anyone to know he is the one looking for turquoise," answered Salah.

"Oblonsky is unsavory Salah. I don't like him. No one does. It would be better for Ms. Joyce to stay away from him. She would not like a repeat of that Montana business."

"It is difficult to tell Ms. Joyce what to do," replied Salah, eliciting chuckles from General Latif.

"Then so be it. Why do I have the feeling I will be useful to Ms. Joyce in the not-too-distant future? Let's see what we can do about Oblonsky's schedule."

Latif pressed a button on his phone and barked instructions to his assistant. When he stopped talking to her, he addressed Salah again.

"Stop by Osama Hassan's desk on your way out. He'll tell you what we have on the Russian's schedule, and make arrangements to get you any ongoing information you might need. And relay my best wishes to Ms. Joyce and Mr. Tillard."

#

Salah phoned Libby that night, late in Cairo but mid-day in Denver. He told her about his meetings with Dr. Barakat and General Latif. Libby remembered the handsome General with the mustache from the Sinai when they gathered to celebrate the gas flow from Jake's first well. Moreover, she remembered the role he played in her rescue and the praise given him by Jake. She knew he fancied her, and wondered if that swayed his decision to help them now.

"Boris Oblonsky's private jet has filed a flight plan to arrive at Sharm el Sheikh in two weeks, on February fifth," said Salah. "It is good for you that Egypt requires such advanced notification to ensure one can fly into the country. General Latif was happy to help, but said that Oblonsky is a nasty person, and you should stay away. I think he's worried about you."

"I would expect nothing less of the General," said Libby. "And I'd expect a Russian Oligarch to be unsavory. I'll be careful. Salah, please make bookings for Jake and me. One room. A suite. Nights of the third and fourth at the Mena House. The next four nights at the Movenpick in Sharm. Then back to Cairo for a couple nights. Please put together the necessary meet-and-greets, cars, drivers, and all the rest. We'll meet you on the fourth in Cairo. You don't need to come to Sharm."

"Your wish is my command, madame."

"Thank you Salah. You're the best."

Libby hung up, leaned back in her chair, and got tingles

anticipating the trip. The plan was ambitious and maybe even outrageous. She could not guarantee a positive outcome but felt the journey at least would be fun. She considered whether or not to tell Jake what she was planning, but decided it best not to. He would find out afterwards, one way or another.

Salah el Gindi hung up and poured himself a scotch. 'What does she plan to do?' he pondered. Salah agreed with Latif that Russians were never good to deal with, and wondered why so many countries and people did just that. He made a mental note to continue researching Boris Oblonsky, his cereal and rubber imports, as well as everything he was involved with in Egypt.

CHAPTER 24

GENERAL Richard A. Radisson was sitting across the conference table from the President, taking part in the weekly White House intelligence briefing. His title was 'Deputy Director of the CIA for Operations', and he did not normally attend these sessions. The Director, however, was indisposed, recovering from his second heart attack at Walter Reed Medical Center. Radisson had been approached by the previous President for consideration to the post of Director but declined, saying it was too political and he preferred the operations role. Nevertheless here he was, in the political hot seat, updating the President.

"Thanks Dick," said President Newton. "I appreciate you filling in for Neal. I've got a new request for you guys."

"What do you need, sir?"

"Ever more frequently, you guys mention the Russian 'Oligarchs'. I'm concerned by the increased power of this group. Every time that term comes up, there is nothing good associated with the group. What are you doing about them?"

"We don't have an open investigation, sir. We gather intel when it comes our way and process it through normal channels. We think there are currently less than a dozen business moguls we'd call Oligarchs. The first ones rose to prominence during Gorbachev's 'market liberalization' in the late 80's. When the Soviet Union dissolved, most state assets were in limbo. Inside deals were done with a privileged few, who became wildly rich. This decade, during Yeltsin's rule, these businessmen gained increasing political power and a vicious reenforcing loop now exists."

"I need to pay more attention to this," said the President. "Some of these guys are buying up assets here in the US, in the UK, and elsewhere. Real estate and small businesses. It reeks of money laundering and it could become an issue with national security. I want you to dig deeper, find out which ones are a threat, and recommend actions we might take to mitigate any threats."

"Are there any specific incidents which elevated this in your mind, Mr. President?"

President Newton snickered.

"Yeah there's one in particular. My wife and daughter were at our condo in Florida, which is a pretty nice place. You know, twenty-seventh floor, on the beach, classy to the point of being stuffy if you ask me. Apparently one of the penthouse units above ours was purchased by a rich Russian, who is prone to wearing Speedos at the pool. My wife says his physique doesn't support Speedos. But what bothered my wife was the very young model in the thong bathing suit that he had hanging off his arm. I know it's a silly reason to launch a CIA investigation, but I like to keep my wife happy. Let me know what you find out next week."

"Yes sir."

Dick Radisson was never one for frivolous travel but could foresee a trip to Miami in the near future.

CHAPTER 25

LIBBY stretched out in seat 1A, next to the window at the front of First Class on BA flight 400 from London Heathrow to Cairo. Jake's frequent flyer program had achieved lifetime gold status before he retired from Reacher Oil, and he was reaping some of the benefits as he pushed towards platinum. The plane was approaching the northern coast of Egypt, indeed of Africa, and about to leave the waters of the Mediterranean behind, replacing blue water below for brown desert and irrigated green space.

"That must be Alexandria," Libby pointed out her window.

Jake leaned over her and looked down at a large sprawling city. They had started their descent but were still at twenty thousand feet, from where one could see the enormous wedge-shaped splotch of green where the Nile spread out into distributary branches. Everything inside the river valley was irrigated and green, including fields of that famous Egyptian cotton loved around the world.

On the coast beneath them was a large city which she correctly identified as the second largest city in Egypt. That was soon left behind and as they got closer to Cairo and closer to the ground she saw an intense pollution cloud almost obscuring the surface below. The green area shrunk until it was a thin ribbon, limited to one or two miles on either side of the Nile, now constrained to one channel. The Boeing approached Cairo from the west, banking on final approach so Libby had a perfect view of the Giza pyramids, their tops sticking out of the brown haze. It was nearly sunset, and bright pink and orange hues dominated the sky. Jake had told her the only benefit of pollution and desert dust was beautiful sunsets.

The Mena House hotel was becoming familiar and soothing now to Libby, and she felt comfort as they drove up the ramp to the entry. The costumed doormen, hibiscus drink, warm towels this time of year instead of cold, Indian dinner, and luxurious room put them both in a good mood. Jetlag overtook them early, and they slept soundly until three in the morning when that same time zone phenomenon had them bolting up in bed with no hope of regaining sleep.

"I can't get back to sleep," said Libby.

"You've ruined any chance I had," Jake sighed. "Even though I took an Ambien, once you wake me up that's it."

"Sorry lover. Maybe I can make it up to you. I've got a good alternative plan," Libby whispered before softly kissing his neck and ear, and moving her hand downwards.

"Are you proposing what I think you're proposing," said Jake as Libby ducked under the covers and kissed another spot that got Jake's instant attention.

He let her continue until he thought he had better take control of things before it was too late. He pulled her back up and kissed her hard. Naked, she straddled him, both of them responding to her new position. He reached up and grabbed one of her breasts. She softly moaned as they made love, a hurried and passionate act. They lay next to each other afterwards and unexpectedly fell back asleep. Jake would say later that morning that he discovered a substitute for Ambien.

#

Salah el Gindi picked them up promptly at ten o'clock, bound for the Mineral Wealth offices. It had taken Jake and David Li more time than anticipated to figure out just where they wanted the claims, so el Gindi had not been able to file them yet. Jake and Libby would do it today with Salah. Together they walked into the Egyptian Mineral Resources Authority wing, following el Gindi to the office of Dr. Hassan Barakat. It was the first time Jake and Libby would meet him; they were not bothered that it took more than a half hour for him to appear.

"Dr. Barakat, may I introduce Mr. Jake Tillard and Ms. Libby Joyce. Jake and Libby, this is my friend Dr. Hassan Barakat."

They shook hands and traded pleasantries. Since it was still Ramadan, no tea or cookies were offered. El Gindi had been especially insistent on meeting Barakat in the morning, before tiredness and irritability set in with the Egyptians who observed Ramadan fasting. Finally, they got down to business.

"What can I do for you today," asked Barakat.

Salah slid a folder across his desk and Barakat removed a few dozen sheets of paper. He put on reading glasses and flipped through the documents, which were in dual language with an Arabic column on the right side and English on the left. He took his time and looked up after he got to the last page.

"You are filing ten claims" he said.

"Yes Hassan. As you know we did a lot of work to narrow down the location of the ore deposit. Fieldwork for a year. Airborne studies and ground sensing for six months. Diamond core drilling after that. You've kept records of all the money we've spent. It all points to a large body of rock we hope lies beneath these claims."

"We're ready to go into the next phase," Jake jumped in. He slid two checks across the desk to Barakat.

"Here are two bank drafts to go along with the paperwork. The first is for the filing fees. We hoped to keep the number of claims to a minimum, and ten is that minimum. The second draft is the security deposit as per regulations, to cover environmental and flight risk. I assure you we plan to start executing phase one within months and will guarantee clean-up if we leave. I hope that is not for many decades."

"Thank you Mr. Tillard. Everything looks in order. I will start processing these applications immediately. It will take our office three or four days to finish, then they need to be ratified by the governing body. That is a usually a rubber stamp, which happens in a meeting once a month. The next meeting is two weeks from tomorrow. At that time it will be official."

"Thank you Hassan," said el Gindi.

"You are all welcome. I wish you luck with your venture. Egypt has not had a gold mine in many years. It is always nice to see someone interested in our far reaches. The Sinai and the Western Desert are both depressed areas. Each could use some economic good news."

Salah started to rise but Barakat waved him back.

"Before you leave my friends I wanted to share something with you. Two days ago I was visited by two men inquiring about the Sinai. I can't tell you their names of course but thought you should know."

"Were they Russian?" asked el Gindi.

"*Mumpkin,*" maybe, answered Barakat. "One was a geologist, with a business card saying he had a PhD. His English was decent but his accent not quite Russian. And he was not a handsome man at all."

That was all they could get out of Dr. Barakat , but as they traveled back to their hotel Jake pondered whether these Russians were behind the earlier claims. He wondered just who the PhD geologist was.

CHAPTER 26

HOLDING hands, Jake and Libby stepped off the reef edge at Ras Nasrani. Their BCD's kept them afloat while they did last minute checks of each other's gear before blowing air and sinking slowly down the reef wall. Their dive plan had them following the reef north between sixty and seventy feet, into the current, until one of them had just five hundred psi left in their tank, then turning around and finning back at a depth of about thirty feet.

The reef here was vibrant, a mix of hard corals like Acropora, and soft corals including giant Gorgonia sea fans that grew to over four feet across. Colorful reef fish were abundant, and there were all sorts of smaller things to notice. Jake pointed out two large parrotfish nibbling on coral then pointed to an orange and white striped clown fish who kept ducking in and out of a clump of purple sea anemone, waving in the current. A moray eel slinked in and out of holes in the hard reef, a sea turtle lounged off to one side, and a pair of rays four feet across cruised above them. After they turned around, on the way back a large grouper that divers had named 'Fred' ate a hard-boiled egg out of Jake's hand. Jake tried to give another egg to Libby but she would not take the risk of putting the egg in the fish's mouth. She knew a grouper had sharp teeth and could easily bite off a finger.

Most dives in this area encountered white or black tipped reef sharks, and occasionally a hammerhead. On this dive they saw just one nurse shark sleeping on a sandy patch between reef fingers in the spur-and-groove area. Both Libby and Jake enjoyed the peacefulness of being submerged, their worldly worries temporarily at bay. After fifty minutes they surfaced and walked back across the reef table to the beach.

"Good dive," said Jake as he removed his mask and snorkel, and ran his fingers through wet hair.

"Yep," answered Libby, before setting off on a long monologue reviewing everything she had seen.

After removing their dive gear and stowing it in the back of the Suburban, they settled down on a blanket, with two Stella beers. The sun was strong and felt good as it warmed their still damp bodies. Libby reached across the blanket and searched for Jake's hand. Finding it and clasping it was all the invitation he needed to pull her to him and kiss her. This led to things that one should not do on a public beach, particularly in a Moslem country. In the partial screen of the car they quickly made love, Jake pulling his bathing trunks partway down and pushing Libby's suit to one side. The danger of this act was not lost on Libby, who surprised even herself by converting that danger into desire. They just finished when a plane took off almost overhead.

#

The next day they went to the pool after a leisurely morning in the room. Although it was not yet noon, Jake watched Libby waiting at the tiki bar for a couple of beers, admiring the new bikini she bought specifically for this trip. Earlier, when Jake told her in the room he thought it made her look particularly sexy, she smiled coyly and said that is what she had hoped.

Libby planned this stay in Sharm el Sheikh for one reason only, and she just saw that reason walk past the tiki bar towards the beach. Boris Oblonsky was wearing nothing but a speedo bathing suit, a thick gold chain around his neck, a heavy gold watch around his wrist, and a much, much younger blond on his arm. Libby was surprised he looked as sexy as he did, something she did not expect of a Russian his age. Fairly tall, slim, and with a muscular build, he had a chiseled face with a prominent chin. The girl was everything a man would want in a weekend fling; thin, blond, enhanced breasts, tiny bikini, and tanned. Libby guessed she was an expensive paid escort. As they headed for the beach, Libby grabbed the beers and walked back to Jake. Beer was not Jake's favorite beverage, but water and ice were still risky in Egypt, even here at the Movenpick. Slushy drinks were tempting, but Jake steered clear. During his six years in Egypt, he had suffered the Pharaoh's Revenge several times, including two confirmed cases of giardia. Fortunately he had never suffered from schistosomiasis or any of the other really bad parasites known to exist here. He was now careful with what he ate and drank.

Stella Beer, brewed in Egypt, was famous for its T-shirt that read 'That which does not kill you makes you stronger'. It was not a good beer but at least came in large bottles and was drinkable if served very cold. The Movenpick had perfected the temperature aspect. Libby handed Jake a beer but did not sit down.

"I'm going to wander around. I haven't explored the hotel grounds yet," she said.

"I was just getting comfortable and now I've got a beer," Jake complained, anticipating that she would want his company.

"No worries my dear. You stay here. I kinda want some solitude to contemplate things anyway. I won't be long."

"Well don't get into trouble. I'll be right here."

She picked up her beach bag, and with Stella in hand weaved between cinder block room clusters before emerging on the beach. She located Boris and friend in lounge chairs to her left, and leisurely strolled in front of them, stopping at an available lounger. A beach boy ran up, opened the umbrella, spread towels on the lounge chair, and placed a sweating bottle of Baraka water on the small adjacent table. He casually asked if he could get her anything else, as he gazed past her to take in the Russian blond.

"No thank you. Maybe later," Libby answered while also peering towards the couple.

After a suitable amount of time, Libby got up and walked to the edge of the water, careful to veer in front of Oblonsky on her way. If she guessed correctly, the Oligarch would notice her yellow bikini and would approach her. She worried that she could not compare to the young prostitute, but it took less than five minutes for him to approach her.

"Are you American?" asked Oblonsky in heavily accented English.

"Yes. How did you guess," answered Libby.

"You have that look," he said. "Healthy. Confident. Very sexy."

Libby grinned and turned to face him, watching his eyes drop to her chest. Libby was all natural and small at the top compared to his companion. But she anticipated this meeting and made sure her nipples were stiff and on display, something she thought would get his attention. He did not disappoint her.

"You heard me talking to the beach attendant, right? Do you always walk up to strange women and start conversations?"

"Only beautiful women."

"Ah, you find me attractive. Thank you. But I think you already have an attractive woman lying just over there," said Libby, nodding her head in the direction of his well-endowed companion.

Oblonsky shrugged, a handsome smile spreading across the chiseled face. Libby could not help but notice that he was quite attractive and very masculine.

"Life is good, but can always be better. I am an eternal optimist. Happiness loves company. Besides she is Russian."

"Don't you like Russian women?" Libby quizzed.

"Oh I do. I like all women. But I am Russian. She is not so exotic."

"I hardly think I'm exotic," said Libby.

"I disagree. You are very exotic. And the more we talk, I definitely find you intriguing."

Libby ran her hand through her hair and then put her left hand on her hip. She took a drink from her beer bottle.

"It took just one look at you for me to decide," said Oblonsky.

"Decide what?"

"That I wanted you. That you would be fun to be with."

"I see. So would you like to take me to bed?" asked Libby.

"Ah, definitely American. Few others would be so direct. So what if I said yes?"

"Then I would need to know the terms of the deal."

"We could talk about that," he said.

"What about your friend?"

"Don't worry about her. She could disappear. Or even join us if you wished."

Libby reached into her bikini top and extracted one of her business cards. She offered it to Oblonsky, smiling and watching as he took it. His smile faded as he read it. Libby did not say anything but waited for him to look up and speak.

"Ms. Libby Joyce. CEO Pimple Creek Enterprises. That is a funny name."

"Libby?"

"No, not your name. Your company name. What do you do Ms. Joyce? What is this Pimple Creek?"

The Russian looked annoyed.

"That is for you to find out Mr. Oblonsky. But to continue our conversation, you can screw me with just one condition. You must first double my personal net worth, wire-transferred into a Swiss account. My guess is you're no stranger to paying for sex. I imagine you have people who can find out how much I will cost and then you can decide if I am worth it. Everyone has his or her price. You can give me your answer tomorrow, say lunch at two o'clock? Arrange a table next to the waterfall at the large pool. I'll see you there."

Libby left Boris Oblonsky standing by the water, staring after her as she collected her things and walked away. She imagined not many people talked to him in such a forward manner. Oblonsky could not see her smile as she walked away, but the whore from Moscow could. Libby thought she saw a smile cross the young blond's face. Perhaps she wondered if Libby would screw her man, in more ways than one. She probably hoped so.

Oblonsky walked back to the blond and ordered her to stay there, saying that he would return. Libby, back by the pool, watched from beside Jake as the Oligarch strode past on the way to his room. Libby thought he still looked irritated, but she was uncertain if that was a normal expression for him. Oblonsky was undoubtedly going to contact his Moscow office, giving orders to find out anything they could on Libby Joyce and Pimple Creek Enterprise.

"Another Stella, Jake?" she asked.

"How about a Cuba libre? No ice. They keep the rum chilled and the Coke cold."

"That sounds about right," she replied. "Time for a drink upgrade."

Libby decided it was time to tell Jake what she was doing, which made for an interesting dinner that night. At first he was upset and angry. Partly because she had embarked on this journey without consulting him, and partly because he was jealous and did not like her flirting. More so because of who it was she approached and the potential danger. Jake had enough of dealing with unsavory characters. That was dealing with Egyptians, Israelis, and Americans. He thought Russians were worse. He did not think Libby should involve this Oligarch no matter how badly they needed funding. As they talked it through however, he understood her strategy but still felt it unwise and irresponsible. He knew Libby could take care of herself and also realized she would continue down this path regardless of what he said. It was part of why he loved her.

#

Oblonsky was late arriving for lunch at the private table he had arranged poolside. Libby anticipated this and made sure she arrived even later. The games had begun.

"Good afternoon Ms. Joyce," he said, pulling out her chair.

She noticed a large Russian-looking man at a small table behind them, realizing the billionaire probably never went anywhere without a bodyguard. She remembered seeing the same man on the beach yesterday, the only person there wearing more than a swimsuit. She thought if she was worth over a billion dollars, she would have protection as well.

"Good afternoon Mr. Oblonsky."

"I've taken the liberty of ordering for you, I hope you don't mind,"

"How gentlemanly. I'd expect nothing less from a man like you," she said.

"What kind of man am I?"

"I think you are a very wealthy man, are you not? An Oligarch."

"Yes, but you might have misconceptions as to what that means."

"Perhaps. Why not set me straight."

"On the definition of an Oligarch let me say there is nothing bad about the term. I believe it was coined by Aristotle referring to a small group that governed. It was a political term and is still sometimes used that way. A newer use for the term is in reference to certain very wealthy private citizens, not part of government, who control business empires. There is nothing inherently bad about this use. Unfortunately, some of my peers have involved themselves in politics and organized crime, giving the rest of us a bad reputation."

"So you're a good Oligarch. That's nice. And what have you decided about taking me to bed?"

"Direct again. I like it. I like you. You are certainly most alluring both physically and intellectually. But your offer is too rich for this Oligarch. One might almost say that you are an Oligarch in your own right."

"Not really Boris. Do you mind if I call you Boris?"

"Please. May I call you Libby? Unlike your company name, I find your given name to be quite pretty."

"Certainly, and although you're quite attractive and charming yourself, I'm glad we will not go to bed. I have a much more interesting offer for you."

"I wondered what your real goal was in meeting me. I'm not sure how anything could be much more interesting than sex with you." Oblonsky paused but Libby did not break the silence. "OK, you have my attention. But can we get to know each other first?"

"I'm not sure you have the patience Boris. I think you'd dedicate more time to chit chat if we were in business together first. Do you agree?"

"Why not."

"Through a Latvian company you've filed mining claims not far from here, targeting turquoise. Correct?"

Libby took another sip of the mimosa Oblonsky had ordered for her, and that the waiter seemed to continually top off. It was not her favorite drink but tasted good in the heat of the day.

"How did you attach my name to those claims?" he asked suspiciously.

"Not difficult Boris. It took a little money but more importantly friends in the right places. International business is new for me, but it's not much different than Wyoming. You're right, the hard part was figuring out that you are behind those claims. The easier part was determining that you've got no chance of finding turquoise. First and foremost, as you've likely discovered, I'm a geologist. My partner is also a geologist and we've done our due diligence. No turquoise. Instead gold and copper."

Oblonsky's eyebrows went up at the mention of gold. 'Not a poker player,' thought Libby. She knew the Russian had interests in various mining ventures including diamonds, nickel, platinum, and sapphires. No gold mine. She thought gold might entice him.

"My people tell me there is turquoise here. We have an expert from one of your universities who read it on a stone tablet."

"A stone tablet? Really? You've been exploring out there with a lick and a promise," said Libby.

"I don't understand this lick and a promise," Oblonsky replied.

"It means haphazardly Boris. From what I've learned, your men have been all over the place, but have approached their work inconsistently. You must realize that an archeologist knows little about mining.""

"Maybe you're right. So, gold is good," replied Oblonsky. "Tell me more."

"The first thing you should know is it won't lie under your claims. You located those based on a pile of cores. Who knows where those cores came from. The gold will lie under claims that Pimple Creek just filed. We've locked up the full extent of the deposit."

They spent the afternoon discussing a number of things. The geology of the area where Libby expected to find gold. The fieldwork, coring, and other efforts GusCo made to narrow down the target. The analyses and projections for mineralization. The plans for developing and extracting the deposit. Then they each reviewed their holdings in a global sense. Libby spent the most time on her Bessie T mine in Wyoming because of similarities to the Sinai, but covered her other two mines, oil ventures, and commercial buildings. Oblonsky gave a whirlwind tour of his business empire, crowned by a diamond mine and oil field in Siberia, but ranging from cut flowers out of Kenya to construction across Russia and Eastern Europe, to fisheries in Kamchatka, and more. He also covered his export deals to Egypt, to which Libby informed him his reputation in Egypt was not the best. He said that happened in business. She told him it might be a liability if they joined forces.

"Let's go diving tomorrow," Oblonsky said, changing the topic. "Bring your partner. We will have fun. I've rented the yacht you see in the harbor. It was too far to bring mine from the Mediterranean for such a short time. This one is small but perfect for diving. I know you dove the other day at Ras Nasrani. Have you been down on the Thistlegorm wreck?"

"No, I've not heard of it."

"It's my favorite wreck dive in the world. A World War II British supply ship, sunk with only two bombs. You'll see."

"What time?"

"Meet in the lobby at eight. The boat has all the gear. Everything we need. Except a swimsuit, that is if you care to wear one. That's up to you. We will discuss your proposal after the dive."

By the time Libby rejoined Jake poolside, it was happy hour.

"Is it Stella time, or Cuba libre time," asked Jake as Libby settled into her lounger.

"Definitely better than Stella time, not yet sure about the libre," she replied. "Let's be optimistic and order a couple anyway."

She reviewed her meeting with Oblonsky and told Jake about the dive plan for the next day. They spent the evening discussing possible business structures for getting Oblonsky's money while ensuring they did not get taken advantage of by the Russian. Their conversation with him would be exploratory only. Formal negotiations would come later, led by Libby's head negotiator.

"I'm glad you won't be going to bed with him," said Jake wryly. "Let's get room service and spend the evening satisfying any pent-up desires you may have."

"He is quite handsome," she said smiling and putting her arms around him.

CHAPTER 27

THE NASHWA III out of Alexandria was a small but luxurious yacht. A crew of six in white, starched uniforms lined up as they embarked. The captain shook everyone's hand vigorously and welcomed them on board. Ten minutes later, leaning on the stern rail of the upper deck, Jake watched the shore fade away as they left Naama Bay, the low, brown, dusty landscape giving way to brilliant turquoise water. Just below him on the main deck, one of the crew let out two fishing lines to troll while cruising. As always, the sun had the sky to itself, which in February made for very pleasant days. Jake turned to join Libby and Boris munching casually on gravlax, caviar, and other morsels. Since they would be diving, there was no alcohol but various fresh juices to drink. The boat took them around the southern tip of the Sinai, from the Gulf of Aqaba to the Gulf of Suez, traveling through Ras Mohammed Natural Reserve. As they turned north, Jake got up and again looked over the stern rail. The crew member had reeled in the trolling lines after catching two yellowfin tuna. He was now using a very long pole to cast an umbrella-shaped lure sideways out from the boat towards a shoal which imparted a light aqua color to the water.

"What are you fishing for?" asked Jake.

"See the ripple on the water?" responded the crew member, pointing.

"That little bit way out there?" asked Jake, squinting to see the subtle feature.

"Yes sir. Calamari," he said as he cast the lure at least forty yards from the boat.

"You're fishing for calamari with a lure?"

"Yes sir."

Jake had never seen that before, and honestly doubted its potential, when he heard the reel make that unmistakable sound of a line being pulled out against the drag. The man reeled in the line and eventually landed a two-foot-long squid. He held it up proudly, big smile with yellowish, discolored teeth and an almost black complexion.

"See. Calamari. For lunch."

"Always something new in Egypt," Jake muttered. He liked calamari.

Finding the location of the Thistlegorm was not trivial, but the captain had brought divers to the spot many times before and finally gave the warning to get ready to dive. Jake had read the printed sheet of paper on board while cruising out. The SS Thistlegorm was a British Merchant Navy ship sunk on October 6, 1941 by two German Heinkel HE 111 bombers. It was anchored, waiting to enter the Suez Canal en route to Alexandria with a full cargo of munitions and vehicles. Nine men died in the initial blast, but thirty-two escaped before the on-board munitions exploded, breaking the ship in two. The wreck lay undisturbed for years until Jacques Cousteau discovered her in the early 1950's, relying on local fishermen and written war records. An article in a 1956 issue of National Geographic announced it to the world, but the ship remained largely untouched until Sharm el Sheikh developed into a dive center just a few years ago. It was an ideal wreck dive, as the ship settled upright, in two main pieces, on sand about one hundred feet down. Sport divers could access most of it without special gear.

"I've heard about this dive for years," said Jake. "But we could never get a boat captain to take us. Said it was too difficult to find."

"I'm glad I could make it happen," said Oblonsky. "It's my favorite. The BSA motorcycles are unbelievable. You will see."

"What's the dive plan?" Libby asked the ship's dive master. Libby was the least experienced diver and a bit nervous, although she would never admit it.

"The ship is in two pieces, but is nearly four hundred feet long," Karim said. "The shallowest piece, an antenna, is forty feet down, and the deepest piece, the propeller, is at a hundred. The currents are usually very strong, so there will be silt in the water. I think today's visibility will be OK. Don't drift away and if you have to, hold onto a piece of the ship. We will hold the anchor line when we descend;

don't let go. I want everyone to stay together, especially when we go inside the ship. We will not enter any confined rooms so there will always be a path to the surface in case of trouble. You will see good things without taking any risk. Lots of divers enter various rooms and cabins looking for things to steal. I know one man who has six place settings of china from the dining room. It is illegal to remove anything and I will not let you take anything out."

Karim looked from one of them to the other, to reinforce that he was serious about this.

"We will follow the mooring line down to the main deck; I tell you again that you need to hang onto the line because of the current. I do not want to chase you, or have you disappear. The same when we surface at the end of the dive. When we get down to the ship, we will swim around the bow, looking at coral and fish, then enter Hold number one. Here you will see many BSA motorbikes, some Bedford trucks, Morris autos, rifles, and many boots and shoes. Please try not to touch them. We will not go into Hold Three where there are bombs, grenades, and anti-tank mines."

Libby interrupted him, "Is it safe with all those bombs?"

"Nothing has blown up since 1941, so I would think so," answered Oblonsky. Libby found the response somewhat lacking.

"We'll come out of Hold One when you're ready and swim along the deck of the ship towards the stern. Take a look at the damage where it broke apart and notice how the steel was peeled and bent by the blast. At the stern you can see two machine gun turrets. Then we'll swim off the side to see a tank and a railroad locomotive that fell off the deck when the ship sank. Our maximum depth will be ninety-five feet. On the way back we'll rise slowly along the deck as we look at all the fish and coral. Look for a crocodile fish on the deck."

They donned wetsuits and equipment and entered the water by stepping off the rear dive platform. As predicted the current was strong and they looked like four flags in a stiff breeze attached to the mooring line as they descended. The silt was worse than at Ras Nasrani but not so bad you could not see. Jake had over a hundred dives on his card, but Libby was a relative newcomer to the sport. She felt nervous as they entered Hold One and began exploring the motorbikes. The dive went as planned however, and before long they were back on board the Nashwa III with Karim opening a bottle of Dom Perignon. He gave a glass to each of them.

"Alas we can only do one dive today," said Oblonsky. "Normally we do an overnight trip here and do multiple dives. To celebrate your first time we will drink champagne. To be followed by Russian vodka of course. But first, *Nasdrovya.*"

"That was absolutely fantastic," Jake said of the dive. "I've done the bottle wreck and several others in the Gulf, but this is the best. Better than Truk Lagoon."

"The colors were so vibrant near the top," added Libby. "Both soft and hard corals are growing on the metal all over. I'm surprised that much has grown in the short time since the ship sank."

"That's because the currents are strong," said Karim. "Most wrecks are much deeper and less colorful. You saw how the colors faded as we got deeper. We are lucky for color here."

"And my god the fish," said Libby. "I saw tons of small reef fish along with barracuda, snapper, and jacks. What were those others in the big school?"

"You probably mean batfish. They're usually here. Very nice. I know you probably saw a number of scorpionfish and our resident turtle, but did you see the crocodile fish?"

"I did," answered Jake. "He was resting on the main deck just as we crossed the big crack. What I couldn't believe was the preservation of the cargo. The bikes still had their seats, the boots looked like you could pull them on, and there were even some clothes that haven't deteriorated."

Boris chimed in, "Libby, I saw you looking at a nudibranch for a long time. I think you found the critter more interesting than the rifles. I thought we were going to have to leave you there. How long do you think you stared at that little guy?"

"I've got no idea. I just didn't want to say goodbye. I've never seen such a colorful little animal like that before. It's amazing what lives down there."

"Well, I think we've earned lunch," said Oblonsky. "Let's change and meet in the dining room."

Lunch was filled with social conversation. Jake was relentless in asking Oblonsky about his business dealings, but the Oligarch was adept at evading anything of substance. He was, thought Libby, entirely charming. Jake and Libby learned much about the other man, and vice versa. Not unexpectedly, lunch was superb, especially the uber-fresh calamari, lightly pan fried with lemon, salt, and pepper. Some of the yellowtail was served sashimi style with wasabi, and some was seared and served over a bed of lettuce with pickled ginger. Jake avoided the lettuce but ate the tuna.

During the three-hour cruise back to Sharm they talked business. By the time they docked, a memorandum-of-understanding had been scribbled which would guide future meetings to create a partnership. Basically, Oblonsky through BFC Co would fund all front-end loading required for development in return for a forty percent working interest. His investment would be paid back in full out of profit once the mine was operational. After payback, he would participate to his interest against the sixty percent owned by GusCo. Jake and Libby would retain control. There were many details to be ironed out and they committed to work on the agreement in Moscow.

Back at the Movenpick, Oblonsky bade the others farewell as he was departing Egypt that evening on his personal jet.

"It's been a pleasure," he said, taking Libby's hand and kissing it, a gleam in his eye. "Maybe not as pleasurable as I first imagined, but certainly productive."

"Thank you for your hospitality and for introducing us to the Thistlegorm," said Libby.

"Glad to meet you Boris," said Jake shaking his hand. "I'll have our colleague Peter Owens contact Victor Popov to continue negotiations. I look forward to seeing you in Moscow soon, a place I've never been."

"I will show you the best sites," said Oblonsky. "Schedule a few days to see the place. It's a wonderful city with the best culture in the world."

As they walked back to their room, Libby told Jake she was happy with the day.

"The dive or the deal?" asked Jake.

"The dive was indisputably great. But you know I mean the deal. Don't you think it went well? I think we've just solved our funding problem with only one partner."

"The devil's in the details Libby. Negotiations can go awry. Egos can take over. Russians are unpredictable. But we'll see how it goes. How about a swim in the pool?"

"I think we've had enough water for one day. Instead, how about we order room service and have it in bed?"

"That sounds like a nice end to the day," he grinned.

CHAPTER 28

AEROFLOT flight 401 passed over the Ural Mountains on its flight path east from Moscow's Domodedovo airport to Yakutsk. This was Jake's first time flying in the Tupolev TU-134 jet. He researched the plane after he booked and found it was prone to stability problems, as its design was based on early fighter jets the Soviets designed for performance and not necessarily safety. The latest crash of a commercial TU-134 was two years ago in Siberia, killing all ninety-four people on board. Aeroflot did not fly that plane out of the Soviet Union due to certification issues. Jake wished he had not researched the plane, but other choices were poor flying to Mirny.

He enjoyed the take-off however, which had an overly energetic steep trajectory, pushing him back in his seat with more g-force than normal. He sat back and drank a Russian beer as he watched the endless forest, rivers, and lakes pass underneath. At Yakutsk he waited three hours for his connecting flight on a regional airliner to Mirny, a small town that existed solely for the diamond mine, owned jointly by the Russian government and Boris Oblonsky. The commuter plane was scarier than the Tupolev.

Mirny was far enough north that it was still light when he landed at eleven o'clock that night. On final approach Jake stared out the window at the huge circular open pit dominating the landscape, seemingly eager to take over both the town perched on one side and the runway on the other. It was a perfect circle, like nothing Jake had ever seen. With the sun as low as it was in the sky, no light reached inside and the pit looked like a black hole. Once inside the small terminal building, he claimed his bag and found a person holding a sign with his name. The man spoke no English but carried Jake's bag to a black car and drove him to the town's only hotel, a single story, dingy-looking place surrounded by groves of birch trees. Even at this hour, men in dark clothes sat in the lobby chatting, drinking vodka, and playing chess. On the way to his room, he passed a large lady sitting on a chair behind a small wooden desk at the end of the hall, presumably making notes on who came and went throughout the night. She did not say anything when Jake attempted to say hello in Russian. His bed was too soft but Jake fell asleep immediately and slept until his alarm buzzed at seven o'clock.

He showered, noticing a large amount of water pressure but a small amount of heat, making him glad it was not winter. Breakfast was a buffet of cold meats, cheeses, fish, and breads. Canned juices and canned fruit. Instant coffee or tea. Not a culinary treat. Halfway through his meal, a man walked into the dining room, looked around, and walked straight towards Jake.

"Mr. Tillard?"

"Yes, I'm Jake Tillard. Are you Mr. Popov?"

"I am Popov. I sit?" asked Popov, not waiting for an answer and plopping down into the chair opposite Jake. "One good part of job is food."

Jake did not consider this buffet a benefit but did not mind sharing his table with the man. From conversations with Oblonsky, he knew Popov was the Oligarch's right-hand man, and had flown to Mirny to show Jake the mine and pave the way for negotiations on the Sinai contract. As Popov poured hot water into a cup with instant coffee and three sugars, they chatted and ate. Jake quickly developed a dislike for the man, who seemed coarse and rude. It was difficult to take his eyes off Popov's eyebrows. Jake also did not like that Popov had a pistol of some sort in a holster inside his coat. They finished eating and Jake went to his room before meeting back in the lobby. Popov was talking with a very small rotund man, who spoke Russian in an animated manner with his hands.

"This Denis Morozof," said Popov when Jake approached. "In charge of mine and guide today."

"English not good," said Morozof. "Welcome Mirny. Good people. Good diamonds."

That was the last English Jake would hear him speak until they said goodbye at the end of the day. Popov told Jake that Morozof had worked at the mine since its beginning, starting as a truck driver.

He was actually a degreed engineer and had quickly climbed the corporate ladder. He was promoted to Director of the Mine five years ago. Jake tried to imagine spending decades in this isolated town. He could not.

"I will be translator," said Popov. "We go."

They climbed into a large truck and drove three miles to the mine headquarters, passing most of the town on the way. He saw dull four-story cement apartment blocks, large diameter insulated pipes running alongside the streets which brought central steam heat to virtually every building in town, statues at several roundabouts celebrating Stalin and other important Soviet men, and people dressed in dark drab clothing walking to who knew where. The bleak infrastructure was interrupted by green grass and thousands of daffodils, marking the arrival of spring. Westerners did not realize that summers in Siberia could be very warm, with temperatures surpassing a hundred degrees Fahrenheit. Most only thought of winter, when temperatures commonly plunged to minus forty. With near constant daylight, summers were a happy time for these people who never seemed to wear a happy face. Their truck passed through a gate into a fenced compound, the guard saluting as they cruised through without stopping.

Jake was reading the brochure he found on his seat when he entered the car. The kimberlite pipe that contained the diamonds was discovered in 1955 and production from the mine started two years later. At that time in Soviet history, things were bleak after WWII, and geological expeditions blanketed the whole country including vast Siberia regions. Expedition geologists Yuri Khabardin, Ekaterina Elagina, and Viktor Avdeenko found what was the second kimberlite in the Soviet Union; they received the Lenin Prize for their efforts. Production proved challenging with engineers using dynamite and jet engines in the winter to melt permafrost so they could gain access to the diamond-bearing rock. Summers were worse, when melting permafrost created swampy conditions; indeed most structures were built on pilings so they did not sink into the mushy ground. By the 1960's, Mirny was producing more than ten million carats per year with some twenty percent of that gem grade.

The brochure description continued but they arrived at the mine headquarters and Jake had to get out.

"We have tea, then drive to mine," said Popov.

Tea turned out to be a euphemism for a propaganda session. After perusing glass cases filled with awards, photos, and mementos, the men sat in a conference room to watch a promotional film on the mine. It was in Russian, but had English subtitles, which were only somewhat comprehensible. Nevertheless, Jake was impressed and looked forward to the tour. He only wondered why Oblonsky wanted him to tour this mine. Their potential gold mine in Egypt would have little in common with the Mirny diamond pit.

As they drove downwards in ever-tightening circles, they passed enormous trucks hauling ore and waste rock to the surface. Every so often they passed crews setting charges, loading trucks, and doing what they did twenty-four hours of every day of the year. Jake noticed most of the workers looked oriental, and wondered if the locals in this part of the country had Asian features. Finally they reached the bottom of the pit, where activity was highest. They got out of the truck, put on hard hats, and walked around.

"It's an unbelievable view from down here," said Jake.

"Yes," replied Popov, "sky very high."

Jake thought the sky was as high as it always was, but it was like looking at it down the barrel of a musket. The walls of the pit were colorful, as opposed to virtually all of the buildings, cars, and people. The scale was so enormous that the walls looked smooth. Indeed it was like sitting at the bottom of a giant funnel. If not for the corkscrew road, one could never get out, the walls being so steep as to be unscalable.

"The colors are what I notice," Jake said. "I thought kimberlite was a dark rock but the walls are shades of brown, gray, rust, and yellow. I suppose it's due to minerals leaching out of the basic kimberlite rock."

Popov explained the workings of the mine. Jake knew most of what Popov told him, that kimberlite pipes were narrow, circular columns, formed when molten, slushy rock very deep in the earth's crust pushed to the surface. Jake drifted off momentarily and remembered when he was at Stanford thinking of kimberlites basically as pimples. He mused how a diamond mine would be the perfect thing for Pimple Creek to operate. He refocused on what Popov was saying. Kimberlite pipes always pushed through the crust in a discrete column, not dispersing out to the sides, or sending out veins and dikes like basalt intrusions. The diamonds in these rocks formed at very deep levels under extreme pressures and temperatures, then hitched a ride to the surface within the kimberlite.

Popov continued and Jake found it taxing to listen for any length of time because of his accent. An open pit worked well here but required a lot of waste rock to be moved. Since they were not far from a stranded oil field, a small refinery was built to make diesel fuel that powered the equipment. This cheap fuel helped make the open pit economic. Most diamond mines start as open pit, but switch to underground when the pits get past fifteen hundred feet deep. A whistle sounded and Morozof pointed to trucks halfway up the pit where workers scurried about.

"Ready to blast," said Popov.

Jake was not sure about being below the blast zone but watched mesmerized when the explosion occurred. It was very contained and orderly, and loading of rock into trucks began almost immediately.

"What you notice about workers?" asked Popov, translating what Morozof had just said.

"They look Asian," said Jake. "Are the people in this part of Siberia Asianic?"

"Not Russians. These workers from China. Boris wanted you see yourself,"

"Why China?"

"Cheap," answered Popov. "Chinese built railroads in United States. Good labor. Cheap price. Same thing here now. Better workers than local people. Local people lazy. Hard to control. Chinese workers have wives open Chinese restaurants. Is wonderful."

"Why did Boris want me to see this?"

Popov shrugged. "Ask him."

Morozof pushed Jake and others into a clump and had the driver take pictures of them with the mining activity in the background.

Finally he made a big flourish out of removing something from his jacket pocket. Jake could not understand what he was saying but he took a long time saying it, all the while looking into the video camera recording the event. Finally, he presented a small velvet bag to Jake as he shouted at the man in Russian to keep taking pictures.

"Open please," Popov translated again.

Jake undid the string and pulled out a small box. Inside was a dark nondescript rock the size of a golf ball. Half embedded in it and seemingly hanging off the side was an octahedron the size of a large pencil eraser, looking like two pyramids stuck together. It was glassy looking, a bit frosty, translucent with a yellow tint. As Jake held it up to his eye, cameras clicked.

"Maybe eight carat," said Popov. "Gem quality but yellow."

"It's beautiful," said Jake. "I've never seen a raw diamond. This will fit well in my rock collection. Although I fear it's worth more than most of my other specimens."

"Worth something. Not much," stated Popov with a wave of his hand. "Ten million carats per year here. Yellow mostly for industry. Grinding. Not favorite for women."

Nevertheless Jake kept it in a safe spot, and looked forward to showing it to Libby. Maybe he would even give it to her if things went that way.

CHAPTER 29

NIZHNEVARTOVSK is much bigger than Mirny, with more than two hundred thousand inhabitants, most working the giant Samotlor oil field discovered in the 1960's. Before that it was a small village, founded around 1905 to supply firewood to merchant ships on the Ob river. Samotlor changed all that, becoming the largest oil field in the Soviet Union and the sixth largest in the world. More than fifteen thousand wells were drilled, and field production peaked at seven million barrels per day in 1980. Jake knew about the field from his university studies and was excited to visit. He thought Boris Oblonsky might own an interest in the field, which was mostly owned by the government. It was hard to ascertain this sort of information now that the country was privatizing, and ownership changes occurred daily. In any case, Oblonsky's company supplied many of the services that drilled the wells and kept field operations going. Samotlor was Oblonsky's biggest source of revenue.

Jake's flight from Mirny was memorable, traveling with Viktor Popov on Oblonsky's private jet. They covered the twelve hundred miles in little more than two hours, about a quarter of the time it would have taken to fly commercial. It was nice to avoid airport check-in, security, and connections. It was even nicer to have a cute flight attendant pamper you; he and Popov managed to put down a half dozen drinks in between Russian snacks. The young lady offered to introduce Jake to the Mile-High Club but he politely declined. Popov asked him if he was gay, then told him he was foolish.

The air distance between those cities was exactly half the distance between Los Angeles and New York City, yet Mirny was not close to the Pacific, and Nizhnevartovsk was still east of the Urals, way east of Moscow. The Soviet Union was a big beast of a country. Jake watched out the window as they approached Nizhnevartovsk.

The terrane was flat and completely covered by forest, dotted with innumerable lakes and cut by many streams and one big river. The oil field covered almost seven hundred square miles, half the size of Rhode Island, and stuck out prominently from the air. A large portion of it was in marshland and taiga, now harboring hundreds of man-made islands housing drill sites. The non-watery portions had been stripped of trees, with roads crisscrossing everywhere, and blighted clearings in between. Jake marveled at the challenge that had been overcome in developing such a field in what was basically a swamp.

Oblonsky arranged a morning tour the next day for Jake, following a late morning breakfast at the hotel. The hotel was two stories, mostly wood, set in a pleasant grove of birch trees. The interior was hunting lodge motif with dark wood, carpets on wood flooring, subdued lighting, taxidermy fish and game on the walls, and heavy appointments. In spite of being more welcoming than the Mirny hotel, there was still the fat lady in the hall keeping track of guests. Breakfast was better than in Mirny. Fresh baked pastries, smoked meats, sausages, yoghurts, and a local delicacy of shaved frozen fish from the Ob. Caviar and potato pancakes, as well as a manned omelet bar. Still the watery canned juices and instant coffee. As he finished eating, a very short man in a chauffeur's outfit walked up and introduced himself as Alexei, his guide for the morning. Alexei was not only short but slightly built, with eyes close set and slightly crossed, a long narrow nose, and fly-away shaggy hair. His English was very good, a result of his studies at Moscow University. Walking to the car, Jake learned Alexei was twenty-six years old, was raised in Kazakhstan, and wanted a job as government interpreter so he could travel overseas and see the world. Alexei urged Jake to correct any flaws in his English so he could continue to improve. He said he did not encounter many Americans.

Their first stop, not far from the hotel, was the Ob River. A broad path lined with pavers ran along the western bank of the river with a retaining wall that stretched as far as Jake could see, five kilometers according to Alexei. Joggers and walkers were out in force, enjoying a beautiful, sunny day. The river itself was quite broad, more than a hundred yards across at this point, with several large boats heading in both directions. Jake wondered where they were coming from and going to, as he knew the Ob flowed into the Arctic Ocean. A number of old men on the bank were casting hooks with very long poles. Alexei did not linger but set off to the next stop, the park in downtown Nizhnevartovsk.

"In the summer there is mostly people-watching here," said Alexei as they strolled around the grassy area. "Sometimes art fairs, sometimes music performances, always children playing. Personally I like it better in winter. We build ice sculptures and ice houses. They are lit with colored lights. It is dark most of the day. Over there we make ice for hockey. The best time of the year is 'White Nights', a festival lasting two days with folk traditions, exhibitions, and music. It is very romantic with many couples strolling all night. This has happened since 1976. Everyone in town comes and stays long after midnight. Even children."

"Who is this?" asked Jake as they passed yet another statue.

"This is the Tatar poet Musa Dzhalil, a hero of the Soviet Union. He fought in the underground against fascism, was captured by the gestapo in 1943, and died by guillotine in 1944. While he was in prison, he wrote poems and left them with other prisoners. After he was dead they brought these poems together. There is a book with over a hundred of his prison poems, translated into more than sixty languages. You see monuments to him all over Russia and Tatarstan."

Jake did not know what Tatarstan was or where it was, and did not ask. They drove past the Palace of the Arts, the Museum of History of the Russian Life, the Drama Theater, the Alley of Honor of Aviation Equipment, several other cultural venues, and many more monuments and statues, before stopping at the restaurant where Boris would meet Jake.

"Is the name of this restaurant 'Pectopah'?" asked Jake.

Alexei chuckled and said, "No. The word you see, '*pectopah*' in Cyrillic means 'restaurant' and is pronounced '*restauran*'. Obviously you do not know Cyrillic. We have many of the same letters as you, but some are pronounced different, and some mean a different letter. For example, our Cyrillic '*P*' is your 'R' and is pronounced like your 'R'. The Cyrillic '*H*' is your 'N', pronounced like your 'N'. Many foreigners seem confused by this. I had a visitor once who got lost in Moscow and called me to pick her up. I needed to know where she was, so I asked her to look around and read a sign. She said she was at a busy street corner and there was a sign saying '*pectopah*'. She pronounced it like they were Western letters, just as you did. I laughed because there are over five thousand restaurants in Moscow, many with that sign. I finally found her, but only after she gave her phone to someone on the street who told me where she was."

Boris Oblonsky was waiting for Jake at a four-top on a wooden balcony overlooking the main floor of the restaurant. Viktor Popov sat to his right and an oriental-looking man sat to his left. Classical music wafted up from the main floor, where a quartet dressed in period attire played Rachmaninoff on a rotating disk in the middle of the room. A young, pretty woman sat beside a large harp, alongside two violinists and a cellist. The restaurant looked half-full, but they were the only ones on the balcony except for the five wait staff also dressed in period clothes, including white wigs. As Jake approached, Oblonsky extended a hand and introduced his guest.

"Welcome, Mr. Tillard. It's nice to see you again. I hope you have enjoyed your visit to Russia so far. This is Mr. Wang Yong, a business partner. You already know Viktor Popov. Sit please. Tell me how was your visit to Mirny? Did you enjoy the diamond mine?"

"Mirny was fascinating. Thank you for arranging the visit. It was the first city I've seen in Siberia and that alone was interesting. How your countrymen managed to find anything of interest out there with the trees, swamps, freezing, and thawing is truly remarkable. I found it all overwhelming, the houses on stilts, the elevated roads, even the central heating running every which way. I'd seen open pit mines before but never a diamond mine. It was incredible in every way. From the air it looks like a perfect circle. From the bottom it looks like a kaleidoscopic funnel. The rocks of the kimberlite pipe are quite interesting as well, and thank you for the souvenir."

"Ah yes, the diamond. You are welcome. I collect them because personally I find them more beautiful than when they are cut. It is amazing what the earth can produce. And how do you find Nizhnevartovsk?"

"Different than I expected. Warmer, prettier, more cultured, bigger. Definitely more of a city than Mirny. You have everything here. A symphony, culture center, museums, parks, sports arena, restaurants, bars. Everything a small city should have. The Ob is impressive, and it seems your residents make the most of it. The people look very healthy and happy. I don't think most Americans picture Siberia like this."

"Unfortunately, our countries do not share a cultural good will. Most Russians are suspicious of Westerners, and of Americans in particular. I believe the same can be said of American's view towards Russia. Both governments are to blame and I don't see that changing. History is what it is and cannot be taken back. Sometimes it wears off as time goes forward. Sometimes things continue unchanged. Maybe in a generation or two our countries will be closer, but I don't see anyone trying to make that happen. Perhaps we businessmen can have an impact. I have been to your country and find it completely different from what we were taught in school and what we're told in our newspapers. Enjoy your time here Mr. Tillard and share what you observe with your friends back home. Viktor will accompany you tomorrow on a tour of Samotlor. It is the crown jewel of Russia and also of my business empire. But now we talk about Egypt."

Champagne flutes were filled and Oblonsky offered a toast, the first of many that evening, in true Russian fashion. Jake noticed it was Veuve Clicquot, which he thought was impossible to get in Russia.

"To business deals in spite of the obstacles," said Oblonsky.

"To business deals," repeated the other gentlemen. Jake was thankful so much of the world spoke English.

"I'm happy we meet again Jake," said Oblonsky. "Ms. Joyce and I forged a basic agreement on the beach and the three of us took it further on the yacht, but we need to move that understanding to a contract. I have extensive experience with mining, as you saw in Mirny. It's my opinion that our future mine in Sinai will require much up-front work and funding. I asked Mr. Wang to join us for that reason. He's with a prominent Chinese business that has interests across the globe including in Russia, with me. For example, Wang supplies most of the workers you saw at Mirny."

Jake studied Wang Yong's features. He had limited history with Chinese, but thought the man was likely from northern China, probably Han. He was taller than an average Chinese man, with a round pale face, flat features, thin lips, expansive yet sparse eyebrows, and short black hair. His suit was impeccable, and he wore a Rolex on his wrist, with no rings of any sort. His English was better than Oblonsky's.

"Thank you for meeting with me," said Wang. "Mr. Oblonsky has told me about your Sinai prospect. It sounds very interesting. Something that our company might like to be part of. We have no business now in Egypt."

"It seems to me," said Oblonsky, "that we could use help from Mr. Wang. The time and money required before we see revenue out of that mine is large. You know I have years of experience in Egypt, and know that Egyptian workers are not good. From what I hear you learned the same thing at your gas field. Also, you have years of living and working in Egypt, so you must agree that the people there are quite lazy."

"I can agree to some extent," answered Jake carefully. "Egyptian workers present challenges but they are a necessary part of finalizing contracts with the government. Not all of them are lazy. In fact, I love the Egyptian people very much and enjoy working with them. It's a matter of trust and relationships."

"Wang can supply workers at lower cost than locals. They will be twice as productive."

"In a remote area like yours," added Wang, "you will need to build a camp. If you use Egyptians, you will need a rotation system with men coming and going every month. They will go back to their families and may or may not always return to work. They will have any number of excuses. My workers will stay and live at the mine full time, with two weeks off each year to go home. You can do maintenance at that time with contractors and specialized staff so you lose very little operational time. Such arrangements work well and I have done it in Africa and Asia."

The conversation continued with Oblonsky making it clear he wanted Wang involved in the business. Not only could he supply

Chinese workers, but he could supply much of the mining equipment needed at a discount. Jake deduced correctly that this was a way for Oblonsky to pay less. Jake saw it as a complication but was intrigued by the potential cost savings. Most of that savings would flow to Oblonsky but the whole venture would ultimately benefit. Near the end of their meal, Oblonsky suggested a three-way partnership, each having a one-third working interest. Jake balked at this idea and stood fast to the concept of GusCo keeping control with a fifty-one percent interest, and the other two each having twenty-four and a half percent.

"You have deviated from your handshake deal in the Sinai," said Jake.

"Things evolve," shrugged Oblonsky. "Prices for commodities are heading down and we need to plan now to manage our cost structure."

"Chinese miners are very good," said Wang. "They work hard, work long, and work with no complaints. Life in China these days is difficult for the average person, so many are willing to work in other countries. They do not spend much and send most of their earnings home to their families. They are used to my equipment and are very productive."

"Where did you learn your excellent English Mr. Wang?" asked Jake.

"I had the pleasure of attending the Thunderbird Global Management School in Arizona. I got a very good education and ate lots of Mexican food. I grew up in the Sichuan province of China, which is known for spicy food, so it is natural I would like your Tex-Mex. I have a case of Tabasco sauce in my house. The best part of Thunderbird was making contacts. In my class alone there were students from over thirty countries, many of them the sons of rulers or top bureaucrats. We all ended up back in our own countries and most did very well. I am now doing business with three of my classmates in Africa. The Lim family had its own contacts in Asia."

"Mr. Oblonsky, I need to discuss this with my partner," said Jake. "I can say now that I will not agree to losing control, so you need to think of another solution. I suggest we meet again in two weeks to continue negotiations."

"Roman Novikov and I will be in London in two weeks finalizing another project. Would that be an agreeable location? Mr. Wang and I are spending the next few days together and we can explore options from our side. If we get closer to agreement in London then we can all meet again with Wang to sign papers. Now we eat. I asked the chef to put together a classic menu. He is a wonderfully talented chef I brought from Moscow."

The music continued, having settled for the moment on Tchaikovsky, which Jake preferred to the earlier Rachmaninoff. The first course was black Beluga caviar, served to each individually in silver vessels sitting on a bed of ice. Aspic and pate was second. Finally, the main course was bear, sliced thin, cooked medium, and served with gooseberry salsa and a rich reduction. It was the most delicious bear Jake had ever eaten.

CHAPTER 30

THE Dorchester Hotel, completed in 1931, stands on the site of the earlier Dorchester House, which served as the American Embassy from 1910 until it was used as a hospital during WWII. Before even that, the name 'Dorchester House' was first assigned to a house on exactly the same location purchased by Joseph Damer, Earl of Dorchester, back in 1792. The site and the building in Mayfair had a long history; the current hotel is known for its luxury and has hosted royalty, celebrities, writers, and artists. General Eisenhower stayed here while planning the Normandy invasion. Jake and Libby chose not to book the Eisenhower suite, rather settling into a normal room, itself tagged with an absurdly high price.

"You get what you pay for," exclaimed Libby, nibbling on a piece of toast. "But I'm not sure I'd pay anything for this marmalade."

"It's not my favorite either," Jake replied. "But I think Marmite is worse."

"Is that this stuff here," asked Libby, picking up a small oval-shaped jar of dark looking paste.

"Yep. Spread a bit on your toast and tell me what you think."

Libby opened the jar and sniffed, wrinkling her nose immediately. She spread a little on a piece of toast and put it in her mouth.

"I kinda like it," she said.

"You're kidding me," Jake replied.

"Yes I am," she laughed. "That's disgusting."

"It's apparently yeast extract," said Jake. "A German guy invented it in the last century, making it from brewer's yeast. How it ever got popular is a mystery to me, but Brits and Australians love the stuff."

#

Peter Owens and Janet Robinson were sitting at a table waiting for them. Since it was raining, the maître d' had moved their reservation from the Dorchester Terrace inside to the Grill.

"A rainy day in London, who would have thought," Owens stood and shook hands with Jake and Libby. The Pimple Creek negotiator had been to London in his prior career working for a large multinational company. It was the first visit for Libby and Robinson.

"That's why they have umbrellas in your rooms, near the front door, and for sale in virtually any quick-stop store," said Jake. "For me rain in London has a certain charm. Strolling beside the lake in St. James Park, walking along the Thames, or strolling down any cobblestone lane in a drizzle can be romantic. Makes a pub visit more enjoyable. Is everyone enjoying the hotel?"

"Absolutely," said Owens. "Beats where I stayed last time, when it was on my own dime."

"Let's get down to business," said Jake after they ordered lunch.

Owens brought them up to speed with information from a private investigator he used from time to time. The dope he found on Wang Yong and Roman Novikov was quite interesting.

"Wang is what Oblonsky said he is," continued Peter. "Basically COO of several companies under the control of the Lim family, currently led by Philip Lim. Wang's father was influential in the Communist party and the son grew up privileged, whatever that meant in China at the time. Interestingly, his father sent him to the Thunderbird School of Global Management in Phoenix for a western education. Not what I'd expect from a communist party faithful but it worked for the son. He graduated near the top of his class and was employed immediately by Chou Lim, Philip's father. Wang ran a series of coal mines in China before working his way up in the organization. Apparently he's ruthless, like most successful Chinese businessmen, but has done nothing illegal as far as I could tell. There are rumors circulating about shady activities, but no one's made anything stick. The Lim family has authorities on the backdoor payroll who shield Wang and others from prosecution. I think our negotiations with him might be difficult and we need to be alert."

"How involved are his dealings with Oblonsky?"

"They've got six projects together, three of them Russian mines. Two of the businesses involve Russia-Chinese trade. The first project we can find that they did together was around 1980. A timber venture east of Lake Baikal, supplying lumber by train to northern China. That was way back in Soviet days, so things were definitely different. It went fine for a few years then something happened and it dissolved. I'm not sure what happened. The mines came after that."

"Personal data?" asked Libby.

"Wife of thirty some years, lives in Shanghai. Two kids, both grown and involved in business outside the Lim empire. Seems to have a mistress in Singapore, where he spends a great deal of his time."

"Does he operate alone?" asked Jake.

"He's got a close associate named Liu Ling who handles a lot of his day-to-day operations. While Wang's not connected to the Lim family by blood, Liu is, sort of. She's the illegitimate daughter of Chou Lim, so she's Philip Lim's half-sister. The father, Chou, heavy into the Party before starting his business empire, met an unfortunate death while boating. Officially his death was labelled an accident, but there are alternate explanations. This all happened over a decade ago. Philip supposedly did not get along with his father and had very different opinions on what direction to take the company. Chou's demise vaulted Philip to the top of the empire and it's been wildly successful ever since. Liu Ling was not a factor in the company prior to their father's passing, but she is today. There were rumors that Liu and Philip had an incestuous relationship, but who knows if that's true."

"OK," said Jake. "What did you find out about Novikov?"

"Smart guy. I imagine you'll like him, at least on paper. Of course he's a geologist. Born in Ganja, Azerbaijan, which was called Kirovabad during the Soviet period. His family moved to Baku when he was small, and he eventually earned a PhD from the Russian State Geological Prospecting Institute."

Jake looked up when he heard 'PhD'. This might be the man who visited Barakat in Egypt. Jake wanted as much information as he could get on Novikov.

"Any idea what he looks like?"

"I don't have a picture with me, but I seem to remember he wasn't a handsome guy."

"He's probably the Russian that visited Barakat in Egypt."

"He seems to be a scientist with peripheral regard for politics and such, but he has the trust of Oblonsky. Novikov sort of mirrors Janet here. Chief geologist for Oblonsky's holdings as well as mine foreman for his nickel mine north of the Arctic Circle. A pretty no-nonsense type and maybe a 'yes man' to the boss."

"Any personal stuff on him?"

"Not much. Divorced years ago, confirmed bachelor now. Seems to like the women and definitely likes the vodka. Not very handsome as I've said. In general, Azeris don't care much for Russians but since they all speak Russki I guess hitching onto a Russian company works for some of them. One more tidbit of interest. Al said there's data showing Novikov spends a serious amount of time with Wang. Ostensibly he's Oblonsky's right-hand man handling business, much like Wang does for the Lim family. So that makes sense. But my source felt there might be something else going on."

"Like what?" asked Jake.

"He's not sure. Just mentioned they spend a lot of time together. On trips and what-not."

"Right. So today we'll talk with Oblonsky and Novikov and see if we can get closer to a deal. Let's meet in the lobby in an hour. Oblonsky's sending a car to take us to his Mayfair flat."

#

The clock on the wall showed the time approaching eight, although it was still light outside. Oblonsky's flat overlooked Grosvenor Square from four stories up, a block from Claridge's. It was decked out in Carrera marble, gold leaf, and mirrors. Heavy furniture completed what Jake thought was outlandishly bad taste, probably a Russian thing, but could have worked for a Saudi Prince as well. The butler had shown them into a large reception room almost five hours earlier, and they had made no progress towards an agreement. Oblonsky himself could not make it to London so it was the four Americans with Novikov, Popov, and another man who came instead of the Oligarch. Marat Bragin, introduced as their accountant, said virtually nothing during the entire session. Novikov did most of the talking but frequently fell back on what he said were limits to his negotiating power. Twice now he had excused himself to phone Oblonsky; those calls did nothing to move things along.

"We are getting nowhere Roman," said Jake, clearly exasperated.

As Owens predicted, Jake and Novikov hit it off initially, spending time trading geology war stories. They agreed that Novikov's time flying in Soviet helicopters in northern Siberia took the prize for most daunting tale. Two crashes, several bears, and the loss of four toes to frostbite beat anything Jake could offer. On the negotiation front, however, things did not go as well.

"That is not true," replied Novikov. "There is progress. We understand each other better now than before."

"That is not the kind of progress we need," Jake answered.

Libby, who had been rather quiet for the last twenty minutes, added, "We have made zero progress."

She stood up and pushed her chair towards the table. Novikov attempted to cool down the situation.

"It is exactly the progress we need," he said. "We talk. We disagree. We meet again. We talk. We drink vodka. Eventually we like each other. Eventually we will agree."

The Americans were learning that negotiations in Russia were different than in the US. Owens was not at all surprised, Jake resigned himself to what he had thought might happen, and Libby was totally discouraged. Novikov motioned to the butler and their glasses were refilled with vodka.

"To our future," toasted Novikov.

"If it ever happens," added Jake.

"*Nasdrovia,*" Libby toasted sarcastically, throwing back the vodka before any of the other. She could not hide her growing resentment towards the Russian negotiation style but was finding a fondness for Russian vodka.

They all knocked back the vodka round and Novikov motioned the butler again.

"You want control," he said. "I understand. Boris and Wang do not want you to have control. You understand. Classic situation. Let

Mr. Owens come to Moscow with me. We will host him until we have an agreement. Nice company apartment. Nice Russian women. We fatten him up on good Russian food. For now let's adjourn to the dining room to eat."

They ate a fantastic dinner prepared by Oblonsky's private chef before calling it a night. Finally they migrated to the door, Marat Bragin making it a point to shake the hand of each of them, starting with Jake and ending with Libby. With the first words since he was introduced hours ago, he thanked them for coming and wished them a good stay in London. When he shook Libby's hand, she felt a piece of paper in his palm, which she discretely deposited in her pocket. Since their hotel was only a few blocks from the flat, they chose to walk while light faded into darkness. Once down the block, Libby took the paper from her pocket and saw it was a business card. Marat Bragin was Chief Accountant for BFC Co. On the back was handwritten a different telephone number along with the words 'call only when desperate'. She stopped walking and showed the card to Jake and Peter Owens.

"You have to see this," she said. "Bragin gave it to me when we left. What do you think?"

"I think," replied Owens, "it's a warning of sorts. Remarkable."

"So what should we do with this, Peter?" asked Jake.

"Keep it safe till shit hits the fan. Hopefully we'll never need it."

The next morning they finalized a negotiation strategy and left Peter Owens to spend a couple days in London before heading to Moscow with Novikov in the private jet. Jake, Libby, and Janet took a black cab to Heathrow airport. They were booked on the Concorde to JFK, connecting to other flights from there. They were somber given the lack of progress.

#

Seven days later, Jake was in his Denver condo when he got a fax from Owens, relaying they reached a deal. In Moscow he was able to fall back on the excuse of limited negotiation room, and Oblonsky had agreed to most of what Jake and Libby wanted. GusCo would retain a forty percent working interest, with BFC Co and Lim Enterprise splitting the other sixty percent. This gave Jake and Libby a higher interest than the other partners but not enough to call the shots solo. GusCo would, however, have a veto and full control in areas of safety, legal compliance, regulatory reporting, export contracts, and pricing. For most capital and operational matters, GusCo would need to convince at least one partner to vote yes.

The fax asked for concurrence and approval to arrange a signing ceremony in early August. If all went well, mining efforts could begin before the end of the year. Jake called Libby and they agreed to meet in her office that afternoon.

#

"It gives us most of what we want but not full control," noted Libby.

"I'm satisfied though," Jake added. "Let's fax back and tell Peter to go ahead."

"OK. Agreed. Have him set up a meeting in New York. I'm tired of spending time on long flights. Let's make them come to us."

"Sounds good. Peter can figure it out."

"Do you really think this'll happen Jake, or will Oblonsky add more hurdles?"

"I think it'll happen. I just wonder what surprises will pop up after we sign. Who'll create problems first. Oblonsky or Wang?"

CHAPTER 31

MANHATTAN was sweltering with temperatures and humidity both in the upper nineties. The sky was clear, and the sun reached into crevasses between the tall buildings. In spite of the weather, Jake and Libby went for a run in Central Park, starting from their hotel near the park's southern end. Their pace turned into a walk by the time they reached The Mall, the heat and humidity beyond miserable. They turned around before reaching the Loeb Boathouse. When they got back to the hotel, they were both sweat-drenched and drained.

"Well that's different than a run in Denver," Libby squawked.

"Not used to the humidity?" Jake grinned.

"They can keep it. The park is nice though. Maybe if I'm here in spring or fall it'd be better."

They argued about who would use the shower first, then decided to get in together, taking time to enjoy each other. Water pressure in New York is never a problem and neither one of them was particularly bothered by using a large quantity of it.

Owens met them in the hotel lobby and they took a cab to the Upper East Side, where the Lim family maintained an office overlooking the Metropolitan Museum. After passing the doorman and a security guy, and taking the elevator up twenty-six floors, they discovered a small space with two offices and a large conference room. No full-time staff, and according to Wang used only sparingly for meetings like this. Oblonsky and Wang were already there when they arrived.

"Welcome," said Wang. "Help yourself to coffee or tea. I ordered bagels, lox, and donuts. You can't find bagels like this anywhere else in the world. Let's keep this meeting informal. Our paralegal is here to help. We all got copies of the agreement reached by our representatives in Moscow. We've gone through them in detail and I hope only small changes remain. Let's go through the main document first and our paralegal will record changes as we agree them. She'll then produce final versions for us to sign. I've taken the liberty of arranging a late dinner tonight, catered inside the Met after it closes. I hope that's OK."

"That all sounds good," replied Jake.

"Fine with me," said Oblonsky, munching on a donut.

They spent the next three hours debating and resolving a myriad of minor details. At the eleventh hour, Oblonsky floated one more thing, which was not at all small. He wanted the new joint venture company to be incorporated in Cyprus, where he held many of his businesses.

"Mr. Oblonsky, we discussed this in Moscow, and I thought we resolved the issue," Owens huffed his annoyance.

"But there are advantages to Cyprus," Oblonsky continued. "The tax rates are very low and there is no capital gains tax. It presents a good opportunity to deal easily with Europe and I have many lawyers there who can handle things."

Jake knew the Oligarch wanted to keep incorporation out of the US to avoid stricter regulations concerning foreign bribes and corruption. They spent a good hour discussing this issue, with Oblonsky throwing out scenarios of operating in Egypt which would benefit from not being handcuffed by US anti-corruption law. Jake and Peter knocked back every scenario and stuck to the message that this was a deal-breaker for GusCo. Oblonsky finally gave in and they agreed to incorporate in Delaware.

#

Dinner was an elaborate presentation of small plates within the Metropolitan Museum of Art. The group from the meeting was there, along with guests invited by Wang, including the Chinese Ambassador, the NYPD Police Commissioner, a few financial bigwigs, and several staff from the museum. Four tables situated around the hall had food, and another was set up as a bar. It was in the Sackler Wing, which housed the Temple of Dandur, a three-story sandstone temple stolen from Egypt and artistically lit to provide an impressive backdrop. In 1978, Ambassador of Egypt Meguib helped dedicate and open the hall, which was used for many events including a never-ending string of fundraisers. Libby thought the room too spacious for their small group but enjoyed wandering among the ancient artifacts.

Robin Descaliers, head curator for the Middle and Near East collection, tinked her wine glass with a knife and announced that she would lead them on a tour of the Egyptology collection. She would include a behind-the-scenes visit to the basement, where most of the museum's collection was stored, waiting for rotation into the public viewing rooms. Many items, she said, would never actually make it out of the basement. Additionally, the majority of the museum holdings were kept offsite, in warehouses largely in New Jersey.

As they walked through one of the main exhibition halls, Oblonsky stopped at a stele. It was rather small, but reminded him of the photograph Novikov showed him of the Sinai stele that guided them towards their turquoise.

"Excuse me Ms. Descaliers, but could you explain this stone tablet to me please."

"I'd be happy to Mr. Oblonsky. But first tell me why you picked this item."

"It looks elaborate yet plain, unlike the treasures you see all around us. Why have it on display instead of in storage?"

"This is referred to as the 'Stele of Horemkhauef'. It's from Upper Egypt during the Middle Kingdom, around 1700 BC. Horemkhauef was an official in charge of measuring fields in the town of Hierakonpolis for taxation purposes and was also a priest in the nearby temple of Horus. I believe this stele was erected in his tomb and that's why it's so well preserved. The stele tells of his mission to procure a statue of Horus from the royal workshops. The engraving itself is somewhat crude, indicating it was made locally."

"Are these stele always found in tombs, or can they be off by themselves in the desert. Like a road sign?"

"Most stelae are attributed to a ruler or important person and are basically grave markers. They're common throughout the Middle East, Greece and thereabouts, but also exist in areas like Tibet and the Mayan world. In Egypt you can find some that were used to depict city boundaries or other demarcations."

Jake saw Oblonsky nod. He did not understand the Oligarch's interest in stele, and thought his question about road signs was odd. He made a mental note to ask Salah and Mohammed if they knew of any stelae in the Sinai.

#

The next morning the message light was lit on the phone in Jake and Libby's suite. Jake called to retrieve the message while Libby began dressing. Evidently the paralegal needed most of the day to complete the documents, and the principals should reconvene at eight o'clock in Wang's office for dinner and a signing ceremony.

As Jake contemplated the change in plans he caught a glimpse of Libby in the bathroom. She had just showered and was wrapped in a towel, her back to him as she brushed her hair and applied make-up. He admired her long legs and the outline of what was beneath the towel. As Jake cleared his throat, Libby looked into the mirror and caught him staring. She smiled at his reflection and turned toward him, dropping her towel. The invitation was not lost on Jake who took pleasure in examining her body as she approached him. Their bodies met and Jake's desire ignited an explosion of passion in both of them. They spent until noon lost in each other, when they were finally interrupted by Owens' phone call inviting them to do some sightseeing in the Big Apple.

They strolled around Greenwich Village, popping into a record shop before stopping for snacks in a trendy corner bistro. They walked across the Brooklyn Bridge and looked back at lower Manhattan, the twin towers of the World Trade Center jutting up higher than anything around.

"We should have dinner at Window's On the World," suggested Owens. "Just the ride up the elevator is worth it. When you get off on the one hundred and tenth floor, there's a collection of huge mineral specimens you two would drool over. The best part's the food which is incredible."

"I'd like that," replied Libby. "Not sure we'll fit it into this trip, but book a table for tomorrow night if you can and maybe we'll make it."

They talked about a ride on the Staten Island Ferry but didn't think they had enough time. Instead, they took a taxi back across the bridge and got a table at Katz's Deli to enjoy kosher pickles and a pastrami sandwich.

"So this is where Sally faked her orgasm in the movie," asked Libby.

"Yes ma'am," replied Jake. "You wanna have a go?"

"Not on your life. Besides I like mine to be real."

Peter Owens blushed at that comment, which did not go unnoticed by Libby. He took a quick bite of his sandwich and washed it down with Dr. Brown's celery soda.

The evening went well and they signed and notarized all the papers. Jake asked Oblonsky why he found the stele at the museum so interesting but got no answer. He was sure the Russian had more than an academic interest in the thing but could not figure out what it was.

CHAPTER 32

RADISSON called a meeting for ten o'clock that night, when normal people would be heading to bed after tucking in their kids. Kawinski was used to unorthodox hours but Sam Oppenheimer, the data junkie, felt put out. Fortunately, Kawinski warned him before they entered Radisson's office to not say anything about the late hour. Oppenheimer was prepared to voice his displeasure, but after looking at Kawinski's expression, did not.

"Have a seat at the table," said Radisson, finishing up some paperwork at his desk.

Oppenheimer had never been in this office before, normally working three floors underground in the data analysis laboratory. Radisson had a wall of windows with a view towards the National Mall and the Washington Monument. His walls were peppered with photographs, framed documents, and a few physical mementos. Oppenheimer had met General Richard A. Radisson before and was therefore not surprised by the height and build of the man when he walked to join them.

"Bottom line?" Radisson asked.

"Two Oligarchs have made significant inroads into the US," replied Kawinski, motioning to Oppenheimer to continue.

"Vladimir Ivanovich started buying properties in New York City three years ago and has remained focused in that city. He has several small companies, mostly jewelry and retail, located in Brooklyn. They are likely fronts for money laundering, and NYPD has him in their sights for connections to the Russian mob. Border Control shows he visits the US once a quarter. Boris Oblonsky has properties in New York, Los Angeles, and Miami. His businesses center on import/export, with a large focus on foodstuffs going back and forth from the US to former Soviet spots like Poland and Lithuania. It's a trade ripe with opportunity for smuggling, and he's on the watch list of both the DEA and US Customs. He only makes it over here once or twice a year."

"What about the others?"

"No real presence yet. A few of them have houses or condos here for personal use. We tracked passport entry and exit of all close and extended family members. Looks like some shopping junkets, a few family holidays, that sort of thing."

"So what do you recommend we do about Ivanovich and Oblonsky?"

"Continue tracking and make sure we've got the full picture. Turn our data over to the FBI for laundering investigations. They'll work with Interpol. If and when we get something concrete, approach Russia through the backdoor at the Embassy and see if they care. It would be better for Russia to handle any prosecution but who knows if they will. There's a good chance these guys are complicit with the government in Moscow. Doing anything outside Russia would be messy and complicated."

Radisson stared out his windows in thought. Kawinski and Oppenheimer sat and silently watched the man. Stan knew they would get specific marching orders.

"Good plan, do it. I'll brief the President at our weekly meeting and suggest he broach the subject with the Russians through the Ambassador. It's not a matter of national security. He can gauge how much of an issue this is for Yeltsin."

"Yes sir," said Kawinski. "Anything else on this?"

"Yeah. Keep an open file on this whole Oligarch topic. Alert me if any of the others up their game on our soil. I'll be damned if I'll let Russian billionaires get a foothold here. We've got enough problems with our own billionaires."

CHAPTER 33

JAKE and David Li pushed their seats upright for landing in Shanghai just before midnight. It had been a long flight from Denver. Jake's philosophy was that jetlag is more manageable if he drank on the plane, yet Li was amazed at how much his colleague had consumed. Even though Jake found his theory did not work, he was reluctant to give up the practice.

"The last time I landed in Shanghai was in the early 80's," Jake said to Li. "There were only a few lights visible under the plane on our final approach. I guess electricity was expensive and no one had the lights on, even at nine o'clock. It was super dark everywhere, like the city didn't even exist. What a difference tonight. Shanghai has twelve million people now, but the real difference must be the standard of living. Back then there were millions of bicycles everywhere. You couldn't cross the street for the bicycles. I'll bet now we'll be unable to cross because of all the cars. Progress. I wish sometimes it wouldn't happen so fast."

Li had never been to Shanghai but knew what Jake meant from talking with his dad. Hong Kong had always been more advanced so he'd been used to modern accoutrements since he was very young. But China itself, especially Shanghai and Beijing, was zooming ahead on the technological front.

They disembarked, claimed bags, cleared customs, and found their meet-and-greet person in the main terminal. Li spoke with him in rapid Mandarin, and Jake was more than happy to have him along. The drive to the hotel was uneventful, although stop and go due to heavy traffic, even at this hour of the night. Jake had been right in predicting there would be a flood of cars on the roads. After checking in, they agreed to meet at nine o'clock.

#

Feng Lang looked happy to see them in his office on the twentieth floor of the Shang Yi building. Feng was short and thin, very old looking, bent over, with wispy thin gray hair, a very large round flat face, and a blotchy complexion. He was dressed in a gray pinstripe suit, white shirt, and dark blue tie. His dominant features were his smile, broad and high, acres of yellowing teeth, and eyes which seemed to twinkle. He greeted Li in Mandarin, the two of them chatting long enough that Jake began to feel awkward. He looked around the office, spartan except for photographs of ships and ports. One wall was largely window, allowing a view of the city and a partial view of the lower reaches of the Yangtze River. Finally Li turned to Jake.

"Mr. Feng apologizes but his English is not good. I have known him since I was a little boy; he is a friend of my father's."

Feng nodded which indicated his English was not non-existent. He shook Jake's hand vigorously and motioned for him to sit. Tea arrived along with very colorful cookies. Li and Feng continued to chat while Jake sipped his tea. He had never been a tea drinker, and did not much like the tea they served in England. This tea tasted better to him for some reason. The conversation between Feng and Li went on for over a half hour. Jake occupied himself with the cookies.

"Mr. Feng again apologizes," said Li, looking at Jake. "We have been rude. He will leave us for a bit to attend to other business while I review what we've discussed."

"No worries," said Jake as they all stood, bowed a bit, and Feng Lang walked out of his office.

"As you know, he's got a big shipping business. He was explaining the business he does with Wang Yong. To summarize it's lucrative but troublesome. Wang's difficult to deal with and has caused problems for Feng. He doesn't honor what he agrees to and has bribed enough government agents that it's impossible to seek any official relief. Wang owes Feng Shipping a lot of money, but the interesting part is Wang's relationship with Oblonsky. Apparently there is very bad blood between Wang and Oblonsky; they pretty much hate each other. Someone named Novikov is in bed with Wang. Somehow, Novikov got involved with one of the Lim daughters. Philip Lim puts pressure on Wang to deal with Oblonsky. Wang puts pressure on Novikov because he knows about the daughter. Novikov manipulates Oblonsky who does deals because he thinks he's getting good prices, but he gets misleading information from Novikov. I don't think Oblonsky knows about Novikov's relationship with the girl, which seems to be an ongoing but infrequent thing."

"Wow, that's twisted," said Jake.

"Not unusual for China," said Li laughing. "There's a long history of affairs and convoluted relationships within the elite. Everyone fucks someone they shouldn't. It's more unusual that a Russian is involved, but not unheard of. Even in the seventeenth century, when Cossacks were used as warriors by the Chinese emperor, there was an appreciation of Russian women in China. I moved out of this part of the world when I was young but kept hearing things from my mother and father. Then at Stanford I minored in Chinese which included reading their literature, analyzing their sociology, and dipping into their philosophies. It's an old and rich culture which had plenty of time to develop intricate nuances. Quite complicated actually. Very hard for Westerners to fathom."

"Whatever, it's beyond me," said Jake. "Back to things that matter, so Novikov holds sway over the entwined business dealings of a Russian Oligarch and a Chinese dynasty?"

"Apparently we geologists wield magical powers," said Li, smiling.

"I don't think it's our discipline David," Jake chuckled as he thought about all David had shared. "Let me see if I can get this straight. In a nutshell, Wang and Boris don't like each other. Novikov may be conflicted. Is there anything else of potential importance you've discovered?"

"Oh yeah. Boris is under investigation in Moscow for tax evasion. I guess that's normal in Russia, but Feng says Boris is being targeted because of something completely different. Regardless, the tax angle is how they'll nail him. Feng thinks he'll go to prison for years."

"Oh boy," said Jake. "That'll complicate things. I guess we'll need another lawyer to tell us what happens if Oblonsky's company is seized. For now, we need to get the start-up money out of Oblonsky and Wang. Is Wang under any investigation?"

"Not that Feng said."

"Ok, that's good. So although Wang is unscrupulous and potentially dangerous, and Oblonsky is heading for prison, we should be fine going forward?"

"Who knows," said Li. "Our biggest worry seems to be Oblonsky's properties being confiscated. But Wang seems to think it's OK to proceed and I don't think we'll ever know as much as him. So maybe we're good. I'd put my money on Wang as opposed to Oblonsky."

"What's on the agenda for the rest of the day?"

"Mr. Feng will be back shortly. Unless you have anything else for him, we should thank him and say goodbye. Then I think you can do some sightseeing."

"I hear walking the Bund is pleasant."

"It is and I think you'll enjoy it. I've arranged for a family friend to show us around town. You'll find Shanghai much different than the last time you were here. I've never been here so I'm excited to see anything. We might meet some interesting people, because my father said it always pays to make acquaintances with people in high places."

"YALLA" Abdel said to Moataz after the moon dropped below the horizon and it became even darker. The NOFORTH man from Fayoum did not really like the Sinai. "The ground here is different than the Western Desert. Don't trip and be quiet. Follow me."

The two young men moved quietly in a crouching posture. They covered the couple hundred yards quickly from where they had hidden to the mining camp, ducking behind the office building. Although it was two o'clock in the morning, they were still wary of anyone who might be awake. Hearing no noise, they continued across the open area to the storage shed where they knew the dynamite was kept. The door had a latch, but no lock, and they easily entered. Abdel switched on his red headlamp so they could see. There were many shelves of supplies, everything from clothing and equipment to food and drinks. They finally found the explosives locker, clearly marked with danger signs. It was secured with two locks.

"Give me the pack," said Abdel.

He slid the pack off of Moataz's back and opened the zipper. He carefully removed a square package wrapped with silver duct tape. It was a crude bomb, and was the first one NOFORTH had ever constructed. Abdel found a place for it behind the explosives locker. He set the rudimentary timer for four hours to give them time to get far away, and to explode before the crew shift occurred. He put the package down and moved several boxes in front of it to conceal it. The two men retraced their steps, finally arriving at their car an hour later. As they drove back to Cairo, Abdel speculated, "*Insha'Allah*, we should be halfway to Cairo before the blast."

"*Insha'Allah*," replied Moataz.

#

Kai finished his morning prayer in the bunkhouse tent which four of the miners called home. He was due to go on tour at eight that morning, his crew relieving the night crew which had put in their twelve-hour shift underground. Kai was a crew leader and as such took responsibility for the drilling, blasting, and mucking of rock along the drift and up to the surface. The first part of his job was planning and procuring the explosives they would need for the day. There were strict protocols on who had access to the explosives locker, how much one could take down the hole each day, and where it was stored underground. Very accurate and specific records were kept, and very few people had access. Kai knew his job and did it well. This was his last year as a miner; he already decided that after twenty-five years of working underground he had saved enough money to retire in China, open a small shop in his town, and enjoy his family that he had seen so little of most of his life. His son and daughter were not yet fifteen as Kai had married late in life. China's one child policy was in effect when his wife became pregnant, but fortunately she gave birth to twins. Under the policy they were allowed to keep both children. Kai's mother helped his wife raise their children until he could afford to return home.

It was pure coincidence and bad luck that Kai opened the explosives locker minutes before the timer instructed the NOFORTH bomb to explode. This explosion set off the dynamite and blasting caps within the locker. Although they had not received the latest shipment of dynamite on schedule, there was still enough to obliterate the storage shed, killing Kai instantly. The blast woke up everyone on the surface. Confused, disoriented workers exited their tents to stand around and ponder the chaos erupting around them. Two of the men fought the few flames that persisted, but for the rest there was nothing to do but stare.

The blast was strong enough that the crew underground felt vibrations. Knowing they were not caused by anything they did in the drift, they hurried to the surface, thinking it was an earthquake, which was not unheard of in this tectonically active part of the world. When the crew got to the surface, they saw debris where the shed previously stood, and joined the others in gaping at the pandemonium.

#

Osama Foda was watching the television news in Alexandria when the story aired. A half dozen men sat up and cheered when the reporter said a storage shed had been totally destroyed at a gold mine in the Sinai. Investigators were on the way to the site and there was no word yet on the cause of the blast. The reporter went on to say that mining was a dangerous occupation and accidents like this were inevitable when dealing with explosives. Osama walked to the fridge and took out a number of Stella bottles, handing one to most of the men. Three of them were strict Moslems and abstained from alcohol, so Osama gave them orange sodas instead.

"To Abdel and Moataz," he said, raising his beer and toasting the men who were just then approaching Alexandria city limits.

The group continued to laugh and talk, discussing the event as a turning point for their cause. When Abdel and Moataz finally joined their colleagues, more toasting and congratulations ensued.

"Shush," yelled one of the men, turning up the volume on the television.

"News just in from the Sinai and the site of the explosion earlier today," said the attractive announcer. "Apparently there was one fatality at the site, a Chinese expatriate employed by the mine. It is not known if this miner had anything to do with the blast, or if he was just in the wrong place at the wrong time."

Osama Fada and the group went quiet.

"Shit," said Fada.

He looked at Abdel and Moataz with a glare no one would want to see. Both men were speechless, staring at the ground.

"You killed a man," Fada said.

"We did not mean to," replied Abdel.

"That is the one thing I cannot condone," said Fada. "How did this happen?"

"I don't know. We snuck into the camp, set the timer on the bomb for four hours, then left. Just like we planned. It went off at the time we planned. We did nothing wrong."

"Shit," said Osama again, unhappy with this new development.

The NOFORTH group met over the next few days, discussing what went wrong in the Sinai and reviewing other plans. Two other operations involving bombs were cancelled and efforts were refocused on protests and publicity. They did not claim responsibility for the explosion and made sure none of the members talked about their involvement. They were all about publicity, but not when it included killing people.

WHEN Jake and the GusCo team evaluated potential mining methods for the gold deposit, they rejected an open pit operation. Janet Robinson had the most hard-rock mining experience and was convinced that the expected distribution of ore lent itself more to an underground mine, having a main shaft with horizontal tunnels called drifts, and upwards-sloping excavations called stopes at various depths. The ore body was essentially tabular, oriented vertically. The richest part was likely fairly deep and narrow so removing overburden would be prohibitively expensive.

Jake and Salah el Gindi came up with the name 'Muat' for the mine, which meant 'favorable' or 'lucky' in Arabic. Jake thought they would need more than their fair share of luck with an operation underground. Ever since he worked a summer in a coal mine, he hated being underground and knew such ventures increased the risk of tragedy. Nevertheless, that is what was needed in the Sinai and that is what was being dug. Jake hoped the Muat would be spared catastrophe, but that hope was dashed six months earlier when the explosion occurred. Ironically, this incident was not underground at all, but on the surface.

Roman Novikov walked along the rail tracks of the drift at the hundred-foot depth level, careful to step on the ties, as the ground between them and off to the side was wet and muddy. In some places, a boot placed in between railroad ties might sink up to six inches in warm, wet mud. Even though they were in the desert, they had hit groundwater at eighty feet, thus requiring a pumping system to keep the mine from flooding. Fortunately the aquifer was weak, with flow through the fractured Precambrian rock slow.

Jake got excited on the elevator ride down the main shaft despite his claustrophobic tendencies, and walking the drift caused his adrenaline to surge. It was seriously satisfying to see his hard work result in physical development. So far he was happy with the progress; this was the first time he toured this drift, which was only fifty feet long so far. The lighting was good, and a constant flow of fresh air pumped through the mine took out some of the humidity. He thought the timbers holding up the roof looked tidy and the wiring and piping that ran along the upper right corner of the drift were neat and precise. The rock on the walls was consolidated and very dark. 'If the rock continues like this', he thought, 'we should have few problems with sloughing'. They continued underground, arriving at the face where three miners drilled in preparation to blast. Novikov shouted at them and they shut down the drills and stood to the side. David Li had accompanied Jake into the mine; he was currently working as Novikov's apprentice and basically as Jake's 'overseer'. He also had primary responsibility for sampling and reporting.

"We use a typical drill pattern,' screamed Novikov, "Because of the type of rock we're using a pyramid cut. We drill twenty-four holes, load them with dynamite, and blast. Very old school. A bit slow but reliable."

"Why don't you use ANFO, ammonium and fuel oil?" asked Jake. "Virtually all surface mining and most underground mining in the US now use that. It's more stable, cheaper, and more dependable than dynamite. New school but you must be familiar with it."

"I am," replied Novikov. "The biggest reason we don't use it here is Egyptian regulation. That ANFO stuff is used by terrorists and it's easy to lose track of. Anyone could scoop a bit and sell it. You can't keep track of it all. Dynamite is more specific. You have a number of sticks, cases, and crates that are easy to count and track. Harder for it to go missing. The other reason is our crew. Chinese invented dynamite and have used it for centuries. All the guys working here have used it for years or decades and are comfortable with it. It might be more expensive but that is what they know."

"If they're so familiar with it, why have we had incidents?" said Jake. "You lost another man last month. That makes two. I saw the report but want the real stories."

"The miner killed last month was unlucky, despite what you named the mine. Muat did not ward off the evil spirits. That had nothing to do with dynamite. The 'official' report we filed said he died when he passed out and fell in front of the ore cart as it was rolling to the shaft. We got two other miners to attest that the man had been feeling poorly for a few days and they saw him just collapse. Bad karma. This story that we made up suited both us and the workers down there at the time. Nobody is at fault for anything. It was just a freak accident. The autopsy could not prove otherwise."

"The real story is that he was working on some wiring along the drift, shocked himself, fell off his ladder, and was run over by the ore cart. He never should have been working on that wiring while ore was moving down the drift. It was unlucky he shocked himself, but the shock and the fall are not what killed him. The ore cart weighed at least five tons and the wheels hit him right in the throat. His head was cut off instantly. The man following the cart saw the head roll off to the side before the cart even passed. If we filed the real story, we would have had weeks of government audits and possibly a shut down. This way we keep working. We sent the body back to China, along with a month's wages for the family."

"This shit has to stop" shouted Jake, angrily poking his finger at Novikov. "We can't tolerate fatalities. You need to make this a higher priority Roman. Do you have any more information on the first fatality from the explosion?"

"Not really. We think that Kai went into the explosives shed around six in the morning to get the dynamite his crew would need that day. We don't know why it blew up. No one was with him and no one saw what happened. It's hard to set that stuff off by accident. He had a lot of experience and was regarded as something of an expert. I don't think we'll ever know what actually happened. Maybe he decided to kill himself, who knows. Fortunately, no one else was hurt. And fortunately, it was only two days before we took delivery of our normal load of explosives. There was not that much in the trailer at the time. If it happened after a delivery it might have taken out half the camp. We've since moved the storage shed further away from the rest of the buildings and tents."

"Did the authorities come up with anything when their investigator came?"

"No. We did our investigation first and could not find anything out of the ordinary. Then the government guy came. There really wasn't much left for him to look at. They found some suspicious pieces, but we never heard back from them. The inspector went over our safety protocols and was happy. It helped that our safety record until then had been excellent. A couple citations for improper protective equipment but everything else was fine."

"Let's try to avoid killing anyone else, OK? David, I want you to spend more time on safety. Make sure all these Chinese guys are wearing the right PPE and doing things by the book. Now let's get out of here and let these guys get back to work."

Jake was ready to get out of the cramped space and back to the surface. They reached the top of the shaft just as a helicopter landed at the pad west of camp. Walking to the supervisor's trailer they saw two people getting out of the chopper. Wang Yong and Liu Ling joined them minutes later, making their first visit to the mine.

"Welcome to the Muat," said Jake when the visitors came into the office.

They greeted each other and grabbed coffee or tea before sitting down. Wang was short on small talk and despite the long trip wanted to start the tour immediately. Jake had never met Liu Ling and was surprised that the woman accompanied Wang. Jake studied her as she walked towards him. Average height, slight build, she was pale with black hair like most Asians. She was dressed in a black pants suit that looked expensive. She had a round, friendly face with very smooth skin, and a pleasant smile. She shook Jake's hand with a very light touch, all the while keeping her almond-shaped eyes focused on his. Jake guessed she was around forty years old, but it was hard for him to tell with Asians.

Wang said they wanted to be back in the helicopter in four hours, as their flight departed Sharm el Sheikh at seven that night. Jake said he would stay in the trailer and catch up on things while Novikov and Li took the two Chinese dignitaries on their tour. One trip underground in a day was enough for Jake and he watched as the others donned their gear. He grabbed Li's arm as they walked towards the exit and whispered to him.

"Stick close to these two and don't let on that you understand Chinese. I want to know if they say anything odd."

"Will do Jake. I've been careful so far not to talk to any of the workers in Chinese. I swear though that I've overheard Roman chatting with one of them in Mandarin."

"Well that's interesting," Jake looked puzzled. "Keep that to yourself. Better catch up with them."

Jake considered Li's last comment as he watched the foursome stroll to the shaft shack. He had not thought of Novikov as the type to speak Chinese.

#

Late that afternoon Jake asked David Li and Novikov to meet before dinner out by their firepit. He got there before them and lit the fire, pouring himself a glass of Old Grand-Dad bourbon which he had brought from the States. Alcohol was strictly forbidden in the mining camp, but he was the boss, so what the heck. When Novikov and Li joined him, he poured a glass for each of them.

"It's not vodka but it's real American whiskey," he said holding up his glass. "Kentucky bred. Fifteen years in cask."

"*Nostrovya,*" said Novikov. "I like bourbon. To what do we owe this breaking of rules?"

"To a successful start of operations. Thank you Roman for your leadership in getting this up and going. Tell me your thoughts? What don't I know yet? Anything we need to worry about?"

"So far so good. It's too bad we had two accidents but that's mining. You don't know what you don't know. Your question is interesting. We get hashish smugglers coming near our area every few weeks. I met with them and told them to stay clear of our operation and we will not bother them. That seems to be working. They sometimes have people with them they are smuggling. Not our concern. I guess my only concern are the young Egyptians we sometimes see. They stay away but watch us, sometimes with binoculars. I asked my hashish smugglers about them and think the people are what you call 'activists'. The smugglers thought they were from Cairo or maybe Alexandria."

"Did anyone use a group name? Like NOFORTH?"
Novikov looked up too quickly at this question.
"No, nothing like that."
"Did they cause any problems for you yet?"
"Not that I know of."
Jake thought back to his conversation on NOFORTH with Salah
el Gindi. The full name was No Foreign Theft, and their goal was
to stop foreign investment in Egypt, particularly in oil and mining.
This group had caused problems around the Seth Field and Jake
hoped they were not targeting the mine now.

As they broke from dinner, Jake asked David Li to take a stroll.
Wang Yong and Liu Ling had left by helicopter after only three
hours on-site, saying how satisfied they were with the operations and
vowing to keep funds flowing. They thanked Novikov for treating
the workers so well and left a small bundle of cash, in US dollars,
to reward the workers to an overnight stay in Sharm el Sheikh.
Jake had purposefully not asked Li to comment on the day while
Novikov was around. They would not be overheard as they walked in
the desert. Jake asked David if he learned anything from the visitors..

"It was difficult to hear what they said to each other without being
intrusive," David said, "especially underground where there's so much
noise. But since they needed to talk loudly to hear each other, I made
out some of their conversation. They switched back and forth from
English to Mandarin. The Mandarin stuff as you would suspect was
the interesting part. I think we might have a problem."

"So what did they say? You can qualify it as you go but tell me
what you think, not only what you heard."

"Novikov definitely speaks Mandarin. Not as good as me but good
enough. Wang was telling Novikov to make the geology look bad.
Do some sabotage to the mine if he needed to. It seems Oblonsky's
in bad shape both financially and politically. Wang wants to make
the mine look bad and force Oblonsky out. I think he wants to get
us out too but I couldn't hear most of that part."

Jake shook his head, muttering "Not good".

"No and there's more. If I got it right, Novikov was talking to
Wang about the Bedouin smugglers that come past every so often.
He thought they might be susceptible to bribes if there was anything

Wang thought they might do. Evidently Novikov has met with them and thinks he has a relationship with them."

"So what did Wang say?"

"He thought about it for a while. I missed the beginning of his answer, but I did hear him say something about hooking the Bedouin up with NOFORTH, and giving them both money. Then I lost the conversation again. I did hear him say Seth Field, so maybe he's getting Novikov to buy their help to do something both here and at the gas field. I don't know."

"Shit," said Jake. "Are you sure Wang told him to get the NOFORTH group on board?"

"Pretty sure. I definitely heard him say to give them money."

"This is becoming messy," said Jake, getting madder by the minute. He thought back to the early days of his gas prospect. He now had different players but similar obstacles.

"But maybe there's a bright side," Li continued. "Liu Ling was silent most of the time. Near the end of the tour, I heard her telling a couple senior workers to not do anything bad. She told them she would protect them as long as they did their job and did not do anything to harm the mine. She gave one of them something I think might have been a business card, telling the guy to contact her if they were ever again asked to do harm."

"So Liu Ling is not on board with all this?" asked Jake.

"It seems so but who knows. It seems clear however that Wang is out for Oblonsky. And possibly you as well."

They continued to walk and talk under the biggest sky outside of Montana. After a half hour they had nothing more to discuss about business and took time to look up. There was no moon and the Milky Way stretched from one horizon to the other.

"So do you like it out here David?"

"The desert has grown on me. At first it seemed just stark and ugly. It was new for me. Now I find it beautiful. The nights are always like this. Billions of stars limited only by what your eye can see. I love the silence interrupted only by animals, or the wind. During the day it's sun and shades of brown. I never knew brown came in so many different colors. Yep, I've grown to appreciate it."

He paused before continuing.

"Mohammed and Abu showed me how to see and appreciate things I would never have noticed myself. They also brought me to meet some local Bedouin. That was really cool having tea with them. They have so little but seem so content. I remember what you told me about your gas field and feeling guilty about how it would change the local socioeconomics. I didn't understand you at the time but do now. I wonder if our mine will be a force for good or a scar on the landscape and local society. Honestly, I don't like having Chinese workers here. It feels like a betrayal of the people who live here."

"Yeah, I feel the same way," said Jake. "I never wanted to bring in Chinese, but it had to happen to get Wang's funding. I hope someday we can change the structure and reverse that decision. Until then we'll try to involve locals when possible and not ruin too much of the desert."

"I hope that happens," said Li. "But it might be unrealistic."

RUBLYOVSKOE Highway runs through a picturesque, wooded area forty-minutes west of Moscow proper, following a road used by Tsars in the sixteenth century. The Romanovs sheltered here, and notables such as Peter the Great and Catherine the Great did pilgrimages to the Savvino-Storoozheysky Monastery in the area. Not far from where Lenin and Stalin had their dachas, Boris Oblonsky built a large house surrounded by an acre of pine and birch. Although he built an eight-foot wall with security cameras around the property, two heavily armed guards continuously roamed his yard to ensure his safety. They supplemented the guards hired to wander the entire neighborhood, a Russian version of Beverly Hills. Oblonsky's neighbors were similarly notorious individuals, and included businessmen, politicians, and celebrities.

The house itself was a twelve thousand square foot faux French chateau, complete with gravel driveway, twelve chimneys, and geometrically trimmed bushes along paths interrupted by gilded fountains. Oblonsky's third wife helped design the property which was only four years old but built to look much older. It was a pleasant evening in May. Oblonsky was meeting with Viktor Popov in the English garden, enjoying dessert and vodka under a sky turning magenta as the sun slowly headed for a short rest before rising six hours later. The conversation was in Russian, spoken in low tones in spite of all the security and isolation. As the Oligarch said numerous times, 'one could never be too careful'.

"So what did our mole say?" asked Oblonsky.

A week ago, the Oligarch sent his right-hand-man to Egypt to meet with Chou Zhou, a miner at the Muat Mine. Chou had arranged to have an accident, deliberately slicing his own leg open with a tool, requiring he be sent to Sharm el Sheikh for medical treatment. With advanced planning and precision timing, Popov flew the private jet from Moscow to Sharm el Sheikh and met Chou in the hospital just after the doctor finished his work. They had only an hour before Chou was driven back to the mine, and Popov got back on his plane.

"Why did you feel the need to plant a mole in the mine?" Popov asked his boss.

"To keep an eye on my investment," answered Oblonsky. "To watch out for any activity that might hurt my position. Basically to watch out for Wang and Tillard. This is a normal thing to do; it's how I built my empire, and it's how I stay alive."

"Have you ever suspected problems with Novikov?"

Oblonsky raised his left eyebrow and looked deeply at Popov. He had not expected this opening. Novikov had been with him for years. He relied upon that man and Popov knew it. He wondered if Popov was plotting against Novikov for his own gain.

"Novikov has been loyal to me for two decades," answered the Oligarch. "I've never suspected him of anything but loyalty. That's why I put him in charge of the operation down there. What are you saying?"

Popov stared back at the Oligarch, waiting a moment before proceeding. He was about to take a big risk, one he hoped would result in a big reward. Oblonsky's face was stolid, his lips pursed, his eyes squinted. He took another sip of vodka and demanded that Popov tell him what he learned.

"Chou noticed a few months back that Novikov seemed to be listening to conversations among the workers. Conversations in Mandarin. He never heard Roman speak it, and could not be sure of anything but he got a strange feeling. When Wang visited the mine last month, Chou overheard Roman and Wang speaking Mandarin underground. They were careful and thought they were alone, but at one point Chou was hidden behind a wall and heard them in Mandarin. Wang talked about taking over the operation. From the bits he could make out, Chou thought Wang was giving Novikov orders to sabotage mining efforts. Like he was Roman's boss. Since then Roman has given some odd orders at the mine,

according to Chou. They've changed the direction of the drift
and Chou thinks they may have veered off the mineralized rock.
At first Chou was upset that Roman was underground so much.
He thought he was not trusted. But then it seemed he was just
meddling."

"I cannot believe Roman would do this. Did you come up with
anything else to back up what Chou alleges? Maybe Chou is playing
us. Did he say he wanted anything from us? More money?"

"No, no, nothing like that. All he did was tell me what I'm telling
you. You know that communications are still impossible from the
mine site, so every time Roman needs to call anyone, he does it from
Sharm. I managed to look at phone records from when Roman
stayed at the Movenpick over the past six months. It's a Swiss-run
hotel, so their records are good. The staff is Egyptian so bribes are
successful. Roman has been there a lot and his call records show that
he phones China more than twice as often as Moscow. Those are
just the calls he initiates."

"So Roman is calling China. Do we know who?"

"Looks like Wang or at least his office. Mostly the main number
but also two others."

"What others?"

"I couldn't find out who owns the other numbers. I have
our security people working on it but it's not easy within China.
Eventually we'll figure it out."

"Did Chou say anything about Tillard and the Americans?"

"Not really, except everyone at the mine likes them. Tillard is
always inquisitive when he visits and asks the workers directly about
things. He gets down to their level, not like a Russian boss. Li is liked
even more. Since he's underground much of the time, the workers
see a lot of him and trust him. Chou thought he heard Roman and
Wang discussing them. Maybe trying to make it seem that Tillard
was behind the sabotage they planned. Perhaps blaming it on Li.
That especially rankled Chou."

"I find it difficult to believe Roman would betray me. Are you
sure he's up to something?"

"It sure looks like it. Sorry to say it seems bad."

"I think we need to do our own planning. I've never condoned disloyalty, and have never liked that Chinese guy. We need to deal with them both. As for the Americans, I like the idea of letting them take the blame. Maybe we should let things run their course and see what Wang does. Then we pin it on Tillard and the woman. It would be nice if I ended this year with sole ownership of the mine."

The Shit Hits the Fan

1997

SHEREMETYEVO Airport was crowded when Jake landed mid-morning, disembarking his Boeing 747 at the terminal built for the 1980 Summer Olympics. Jake thought the place looked a bit tired but maybe that was just the state of Russian infrastructure. The airport was expanding and modernizing to accommodate the increase in air traffic brought by privatization, the latest project to lay another runway littering the whole area with construction trucks and equipment. Confusion was rampant but an efficient process pushed him through customs and immigration quickly, and a man was waiting to guide him to a car.

Little more than an hour later, Jake walked into the Metropol Hotel. This Art Nouveau masterpiece was built at the turn of the century, housing the first headquarters of the new Bolshevik Government. In 1991 it was totally renovated and opened as a five-star luxury hotel. Most of the architectural elements and many original furnishings remained and the hotel had an historic feel. Service was arguably the best in Russia.

Oblonsky had expected both Jake and Libby to come to Moscow, and was disappointed that Libby stayed home, citing too much work. She had relayed that Jake was GusCo's COO and could handle this trip alone. Oblonsky insisted Jake stay at the Metropol and was footing the bill. Although the local economy in Moscow was sorting itself out and prices were generally low, the Metropol was an exception, charging London prices and hoping to suck in as many foreign dollars as possible. The hotel preferred US dollars.

The trip from Denver had been long and Jake was tired. He was glad his meeting was not scheduled to start until dinner. Fighting jetlag, he settled into his room, nibbled at room-service borscht and salad, and went for a short walk. Pausing at the corner outside the

Metropol, he gazed across the street at the Bolshoi Theater, a classical building set beyond a lovely square open to the road. Construction was ubiquitous. Turning to the left, Jake walked through Ploschad Revolyutsi, past the Kazan Cathedral, and into enormous Red Square. He stood for a long time taking in sights he had heard about for so long. In front of him was the magnificent State Historical Museum, a 19th Century masterpiece built of rusty-red sandstone in Russian Medieval style. The plethora of spires, turrets, and merlons gave it a busy look that contrasted against the blue sky dotted with white puffy clouds sailing southwards. The building echoed the complicated architecture of St. Basil's Cathedral at the other end of the square, famous in photos but smaller than Jake expected. Even so, the bright multi-colored onion domes presented a unique sight, the Moskva River just beyond.

In between sat the Kremlin, with its steep-roofed towers, crenulated walls, and gold-domed churches. The warm afternoon had brought out families who were enjoying the day. In addition, small groups of tourists followed guides holding up umbrellas or flags, stopping every so often to hear about one of the sights. Jake walked down the east side of the square which was paved with stones. He glanced into the GUM, the famous glass-roofed shopping mall which was reputedly the only store in Moscow that never ran out of inventory. It had become a mecca for foreign tourists and local elite, with prices to startle. Jake made a mental note to return and buy something for Libby, but now walked back to the hotel for a nap.

#

Dinner was catered into Oblonsky's office on Arbat Street, which Jake learned was less than a ten-minute walk from the Metropol, on the other side of the Kremlin. In spite of that proximity he was chauffeured, a drive which took longer than walking due to congestion and awkward traffic patterns in the area. One advantage of driving was the travelogue given by Dmitry, his English-speaking driver who went into detail on the Lubyanka building that housed both the famous prison and the FSB, the latest version of the KGB. As they drove past the white stone building, he wished Jake never saw the inside, particularly the basement. Dmitry finally pulled the car into the below-ground parking area of 1 Arbat, leaving Jake at an elevator which brought him up to the lobby and security. After passing through a metal detector, he followed a pretty lady to another elevator which spat him directly into Oblonsky's office.

Boris Oblonsky, Wang Yong, Roman Novikov, and Viktor Popov were drinking aperitifs, sitting at a conference table elegantly set for dinner. Jake joined them directly. Several tuxedo-clad, older waiters shuffled food and replenished drinks. The group was watched over by two men Jake guessed were bodyguards, one large Asian-looking man for Wang and one even larger, dour giant for the Russians. No one introduced those two gentlemen and they never said a word. The conversation began light, mostly about the good weather, the renovation-boom in Moscow, and current sports. It transitioned towards the Oligarch and Wang discussing grain exports and problems they had with new government regulations. After dessert, Oblonsky turned conversation to the Muat Mine.

"Roman, give us an update on the Sinai mine."

"Yes sir," replied Novikov, who spent the next ten minutes reciting figures involving feet of drift excavated, tons of ore shipped, and percentage of gold seen. It was all robotic and contained nothing about the problems or challenges which faced every operation.

"This operation has been jinxed since before it began," said Jake. He wanted to provoke the group and see if he could get the undercurrents that David Li discovered out in the open.

"What do you mean?" barked Oblonsky.

"We've never talked about it, but before either of you got involved a large pile of drill core was removed from the site. That core led us to search for gold in the first place. It likely contained important information, but we never got to analyze it all. We took a tiny fraction of the cores in the very beginning and planned to get and study the rest, but that never happened. Mr. Wang, you were not involved back then, but I know Boris was looking for a turquoise mine in the area. Boris, did your people take that core?"

Oblonsky chuckled and waived for the waiter to refill their glasses.

"Bravo, Jake," he said holding up his glass. "To our partner from America. Of course we removed the cores. We were looking for turquoise as you said, before we met each other. We put the cores on a ship in Sharm el Sheikh, bound for Africa. From there we planned to ship them to Yemen and then fly them to Russia for analysis. But they disappeared. The entire ship was lost at sea. No one ever saw the cores, the boat, or the crew again."

"Pirates?" asked Wang. "They've been operating off of Africa for years."

"I don't believe you Boris," said Jake. "You want me to believe that you staked claims out there without working on those cores?"

"I do. We did. We took a chance. It did not pay off but that is life."

"So we don't know who sank the boat?" said Wang.

"We don't," replied Oblonsky. "But Mr. Tillard was premature in saying you were not involved, Wang. You knew I was looking for turquoise there. We talked about that, and I remember you asked a lot of questions. We wanted you to participate but you had no interest. Maybe you really did have an interest. Maybe you took those cores."

"That was a long time ago Boris. I had nothing to do with any cores."

"What about the explosion at the mine? Did you have anything to do with that?" asked Oblonsky.

"Absolutely not," said Wang. "Why would I do that? A man was killed. One of my men. A Chinese miner. I suppose you're going to accuse me of killing my miner who fell off the ladder underground?"

"I wasn't, but it's interesting you brought that up. We've worked together a long time Wang. Tell me, why you are trying to sabotage our gold mine?"

The Oligarch took another drink of vodka and stared into Wang's eyes. Wang stared back without moving a facial muscle. He did not offer anything in defense.

"I have a mole in the mine," continued Oblonsky. "One of your own Chinese workers. It was easy to find one willing to watch and report back to me. It did not even cost me much. I don't think those men like you Wang. Popov paid a visit to the Sinai and learned some interesting things from our mole. You have been telling the Chinese crew to veer off the deposit, substitute the ore in assay sample bags with worthless rock, and make the mine look worse than it really is."

"I have no idea what you're talking about," said Wang, gently placing his wine glass on the table in front of him.

"I believe you do," said Jake. "My man at the mine overheard you telling some of the miners to do these things. You were quite specific in what you wanted. You talked about paying local Bedouin and activists from NOFORTH. All of it designed to get Boris and myself out of the deal."

"Your man Li told you this?" asked Wang, suddenly realizing Li must understand Mandarin.

Jake was getting agitated. He stood up and raised his voice even louder.

"He was born in Hong Kong and speaks Mandarin. It's his first language, for Christ's sake. We made sure no one at the mine knew this, although I have to say I never expected it to pay off so handsomely. We know what you've been doing, trying to get Boris out of the deal by showing that the ore was getting poorer. Driving up costs and introducing minor setbacks. What I don't understand is how you expected to get me out of the deal. After all it's my mine. My idea. My exploration. My baby so to speak. I was never going to give up."

"What else did Li say?" asked Novikov, looking sheepish sitting next to Wang.

"Well that is interesting," said Jake, turning to him. "It seems Li is not the only one unexpectedly fluent in Chinese. Did Boris know you spoke it, and did he know you've been working closely with Wang?"

"I never hid my knowledge of Mandarin," said Novikov. "And of course I work with Wang. He's a partner in this mine and has questions. Just like you."

"As long as we've worked together Roman, I missed the fact that you spoke Chinese," said Oblonsky. "And I certainly did not suspect you were plotting against me with Wang."

Novikov stood up and reached inside his jacket. The sound of the gun filled the air and Jake saw both bodyguards raise their guns, unsure of what to do next since it was Oblonsky who shot Novikov dead. The Russian guard did not want to shoot his boss, and the

Chinese guard decided it did not involve him. Oblonsky never rose from his seat but held the gun in one hand, his vodka in the other.

"Holy shit," Jake yelped, crumpling to duck under the conference table.

"That solves my problem of staff disloyalty," Oblonsky said to Wang. "It does not solve my problem of partner disloyalty."

Wang turned to look at his bodyguard but not before Oblonsky nodded at Popov, who put a bullet in the Chinese guard's head. The large man tilted forward, his face hit the floor, and he bounced once. Popov put another bullet into the back of his head to make sure he was dead.

Jake, still under the table, saw the man hit the floor, then poked his head above the edge of the table to see what was happening. He moved his gaze from Oblonsky to Wang. He felt like vomiting.

"You were going to push me out of this deal," Wang said to Oblonsky.

"Where did you get that idea Wang? We don't like each other but I don't like any of my partners. That doesn't mean I want them all dead. You served a purpose in this partnership. I brought you in to pay our way and provide cheap crew and equipment. Why did you screw it up?"

"I've always hated you," said Wang sneering, realizing his time was running out. He was spitting as he talked. "I worked with you because the Lim family wanted me to. I had to force myself to work with you. I dislike Russians in general, but you I find particularly unrefined and distasteful. You are a thug who will do anything for a ruble. You and the Lims, you're the same. You treat people like shit. Money and power, power and money. I wanted the Sinai mine for myself. To get you and Tillard out, then break with the Lims. That family used me for half my life and I'm sick of it. I've had enough of working for them and putting up with you."

"Well then let me solve that for you," said Oblonsky, putting a bullet into Wang's chest. A large crimson spot grew on his white shirt before the tall Chinese man teetered and fell forward onto the table, breaking china and crystal, and scattering the remains of dessert. As his head came to rest sideways on the table, Jake noticed the stem of a Baccarat wine goblet sticking out of his left eye. He stared at that eye, making no move to stand up, when Oblonsky addressed him.

"I didn't know that you knew," Oblonsky said to Jake, the gun now trained on the American. "Your David Li learned about Wang and his efforts to undermine us and you did not tell me?"

Jake was sweating, staring into the barrel of the pistol. He slowly stood up, feeling even more nauseous.

"I planned to tell you at this meeting, which is what I did. I just didn't know what role you played in this. Why do you think I brought up the missing cores? The cores don't matter at this point, and really didn't matter much ever. We took what we needed in the beginning. I wanted to get the conversation into the open. I thought maybe Wang snatched the cores. It was either him or you. But really I just wanted to start the dialogue about Wang screwing us, and see where he went with it."

"It could have been those protestors who took the core."

"Could have been. But they are after publicity and there was no publicity. I didn't know anything about a boat or shipping the cores out of Egypt. The NOFORTH group would have scattered them across the desert. Or destroyed them with a bulldozer."

"You could've at least told me about Novikov."

"You're right Boris, I could have. Would it have turned out differently?"

"It might've been less messy. Now we have a mess here my friend. I will take care of this, but help clean up. I don't want any staff to see what's happened. We need to hurry."

Oblonsky shouted orders at Popov, who left the room to dismiss that staff. He gave more orders to the bodyguard, who started moving two of the bodies off the oriental carpet onto the parquet floor near the window. Popov came back with very large plastic bags and other materials. Oblonsky barked directions which they followed.

"Viktor, you and Ivan get these bodies into bags. You need to remove the carpet as well. Jake, you gather any evidence and put it in those smaller bags. Put in anything you think might be incriminating. Leave the bags near the bodies. I'll make a call and get someone to come get all this stuff and dispose of it."

"Can you make this go away?" asked Jake.

"Of course. But we need to be quick. We'll do what we can here and then go over to Tverskaya Street and have drinks at my club. We should be seen and get our faces on security footage. The bodies will never be found but there will be an investigation when Wang does not show up at his hotel. Police will come and look in this office. I'll make sure this all stays away from us."

Oblonsky dialed his phone and started speaking in Russian. He turned away from Jake before taking the pistol he used, wiping it clean, and putting it on the table. Popov and the guard wrestled with the bodies while Jake put everything he could into three thick leather bags. The glasses, silverware, papers, and anything else Wang might have touched. His phone which was lying on the floor. Novikov's reading glasses and gun. More silverware and china. Oblonsky was still talking but motioned to Jake, pointing to more things on the table including his gun and a pile of papers. Jake picked these up and added them to a bag, then placed it near the bodies.

"Change of plans," Oblonsky said when he hung up. "Let's leave and go about our business. My men will remove all this. I'll go back to my house. Jake, my driver will take you to the Metropol. Let's have breakfast at your hotel tomorrow at ten."

As Jake got into the sedan, he noticed it was still light in spite of being quite late. Traffic was still heavy, but the one-way flow was in the right direction and he was at the Metropol in less than five minutes. He made his way to the fourth floor, passing the large lady at the desk, who bent over to make a note of his passing. He thought Oblonsky might have things under control but probably only for himself. Jake knew he was in Russia, he was alone, and he needed to get out. He considered going to the US Embassy but from past experience suspected they would not provide the protection he needed. The impulse to vomit had passed, replaced by severe anxiety. He felt his heart racing, and wondered if he would make it out of Russia.

CHAPTER 38

THROUGH the peephole, Jake saw the ugly face of Viktor Popov. He had to open the door, but was understandably reluctant. Taking the metal security chain off the door guard, he turned the doorknob and let the killer into his hotel room. It was the middle of the night.

"Change plan. Must leave now," said Popov in heavily accented English. Jake had grown to dislike this huge, barrel-chested man with gorilla-like arms, pudgy face, and Brezhnev-like eyebrows. The events in Oblonsky's office earlier had reinforced this dislike.

"I thought we were to act normal and have breakfast at ten. My flight isn't until late this evening. Twenty hours from now."

"Flight changed. Come now. Bring things," replied the Russian.

"But you need to tell me why Viktor."

"Boris will tell why. Come now," he repeated.

He was getting nowhere with the man. He was mad but could not challenge the brute with the gun. He opened the closet, took out his small suitcase, and started putting things in it.

"Where am I going Viktor? What should I wear?"

"You leave Russia. Dress for plane."

Jake changed into traveling clothes and continued gathering his belongings.

"No more time. You must be at plane forty minutes."

Five minutes later, the two men walked down the hall, the lady again bending over to make a note. Popov said something to her in Russian and she stopped, looked at him, and pushed her notebook away, sitting back in her seat. They took the elevator down, walked through the lobby of the Metropol, and out the revolving door to a waiting limousine. Jake assumed they would check him out of the hotel at some point and alter the records as to his coming and going. They got in the back, Popov said something to the driver in Russian, and they sped down Teatral'nyy Proyezd past the Bolshoi theater, turned right on Ulitsa Il'inka, past St Basil's, and crossed the Moskva River with the Kremlin fading in the rear. He thought of his earlier walk through Red Square and how upbeat he had felt. His attitude now was completely opposite. Out the window, Jake watched as they raced southwest on Leninski Prospekt en route to Vnukovo Airport.

"Will Boris be on the plane?" asked Jake. "How will I get through immigration?"

"I don't know," replied Popov, who turned and looked out his window.

"All you've told me is that I must leave the country now. No reason why. I'm not feeling comfortable with this. Why shouldn't I just get out of the car?"

"I cannot tell anything. Be patient, it's OK," said Popov.

Jake fumed as he settled back in his seat, realizing he had little choice. A half hour later, the car passed through a security checkpoint and cruised along airport taxiways towards a waiting Gulfstream IV. Jake climbed up the airplane steps as Popov handed his bag to the ground worker for placement in the hold. Boris Oblonsky was waiting for him in one of the front seats.

"What the hell is going on Boris?"

"I am sorry to be rude Mr. Tillard, but I'm afraid the authorities are looking for you. If you don't get out of Russia now you will be in Lubyanka Prison by the end of the day. You are wanted by the FSB as well as the Border Guard Service and the local Moscow police."

"Why are they all looking for me?" Jake asked.

Shocked, Jake dropped into the leather seat.

"It's unfortunate, but you are wanted for murder," replied Oblonsky.

"Murder? Those men in your office? But I didn't kill them. You know that. You have clout. Why didn't you tell them I didn't do anything?"

"Because your fingerprints are on the gun that killed them."

"But I didn't pull the trigger," screamed Jake, slowly coming to the realization of what was happening. "You son-of-a-bitch."

He remembered now how Oblonsky asked him to pick up all the evidence and put it in leather bags. That included the gun Oblonsky himself used to kill Novokov and Wang. He felt naïve for having followed the request, but he was in a state of shock after witnessing the murders. He was mad at not only the Russian, but also himself for being so foolish.

"Don't be upset Mr. Tillard. It's not so bad. Lucky for you I have connections. I am able to get you out of Russia tonight. Immigration is no problem. My plane will fly you to New York, and from there wherever you want to go. With our countries as they are now, I doubt the Russian police will get to you in America. But you will not be able to enter Russia again. If things go bad you could end up with an Interpol Red Notice. I would be careful about traveling abroad in the near future."

"You set me up, you asshole," screamed Jake, enraged. "You had me handle your gun and put it into the bag."

"Yes I did. I also wiped off my fingerprints first. It was, how do you say, a spur-of-the-moment idea. One of my better ones. Bad for you the gun has only your fingerprints on it. It also happens to be a Glock that was reported as stolen in western Montana last year. It is amazing what is possible to buy these days. Interpol will have this information."

"So you planned all this in advance?" asked Jake.

"Not really. I could have gone for years doing business with the Lims. Wang Yong was a jerk, but I knew him. I bought the gun just in case. I never thought I'd use it. But I believe in forward planning. I got it just after starting business with you but I have guns from many countries. I admit it was fortuitous I brought that particular Glock to dinner last night."

"You are a bastard."

"Many would agree," Oblonsky smirked.

"How did the police get the gun? I thought you had your people get rid of the bodies and the evidence."

"I could have done that but the Chinese can be a problem with their tenacity. After you left my office, I changed my mind. I did not get my people to clean up the mess. I called a friend in the FSB instead. He was happy to have a major crime handed to him. It will give him a promotion. Now I have another indebted colleague in the FSB."

"But this is not right," protested Jake.

"Nevertheless this is how it is," said Oblonsky. "I must leave now. I'm taking a big risk helping you like this. It would be unfortunate for you to be found on my plane. You must get out of Russia. There will be no record of you leaving my country. The plane manifest will show no passengers on this flight. It will pick up two of my staff in JFK and bring them home. When you get to the US you will follow directions of the crew how to enter through immigration. We'll talk by phone next week about what will happen to our gold mine. Good luck today, my friend,"

Sarcasm permeated the air. Boris Oblonsky stood up and departed the plane with his bodyguard. The flight attendant immediately pulled up the steps, closed the door, and the Gulfstream taxied towards the runway. Jake could not rationalize what had just happened. He sat back in his seat, preoccupied with his situation, and stared without seeing the pretty attendant. When she asked again what she could bring him, he could not get out any words. As he crossed the Russian border, his thoughts drifted back in time to an earlier involvement with the CIA. Maybe it was time to revisit his old contact there.

CHAPTER 39

AFTER Oblonsky's plane landed at JFK, the pilot asked Jake to wait in the bathroom while the border patrol agent boarded for inspection. The agent never looked in the head and left with more cash than he had before. They cleared customs, refueled, and flew to Denver where Jake took a waiting limo to his condo in Cherry Creek. En route he phoned Libby, who had been expecting him to call for a few days and was growing concerned. Sensing the anger in his voice, she became more anxious, realizing there was a problem. Jake gave her a two-minute synopsis, after which Libby agreed immediately to meet him at his place. She had been working late, and arrived just after midnight. He poured bourbons for both of them and relayed the story in detail.

"Shit Jesus, Jake, maybe we should pull in our horns," said Libby. "That's the most fucked-up stuff I've ever heard, and I've worked the mines for a long time. Thank god you're OK."

"No kidding," Jake said. "I knew going into Moscow that Wang was trouble. David had convinced me of that. What I didn't know was that Oblonsky was worse. I guess I should have realized that. Anyway, it's all water under the bridge now. What we need to do is figure out what to do going forward. We have to get Boris out of the deal."

"I say we bury him. Put him six feet under. Or better yet, a hundred."

"Easier said than done, Libby. The man's Russian. He's smart, suspicious of everyone, and overly cautious. He always has bodyguards with guns."

"Well Russians bleed just like anyone else. We can't touch him in Russia of course, but we do have a mine in Egypt. They just started diggin' at the two-hundred-foot level. They'd never find him down there."

"We'll never get him down there," said Jake. "He's way too careful."

"Then we've got to think outside the box. I can't see him just handing his interest away. I'll bet he's planning to do one of three things. Either get you into that Russian prison after all, tie us up in legal circles so we've got no choice but to back out, or kill us. Seems like he's got leverage after framing you in Moscow. But my guess is he's got to deal with the Chinese first. Killing Wang didn't solve anything on that side."

"That's for sure," said Jake. "How he gets them out of the deal will be telling. We need to retaliate, but I don't think we can do it alone. Might be time to call a friend. Or should I say an ally of convenience."

"You have someone in mind?"

"I thought about this on the plane ride. Who has motivation as strong as us to fuck Oblonsky?"

Libby thought a minute then said, "Well obviously the Chinese? But they started this shit. And I don't think they're our good friends."

"Maybe, but maybe not. You know that old saying, 'The enemy of my enemy is my friend'? It wasn't the Lim family who threw the wrench into this thing, it was Wang himself. I think he was trying to go rogue and get out on his own. That would have been a double blow to the Lims. Let's get David in here and talk about how to approach them. He can be our window into the Chinese mind."

#

It took two days for Li to get to Denver. He landed on Friday night, and they gave him until lunchtime Saturday to recover. As the three of them sat in Libby's office gazing out at the Rockies, Jake told the Moscow story a second time.

"God, Jake," Li said when Jake finished.

"Yeah, it's turned into a fucking disaster," Jake responded. "We need to brainstorm options on how to continue. Libby and I have an idea, but I want to get you involved. See if you have any thoughts."

Li got out of his chair and walked over to the windows. It was a stormy day in Denver, windy, rainy, and cool. He gazed towards the mountains then refocused his eyes on the sidewalk eighteen stories down.

"Some people walking in the rain have no umbrellas and are getting soaked. Others with umbrellas have protection. One poor soul down there just had his umbrella blow inside out and now he's really in trouble. Not dressed for rain and now without his umbrella."

"OK. Well that's interesting, David, but not helpful," Jake countered dismissively.

"No seriously, we need an umbrella," said Li. "A strong one. One that will protect us from the Russians and not blow apart."

"I know you did well at Stanford, David, but I don't remember you being a philosophy major."

"Everyone is a philosopher in a Chinese household. I had Confucius-loving parents who talked like this. They would have written good fortune cookies."

"So where do we find this umbrella?" asked Jake.

"At the Muat I met Liu Ling; do you remember Jake? She accompanied Wang Yong when he visited. She didn't say much, but I overheard her conversations with a couple of the senior miners. She told them not to do the bad things that Wang requested of them. I didn't understand at the time, but I suppose she knew Wang was corrupt. Which implies the Lims might have thought the same thing, and that's why Liu was with him, to thwart his intentions. My father told me that Liu Ling is very close to the Lim family, and maybe that's why she was attached to Wang, to keep an eye on the family business. She probably knows why Wang went missing, and she's maybe not keen on seeing Oblonsky come out of this smelling like roses."

Jake thought about this, and thought back to what his daughter told him a few days ago. Gussie was staying with him for most of the summer.

"Let me ask you something David. My daughter saw me reading something the other day, and saw the surname Liu. She's taking Chinese at that new school of hers, but I'm not sure she got it right. She said it meant 'kill' or 'destroy'."

"Well it's confusing to go from an English translation to a Chinese character. At least it can be a non-unique exercise. In any case, 'kill' is a reasonable interpretation of Liu. The surname is likely a derivative of a Han dynasty name that did indeed mean 'kill'. However I've also heard that Liu can mean 'beautiful flower', so take your pick. The former is more relevant to our Ms. Liu Ling. I'm impressed your daughter has learned that already. She must be quite smart. For certain, Liu has an auspicious name."

"Name notwithstanding, if Liu is a Lim power broker, do you think she can help us extricate the mine from Oblonsky?"

"There's one way to find out. I can ask my father to get us a meeting with Liu. We'd probably need to travel to her."

"Uh-oh, that's not good," said Jake. "I'm not sure I can travel. The Moscow police are looking for me and Oblonsky said I might be on Interpol's watch list. Before I leave the country I need to figure that out."

"Can you do that?" asked Libby.

"Maybe," answered Jake. "I'll try to get hold of Stan Kawinski. David, hang here in Denver for a few days and enjoy yourself, on expense account. I'll let you know when I find out."

Li left the conference room and Libby turned to Jake.

"Stay at my place tonight?"

"I'd like that. Dinner out first?"

"Let's eat in," Libby smiled coyly. "Make some steaks. But not till after we get reacquainted, if that's OK with you?"

"Yeah, I look forward to getting reacquainted," Jake returned her grin. "But first let me see if I can reach Stan."

"Get a wiggle on. It's been a while, and I don't like waiting."

#

When Jake phoned Kawinski, his secretary said that Mr. Kawinski was out of the country. She would send him a message, but she did not expect him back for a week. Stan had helped Jake when he struggled with his gas deal, when he was a CIA agent working for General Dick Radisson at the State Department. Both Kawinski and Radisson were indispensable in handling Israeli criminals and bad elements within the US government who were making Jake's life hell. Jake hoped Stan could tell him if it was safe to travel overseas. Maybe he could help with more than that.

Since Kawinski was unavailable, Jake wondered what to do next. He grabbed his coat and walked to his condo to freshen up before joining Libby at her place. As he trudged through the rain, he thought of David and his umbrella metaphor. He was a nice young guy and maybe his idea of approaching Liu would work. Jake hoped so. His thoughts were suddenly interrupted by his phone.

"Hello."

"Jake. Is that you?"

"It is. Stan?"

"Yep. I'm working so it's got to be quick. I'm in Asia so could lose you any time. Crappy satellite coverage here. What's up?"

"Can I give you the background?"

"Better not now. Just tell me what you need."

Stan was always perceptive and to-the-point. He figured that Jake needed something and that's why he called.

"OK. I got into a situation with a Russian Oligarch named Boris Oblonsky. He got me into hot water and I need to know if I'm on Interpol's radar, and whether I can travel overseas or not."

"Phew boy. I may have heard of that problem, if it was in Moscow. OK, no problem. I know of Oblonsky. Great company you keep," Stan laughed. "I'll get back to you soon and let you know if you can travel."

"Stan, when you get time, also tell me what you can about Oblonsky, OK?"

"Will do Jake. I'll call you later. We'll talk longer. Got to go."

The phone went dead. Jake had no doubt Stan would call him back soon with the information he needed.

CHAPTER 40

THE Airbus A330 flew above Victoria Harbor and Kowloon City, past Bishop Hill, and after the pilot saw a large red and white pattern on Checkerboard Hill, made a right-hand turn below six hundred feet to touch down at Kai Tak Airport. The approach, adjacent to two-thousand-foot-high mountains, could not be done on instruments, and required a manual landing. It was ranked as the sixth most dangerous commercial airport in the world. Hong Kong was building the Chek Lap Kok airport to replace it, but that would not open for at least a year.

Kawinski had indeed phoned Jake the day after his call. Stan asked for more background and Jake gave him a shortened version of what transpired in Russia, backed by an overall summary of the mining venture, partners, and current operation. Stan said there were no warrants for him with Interpol and promised to squash anything that might surface. He had a man in the Embassy in Moscow keeping track of the murder investigation. He had information on Oblonsky and promised to do additional digging on current affairs in the Sinai. He asked if Jake could meet him in Washington D.C. in a couple weeks.

The plane landed in Hong Kong and taxied to the terminal building.

"Well let's hope I make it through customs," Jake said to David as he reached for his bag in the overhead bin.

Their entry into Hong Kong was uneventful as was their taxi ride to the hotel. It was Jake's first time in the city and although he was focused on his agenda, he looked forward to a bit of sightseeing. David met friends of his dad that afternoon, which enabled Jake to explore on his own. He was intrigued by the number of contacts Li's father had in this part of the world and was more than happy to let David foster relationships here. While Li was off on his own, Jake took the Star Ferry and wandered around Kowloon. He loved the Wong Tai Sin Temple and was surprised by how new it was. He strolled through the Temple Street Night Market just as venders were setting up for the evening. By six he was fully exhausted; both Jake and Li went to sleep early.

\#

Liu Ling welcomed Jake and David into the conference room, bowing and presenting a business card to each of them, held with two hands. Jake and David reciprocated. Jake studied the petite meticulous woman, remembering the first time he saw her at the mine, in a conservative jump suit. Today she was dressed in an expensive, conservative, gray, silk dress, hemmed below the knee, with black pumps and a single strand of pearls. She looked elegant.

Liu explained she was meeting them alone because this was an informal meeting. Yesterday at the hotel, David told Jake he hoped Liu would meet them alone. Evidently that would indicate they could be frank and would have a better chance of making real progress. Liu started the conversation on a social level, then tea and cookies were served before Liu began talking about Wang Yong, albeit in a circuitous fashion.

"The Lim family runs some of China's oldest businesses. They are well connected and respected. Hard in business but fair. Business here depends on relationships that have been built through generations. Philip Lim is eighth generation and has led the business empire since his father Chou Lim died over a decade ago in a boating accident. Philip is my half-brother since we share the same father. My mother was a schoolteacher in a small village near Guilin where Chou Lim kept a house for her. My mother loved my father, however they could not marry since he was already married to Philip's mother. My bastard status restricted my access to many things but having such a respected father awarded me other advantages I never would have had growing up in my village. Despite not knowing each other when we were young, Philip and I became close after university and we have each other's trust. That's why he attached me to Wang Yong, to watch out for the family's interests. David Li, your father went to school with Philip and that is why I'm meeting with you today. Did your father tell you any of this?"

"No, he only suggested that we meet and that you might be interested in helping with our current problem."

"Your father phoned Philip who asked me to meet you. I'm uncertain what your father shared with Philip, but he told me nothing of your problem. Philip merely instructed me to listen to you today. Tomorrow I fly to Mongolia with him and if there is anything for us to discuss concerning this matter, we can do so then."

"Should we tell you about our issue?" asked Jake.

"Not yet. First I'll tell you about Wang Yong from the perspective of the Lim Family. Wang worked for the enterprise more than two decades. He and my father, Chou, grew up together and were friends. Wang was involved in many Lim companies and in all the business we do in Russia. Almost half of our Russian business is with Boris Oblonsky. Over the last couple of years, Wang suggested to Philip that Oblonsky was taking advantage of our partnerships and recommended the Russian 'be dealt with'. Philip and the family board disagreed amongst themselves on this, but were coming to the conclusion that Wang was the problem and was as corrupt as Oblonsky. Wang lost the trust of Philip who quite honestly never saw him like our father did. There were some who wanted Wang to be demoted or moved to an insignificant area. Therefore his disappearance was welcomed by some in our company."

"What do you know of Wang's demise?" asked Jake.

"We know he died in Moscow from a gunshot," answered Liu. "We know it was during the time he met with Oblonsky and yourself. We know the Moscow police have a warrant out for your arrest in connection with his death."

Liu stopped talking and silence filled the room. The Chinese woman looked deeply into Jake's eyes and did not move. Neither did Jake flinch or look away. They say the eyes are windows into the soul, and Liu thought into a person's character as well. After an awkward minute, Liu broke the silence.

"You do not look like a killer, Mr. Tillard."

"I'm not sure all killers look the same. Why did you really agree to meet me?"

"The short answer is because Philip asked me to. The longer answer is to learn more about Wang's 'demise' as you put it. The real answer is because we understand here in China that little is as it first appears, especially when it comes to Russians. You Americans think truth and honesty are best practiced in a widespread manner. It is a unique view in the world. One that our culture can't quite understand. Honestly, I wanted to hear your version of the story."

Jake sipped his tea and began at the beginning, with the pile of cores sitting on the desert floor in the southern part of the Sinai. He talked about the geology leading to his conviction that a mineable deposit lay beneath that desert. He traced the history of how Oblonsky and then Wang became involved. He told, in his truthful American way, what happened in that Moscow conference room and what happened since. He left nothing out, being efficient and comprehensive in his explanation. Then it was his turn to be silent and let it sink in with Liu.

"Wang was not without guilt, but did not deserve to be executed," is what she said.

"I don't think Wang was a killer any more than me," replied Jake, "but it doesn't surprise me that Oblonsky is."

Liu sat back, put her graceful hands below her chin, and exhaled a long breath. She looked at the ceiling then shut her eyes.

"No, Wang was not a killer. I worked with him for years. He was unlikable but almost in a good way. I did not have to socialize with him during our many trips. He always treated me with respect, but he liked women and would frequent the brothels. No, Wang's downfall was simply his ambition which led to disloyalty. Our organization will shed no tears for Wang Yong however we will not let his murder go unpunished. Justice must be dealt. Of course you realize we did some investigating prior to your visit. You have a history of being tough but certainly not a killer. We thought it likely that Oblonsky's bodyguard pulled the trigger, not you. We didn't think it was Oblonsky himself. Your story makes sense to me and I shall share it with Philip tomorrow. What do you think should be done?"

"We thought with your help we could get Oblonsky to relinquish his interest in the Muat Mine. Perhaps you could assist us with leverage over him."

"That does not sound like much of a plan. Did you not get any further?"

Jake had hoped they would get to this point. He and Libby were unsure just how far to go in this first meeting. He looked at David who nodded slightly in encouragement.

"GusCo is involved with Oblonsky in only one venture, the Muat, so that is our focus. We recognize that the Lim family has many ventures with him, and our mine is just a small part. Oblonsky framed me for something I had no part in, and that's made me very angry. It seems we both have an interest in going farther than just sorting out the mine. We hope with your help we can detain Boris in Egypt and scare him enough so he agrees to a list of demands. These would include giving up his interest in the Muat, clearing my name in Russia, and compensating the Lims for any business lost."

"All that is fine," replied Liu, "but you are not being hard enough on Mr. Oblonsky. He will need to suffer for his actions. He killed one of our men. You have a saying in English, 'an eye for an eye'. If he is not killed, then he must suffer greatly. I will discuss this tomorrow with Philip. What are your plans?"

"We have a flight back to the States the day after tomorrow, but we're flexible. If you see any reason for us to stay longer, we're happy to do so."

Liu peered out the windows and thought for a moment.

"It's hard to say, but why not postpone your departure? There is much to see and do in Hong Kong. There are many sights, many restaurants. We can meet again on Friday or Saturday. Maybe I will have some news."

That night David and Jake dined at the Jumbo Kingdom, a floating restaurant in Aberdeen Channel. Some would call it a tourist trap, but Jake decided they were tourists, so why not. The typical Cantonese food was good but unremarkable. The beer and the people watching were better, and it was always nice to be on the water. Best of all was reflecting on the meeting with Liu. Jake thanked David for arranging the meeting and hoped the next one would lead to an agreement to deal with Oblonsky.

#

"How was your time in Hong Kong?" asked Liu Ling on Saturday.

"Memorable, in a good way," replied Jake. "It's a dynamic city. You're lucky to live here."

"As long as we can keep China at bay, it will continue to be a good place for business. As you know, the Handover occurred last week, with Britain giving control of Hong Kong to China. We were a British colony for a hundred and fifty-six years. As such we had special privileges and a unique position in Asia. That's now over, and for now we have a special designation within China. When that ends, and it will, things will change here. Like most companies we are planning for that day."

"Will your company stay here?"

"We'll have to see how it goes."

"We've rebooked our departure to tomorrow," said Jake. "Will that be enough time?"

"It should be. I've cleared my schedule for the rest of today. We can discuss what to do about Oblonsky and agree on actions before dinnertime. Philip will join us at dinner. We have some ideas."

They spent the rest of the afternoon planning retribution for the events in Moscow. The severity of what the Lim family wanted to do did not surprise Jake, although the reach of their people and influence did. The plan Liu outlined was in essence similar to what Libby and Jake first conceived, but more convoluted. Dinner with Philip Lim was at a private club, in a private room. Lim looked older than Jake expected, but had the demeanor of someone used to getting his way. He spoke sparingly and carefully. Discussion was all about implementing the plan, which would begin soon. It would bring together the strengths of both organizations.

CHAPTER 41

KAWINSKI sat on a bench midway along the Lincoln Memorial Reflecting Pool. The forecast was for another record hot day, but it was still early morning and quite pleasant. He wore jogging shorts, a Marines tee shirt, and running shoes. He sipped on a Starbucks, watching the clouds reflected in the water. Jake was dressed in similar fashion, but with a Dartmouth shirt. He walked up to Stan and sat next to him; there were a few people milling around, but no one close enough to overhear them.

"Jake Tillard, it's been a while. How've you been?"

"After we last met four years ago, I settled into a good life, developing the Sinai gas field, enjoying my daughter and the ranch in Montana. The good life got interrupted this year."

"How's Marv?"

"Marv's fine, slowing down but still ranching. Libby and I made progress on a relationship but haven't reached the point of commitment. But there's also been dark times, Stan. Do you remember my daughter Gussie?"

"Of course. Cute kid. Pretty little thing. Quick to figure out how to fly a kite."

"Well, she had a horrible accident at the ranch. She's fine now but we almost lost her. I was devastated and blamed myself, my dad, and even Libby. It was a freak horse accident. Anyway, Libby helped me through it and got me focused on a gold prospect in the Sinai. Regrettably, she also got us involved with Russians and Chinese. It seems I've found complications in my business dealings again."

"Jake, I'm sorry to hear about Gussie but glad she's fine. She always had a smile and tons of energy. You've had your share of tragedy, man. I see a lot of that in my job and I know it's tough to bounce back. It must be difficult being a single father while trying to do the business you do."

"Thanks Stan. It is hard. I've put Gussie in a boarding school, which I think is going to be really good for her."

"I'm surprised you and Libby haven't tied the knot."

"I proposed, but she said I wasn't ready. Evidently she thinks I have things to work through, which I guess is true. She also said she didn't want to screw up a good thing. What the hell does that mean anyway?"

"Maybe it means she likes you but likes things the way they are for now. But maybe not forever. Maybe she sees the demons you're fighting. Don't give up on marriage, but get your shit together. The right time'll come."

Stan sipped his coffee and let Jake have some space.

"I've been to D.C. a lot," said Jake, "but I've never sat on the Mall and looked around. It's nice. Peaceful."

"You need to visit when the cherries are out," replied Stan. "I love this spot right here. It's incredible how relaxing D.C. can be, surrounded by the assholes running our government. Washington's an enigma, an insular place populated by some of the worst human beings you can imagine, but somehow the country works. When I sit here and look at the Lincoln Memorial, I'm reminded that not everyone is terrible. After we're done, wander over to the Vietnam Vets Memorial. When it was installed in 1982 it had 57,939 names on it. Not all of them were good people, but most were heroes. A whole bunch of kids caught up in a political nightmare. Do you remember the protests that filled this space during the war? The music? The hippies? The free love? It's sobering to remember those times. But we got through it, and we're probably in a better place because of it. I guess that's progress through adversity."

The men talked about their country and the world. Jake asked Stan what he'd been up to but got little information, which he expected. Stan became close to Jake a few years back but never shared much about his personal life. They finally got around to Jake's new problems.

"About your Oligarch. This is classified, but you'll be interested to know the CIA started investigating Russian Oligarchs last year, on orders from the President. Two of them popped up as potentially

troublesome for our country. One of those is your buddy. The State
Department has a long file on Oblonsky, documenting two ongoing
US investigations and other international ones, but to-date no one's
been able to get anything to stick. The man is rotten but smart and
careful. Why do you keep getting involved with such people Jake?"

"Lucky I guess," he replied sarcastically.

"He's got a labyrinth of businesses, shell companies, and
partnerships spanning the globe. A lot of activity in Malta and
Cyprus, some in the Caribbean. Seems to avoid drugs and guns, but
he's into almost everything else. We track him continuously now, so
if you need to know his plans I can help. I took the liberty of looking
into troubles at your gas field which gave me a chance to reconnect
with our mutual friend General Latif. He indicated that the Egyptian
government thought your security issues were due to NOFORTH.
We track that group along with others linked to terrorism. Much of
what we learn through satellite surveillance we supply to Mubarak's
people. NOFORTH's an odd group, fairly loose, mostly young, and
dispersed in their operations. They take credit for some attacks but
not for others. They publicize certain protests and not others. We
think it's because they're poorly organized. In any case, we give
Egypt everything we get on them. These days, at least, Egypt's on
our side. The General is paying attention to your areas in the Sinai. I
think he has a fond spot for you, or maybe more so for Libby."

"I could use any advance information you get on Oblonsky's
traveling to Egypt," said Jake. "Particularly in the next month or so."

"I'll try," replied Stan. "Can I give you any other help?"

"Maybe, but not now. I'll let you know. Stan, it was nice seeing
you."

"Same here. Take care, Jake. Call me if you need me."

Stan stood up, deposited his coffee cup into a bin next to the
bench, and jogged towards the Lincoln Memorial. Jake watched him
go, then got up and went the other way.

CHAPTER 42

El Tor, Sinai
                                                          September, 1997

MOHAMMED and Salah el Gindi drove slowly into the village
of El Tor, on the southwest coast of the Sinai Peninsula. The village
was founded in the 13th Century, but the area has a much older and
involved history. During the reign of Emperor Diocletian in 284-305
AD, some forty early Christian hermits were murdered by Bedouins
here. Later, in the third century, monks fleeing persecution used the
area, and later still, in the sixth century, the Raithu Monastery was
built by emperor Justinian.

Today what remained was a small village consisting of a market
square with several dusty streets around it, next to a port half filled
with rusting fishing boats. A tall, white minaret caught Salah's
eye along with a light brown water tower, its funnel-shaped upper
part trying but failing to blend into the scenery. Ten miles away
rose mountains of the Raithu Desert which contained Mount St.
Catherine and the Muat Mine. The landscape near the village was
flat and brown. Most of the concrete buildings needed work; maybe
a third were abandoned and crumbling. They passed the South Sinai
Governate building before reaching the Police Officers Club, where
Salah had arranged to meet the local police chief.

"*Sabah al Khair. Izayak Mohammed,*" said Hamdi Hamoud, El Tor's
police chief, as he embraced Mohammed, slapping him on the back.

They served with each other during the Six Day War almost
exactly thirty years earlier. During that short battle, the Israelis
caught the Egyptians by surprise, destroyed nearly all their air force
the first day, and drove the Egyptians out of the Sinai with heavy
casualties. Mohammed helped Hamoud escape to Cairo across the
northern part of the Sinai and Hamoud credited Mohammed with
saving his life that day. They saw each other infrequently in the
decade following, but had not met for the past dozen or more years.

"*El hamdu l'Allah,*" replied Mohammed, who introduced Salah el Gindi to the policeman.

Jake purposely sent Salah and Mohammed to El Tor without him. He knew about Mohammed's relationship with Hamoud and trusted his Bedouin friend to sway the police chief in their direction, without being encumbered by the presence of a *khawaga,* or foreigner. After much reminiscing and more tea, Salah reviewed their exploits at the Muat Mine.

"I know about the mine," said Hamoud. "It's a big thing around here. Not much happens in this part of the world. Your mine is controversial since you hired Chinese miners."

"We had no choice," answered El Gindi. "Our financing is from a Chinese family who insisted on it."

"It's not appreciated by the local people. I think most of them only appear disgruntled, as few of our men would consider working underground. Mining is not in their blood and you would not find enough willing bodies to do that work even if you were to look. The people here wonder if there is something they could do other than working underground. El Tor is going through hard times and some of the men want work."

"That's good because we see a way to make some good jobs here. But we need to take care of something first."

Salah el Gindi told him about their partners and the trouble in Moscow, disclosing how their Chinese partner wanted revenge for the killing of their compatriot. Salah was careful to frame the plan as belonging to the Chinese and avoid attaching it to the Americans. He reviewed the plan to kidnap Boris Oblonsky and hold him hostage. More than anything however, el Gindi spoke about the mine and their business plan for making it profitable. They were considering using El Tor as their export facility to ship ore down the Red Sea to a smelter in Africa. He painted a picture of jobs that could be available to locals, including driving trucks, loading ore, running the shipping business, and catering to miners and other workers.

"Those are jobs our locals might want," said Hamoud. "But I see all this activity as a problem for our local, very small enforcement staff."

El Gindi had anticipated this and smiled. He had discussed the matter of *baksheesh* with Jake. Little was accomplished in Egypt without greasing local palms.

"We agree. Of course we would provide money to hire more police, buy better equipment, and increase your activities. Mohammed and you could calculate how much you need, and I'm sure our management would be reasonable."

"So what do you need me to do?" asked Hamoud. "You've heard of the attack last week in Cairo. Terrorists hit a tourist bus in Tahrir Square outside the Egyptian Museum and killed nine tourists, mostly Germans, and wounded another nineteen. With your funds, and considering these recent attacks, we could provide added security for you."

"That would be good on an ongoing basis, and our funding will help you provide this," said el Gindi. "But we have a more immediate need. Mohammed can go over it with you."

Mohammed ran through the plan to kidnap the Oligarch. They would need police to either help or get out of the way. Hamdi Hamoud had several good suggestions on how to carry out the kidnapping and export of Oblonsky. He had no qualms about getting his officers involved, since he was no fan of Russians. He was glad to help his old friend, and besides, he noted, it would add excitement to a boring job. By the time they finished, the three men had negotiated the amount of money the local police chief would receive, both formally and informally, the number of police who would help the kidnapping effort, and even the boat that would be used to spirit Oblonsky to Africa. They left the Police Officers Club and went with Hamoud to the best fish restaurant in town, a local place next to the port. It was a small, plain building with a kitchen and minimal décor consisting of a half dozen wood tables, but they served the best coral trout Salah had ever tasted. Hamoud joined them in emptying several Stella bottles while they dined.

CHAPTER 43

BORIS Oblonsky's Gulfstream landed at the Sharm el Sheikh airport in late afternoon. He transferred to the Movenpick, took a swim before dinner, and went to sleep early. Apart from his two security men and an assistant, Oblonsky was here alone, having requested a last-minute tour of the Muat on his way to Cairo and then London. Jake learned he was scheduled to visit Egypt from Stan Kawinski and arranged to be there at the same time. He was not sure the Oligarch would visit the mine, but had guessed correctly that he would. With el Gindi's network and contacts, they learned his specific plans for the visit and were ready for him.

The Russian traveled in a small caravan of two Mitsubishi Montero SUVs, the best off-road car for hire in Sharm. Mohammed watched from a dirt road on a small rise as the vehicles climbed the hill out of Na'ama Bay and passed through the first checkpoint, manned by United Nations peacekeepers. He followed them in a non-descript sandy-brown Niva, riding with his cousin Abu and two police officers from El Tor. Mohammed kept the Niva far enough behind the caravan to avoid suspicion, then as they approached the next checkpoint several miles outside town he crept up behind the rear Montero. This stop was manned by Egyptian police, who demanded that all occupants get out of the SUVs. Other than Mohammed's Niva, there were no other cars in sight. The police at the stop motioned for Oblonsky's group to stand together beside the long-arm barrier stretching across the road and asked for papers. While they were getting out, Mohammed and his crew walked to join them. Sensing something was wrong, one of the Russians reached inside his coat and pulled out a pistol. Abu shot him immediately, which dissuaded the other bodyguard from doing the same thing. None of the police did anything, which was not lost on Oblonsky.

The Russians were disarmed and dropped to the ground where they were handcuffed.

"You cannot do this," yelled Oblonsky. "Do you know who I am?"

No one said anything as Oblonsky was man-handled into a police car, his cuffed hands further attached to the door. The dead body was loaded into another police car and taken away. The other two Russians and their drivers were allowed to leave for the Sharm airport with the two Monteros. Since they each had a police escort, none of the Russians would report anything, at least in Egypt. They were grateful to be alive and took off in the Gulfstream as expeditiously as possible to return to Russia, without the Oligarch.

Mohammed traveled in the back seat with Oblonsky, heading west across the lower Sinai to just south of El Tor. During the last hour of the drive the Russian was unconscious, after Mohammed knocked him out to stop the constant tirade of shouting and complaining. As they pulled up to a remote dock, Oblonsky regained consciousness. Mohammed and two sailors wrestled him onto a trawler, where Jake and Stan were waiting. As soon as he caught a glimpse of Jake, he started screaming again, in both Russian and English.

"You're in no position to hurl threats Boris," said Jake. "Shut up and listen. I'm not going with you and you'll want to hear what I have to say."

"I will kill you, you American scum," shouted the Russian.

"Well Boris, you had that chance in Moscow, and I'm going to see that you never have it again. You killed our partner, killed your own comrade, and framed me. Who knows how many people you've had killed. You're a despicable human being. The Chinese want you dead, but I told them you had value alive. We compromised and they've set up a little cruise here to try and work things out. It would benefit you to keep all this in mind."

"Mr. Oblonsky, you don't know me," said Kawinski, moving nearer the Russian, peering directly into his eyes. "I work for the US Government. You are close to being prosecuted by my government for any number of crimes. If you survive this ordeal I urge you to tread lightly on any business in the US and any dealings with US citizens. You won't see me the next time we meet and you should hope that does not happen."

"Libby and I decided you should be three hundred feet underground by now, buried alive," said Jake. "But interventions by the Chinese and this man persuaded us to postpone those plans. They convinced us that you turning up dead or going missing would leave a mess. At this point, Boris, only you can save your life, so I'd suggest you be smart and do whatever the Chinese say."

"I'll kill you Tillard."

"That's not being smart Boris," said Jake as he delivered a left hook which knocked the Russian to the ground. "I may see you again, but if not *"do svidaniya."*

Jake and Stan got off the boat before it left the dock. Two of the mixed Sudanese and Egyptian crew pulled Oblonsky to his feet, took him down into the cabin, and chained him to a bench. They were careful to keep the Russian well secured at all times.

#

Just after the trawler crossed the border into Sudanese waters, it was met by a smaller speedboat containing two Chinese who boarded the trawler and asked that Oblonsky be brought on deck. The Russian was visibly distressed, probably dehydrated, but still full of spunk. He recognized Liu Ling and spat in her direction.

"I demand to be released," he said. "You know who you're dealing with. Wherever you go I'll find you and kill you."

"I don't think so," said Liu.

"You'll pay for this," said Oblonsky to the woman.

"I don't think so Boris. It was quite inconvenient for me to make this trip, but I wanted to handle this personally. You see it's personal to me. I didn't like Wang but he was almost a member of my family. You killed the wrong man."

"Go ahead and kill me now," said the Oligarch.

Liu laughed and walked closer to him. He was chained to the railing, feet and hands zip tied. She took a handful of his hair and jerked his head upwards.

"You knew it would never end that easily. A man who has committed a mistake and does not correct it is making another mistake. Old Chinese saying you should ponder."

Liu nodded to a large Chinese man to the Russian's left. When the man hit Oblonsky with a brass knuckle, Liu could see a tooth fly out of his mouth. A second blow from the other side caught him just below the eye. Blood flowed freely from his mouth.

"We will try to reach an agreement," said Liu.

"Fuck you," replied Oblonsky.

"You are predictable, Boris," she said, turning to the large Chinese man and nodding again.

That man and one of the crew unsecured Oblonsky from the railing, pulled him to his feet, and then tied a rope to his zip-tied hands, bound together in front of him. They wrestled him to the back of the boat and pushed him overboard. The rope was sturdy, about twenty feet long, and the Russian was soon being pulled along in the wake at ten knots. He struggled to keep his head above water and to breathe, turning like a corkscrew. Within minutes he seemed to give up.

"Get him out," ordered Liu. She did not want him dying just yet.

The captain cut the engine and the two men pulled Oblonsky back to the boat, where they used the small crane, usually used to retrieve large fish, to hoist him out of the water and swing him onto the deck. It looked like one shoulder had been dislocated. His coughing turned into a moan. He vomited, then spat several times, and seemed humbler than before.

"I can give you anything you want," he said.

"That's a better attitude," answered Liu. "Let's get down to business then. These men will not hesitate to shoot you if the need arises. They all have guns. Be aware that you are fully expendable."

On Liu's direction Oblonsky was taken below. She heard a scream when they put his shoulder back in its socket. He was allowed to change into dry clothes before being brought back to the deck where a table was set with drinks and snacks.

"Help yourself Boris," Liu said, looking at the man's face. "I'm not sure if you can eat with your jaw in that condition, but you should be able to drink. If you wish I'm sure the chef can make a smoothie. We can be civilized if you cooperate. Remember that although your hands are free, you are not. Your only options here are those I give you. The best you could do if you try to escape is to run and dive over the side into shark-infested waters. You might receive several bullets on the way. We are ten miles offshore. If you do anything threatening, my colleagues will not hesitate to shoot. I have instructions from Philip Lim to leave you in Port Sudan, dead or alive. I can only deliver you alive if you agree to a short list of demands. If we can agree, then we will leave you there and you can find your way home. If we cannot agree, then you will be left dead on the dock. I'm not sure what the local Sudanese police would do with your body when they find it, since it will have no identification, no teeth, no fingers. We have until eight tonight to work this out. That's when we land in Port Sudan."

"You know you won't get away with this, and my people will hunt you down."

"Ah. That is one of the demands. To leave us alone. As I said a few minutes ago, let's begin."

Liu had a list of demands on a piece of paper, along with a file containing legal documents requiring his signature, which she slid across the table. The Oligarch had little choice and knew it. The documents ensured that BFC Co would transfer its ownership in the Muat Mine to the Lim family at no cost. He would divest himself of other interests they had jointly, with the Lim family having first right of refusal for each transaction. Oblonsky signed affidavits clearing Jake Tillard in Russia, and eradicating any possibility of Tillard being prosecuted within Russia. In return he would be alive and not pursued by the Chinese. He would also have Chinese agreement to not jeopardize his plan to export natural gas from Siberia to China, one of his largest future projects. Finally, he agreed to take on a Lim representative as his assistant with access to everything he did, and to not seek retaliation on the Chinese or Americans.

"I think in light of what you've done, this is more than fair," said Liu. "I argued against letting you live, but Philip Lim feels you can be valuable sorting things out. You must remember, Boris, that Russians can be violent, but we Chinese have longer memories, better networks, and a greater capacity for cruelty. If you agree to these terms, you must accept that you will not gain revenge in the future."

"What does Tillard get out of this?" asked Oblonsky.

"The Americans are not as vindictive. I think he'll value most the satisfaction of watching you humiliated. But he gets tangibles as well, which don't concern you at this point. Just know that Tillard is now aligned with the Lim family. He's out of bounds like anyone on our own payroll. The same goes for Ms. Joyce and anyone connected to them. You're not to go near them in any capacity. That means personally, physically, through business, or anything else."

Oblonsky looked at Liu and sneered, knowing there was nothing he could say.

"I need you to sign these documents," said Liu.

"You know these contracts have no legal value, since I'm being coerced to sign them."

"They can be argued to have legal standing, but I'll assure you any dispute that arises between us will not be handled through legal channels. The point of this paper is to document that you agree to our terms. It will be a reminder for you of what you need to remember. If there are any infractions on your part, you won't see the retribution coming. You and your family are all targets. Are we clear Mr. Oblonsky?"

Oblonsky signed the document as the lights of Port Sudan came into view. They docked in port and let the Russian off the boat as it refueled and the sun came up.

"You can't just leave me here," said Oblonsky.

"I'm afraid we don't have visas for Sudan," replied Liu. "We can't step foot on the soil. But a word of advice for you. This is a tough city."

"But I have no identification or money."

"Ah, experiences like this makes one tough, don't you agree?" Liu expressed with a wry smile.

As soon as the trawler was fully refueled, they shoved off leaving the Russian standing on the dock. Liu wondered if he would make it out of Sudan alive. She opened her brief case and deposited the documents, looking forward to getting to Cairo and flying home.

As Liu's boat disappeared around the bend, Oblonsky began walking into the port and soon felt so uncomfortable that he returned to the marina. It was filled with fishing boats and commercial vessels, but had a number of small personal craft off to one side. There were a half dozen larger boats which might be considered small yachts but only one was not buttoned up. The stern showed the name 'Peaches', with registry in Cyprus. He approached that boat and called out to the occupants. Incredibly they spoke Russian and invited Oblonsky aboard.

A week later Liu Ling was in Beijing when she heard that Oblonsky had found his way back to Moscow. She smiled.

All's Well That Ends Well

1998~1999

SNOW was falling over the Front Range, with forecasts predicting twenty to thirty inches. Jake had driven up the mountain out of Denver yesterday as it started, joining Libby in Genesee, promising to stay for the duration. On the way he stopped by the grocery store, laying in provisions for a couple nice meals. They both loved to cook, eat, and drink. Dinner last night had been a feast of Tex-Mex featuring Libby's specialty, carne asada. This morning, after a lazy session of lovemaking, they had Eggs Benedict and mimosas in bed, courtesy of Jake. As they soaked in the hot tub, watching oversized flakes falling, Libby unexpectedly asked.

"How attached are you to the Muat?"

Jake looked at her, trying to gauge where this was going. Her face gave nothing away.

"What do you mean?"

"I mean we got rid of the Russian partner, leaving the Chinese. I'm not sure that's who I want to work with. I know you love Egypt and want to keep working there. You have the Seth Field, which satisfies that need. A gold mine doesn't add much except a bunch of headaches."

"You wanna' get out of the mine?" he asked. "It was your idea from the beginning."

"Yeah, that's true. But I don't know," Libby frowned, looking pensive. "The exciting part is over. For me it's the upfront search. I love finding something. Always have. Producing stuff is fine for cash flow, but not nearly as interesting. That's when all the problems start. We've got a good handle on what we expect to come out of the thing. Maybe we could leverage it into something else?"

Jake had learned to read Libby, and it was obvious she had something up her sleeve. This was not a spur-of-the-moment conversation. Still, she gave away nothing, her poker face intact.

"Obviously you have something in mind. So what is it? Out with it Libby."

She came over and sat on his lap, put her arm around his head, and kissed him. She held his head in both her hands and looked into his eyes. She took one of her hands and coyly moved it into his lap.

"You know me too well," Libby said.

Jake was not having any of this and pushed her hand away.

"Not in the mood?" she said.

Jake pushed her off his lap.

"Not till I figure out what you're up to. Stay on your own side until you tell me what's going on."

"OK but you're a spoilsport. My sense is the Lims wouldn't mind having the Muat all to themselves. On the flip side, we're not particularly happy with some of the things we put up with there, like the Chinese miners, the Chinese supply chain, the Chinese bribes, and so on. I've had Owens looking into Lim holdings around the world. I thought maybe there was something we might swap for."

"You talking another mining property?"

"Could be. Or maybe something else. I don't have any preconceived expectations."

"So what did Peter find?"

"They have extensive holdings globally, which we knew. Peter did some portfolio analysis like he loves to do and boiled it down to three options. They've got some import business into the US that might be lucrative, but I think that's too far out in left field. It might be good business but doesn't have much appeal to me. I doubt it would interest you either. Who the hell wants to import textiles and manufactured shit, besides it's not an area either of us knows. They've a couple rare earths mines in China and control some export there. Peter thought it might work with my RE mine in California. But I don't think we want to partner with them in their own country. Still, maybe there is something we can do in terms of rare earths distribution. Keep that in the back of your mind. So in the end, I narrowed it down to one possibility. They own a silver mine in Idaho called the Silver Queen. Not surprisingly the Lims are having compliance problems, I suspect because of how they cut corners. It's not super successful, but it's in a good mining district with a bunch of history. We'd need to do a ton of due diligence first, but I thought I'd float the subject and see what you thought."

Jake got out of the hot water and sat on the edge of the tub. The outside temperature had risen to near freezing and the snowflakes were fatter. They hit him in the face as he gazed upwards. Libby watched him through the steam as flakes stuck on his hair and mustache, pausing before melting away.

"Interesting," he said. "You're right about one thing. I don't need the Muat to stay involved in Egypt. It's still risky and who knows how profitable it will be. There's always the political risk to consider and right now I'm a one-horse business. The Seth Field's doing well, and I like the angle of gas export to Israel. It's fun to work the marketing there and Jerusalem is always fun to visit. Gas is more comfortable for me. The gold mine is something completely different and I liked the idea of having a mine. You've got a couple of them already so it's not new for you. Frankly I don't care if I have a mine in Egypt or Idaho. It'd be simpler with a mine in Idaho. Better fly fishing anyway."

"The Coeur d'Alene area's beautiful Jake. The Silver Queen's got history. I think it might work. I'll get Peter to dig deeper and let us know what he thinks. OK?"

"Yeah, OK. Could work. I assume you've not mentioned this to anyone?"

"No, of course not. Let's see what Peter finds and then think about what sort of deal we could propose. Maybe take a trip up there next month. I hear there's decent skiing nearby."

"Hell Libby. Let's go next week. A ski trip sounds good. If we wait for Peter we might never take the trip."

CHAPTER 45

SCHWEITZER Mountain ski area opened as a small hill for the residents of Sandpoint, Idaho in 1963. The area grew to accommodate more and better skiers and was now a favorite of 'confident' skiers, with a majority of its terrain rated advanced to expert. Jake and Libby took three successive lifts to the top and paused at the summit, over six thousand feet in elevation, to take in views of the Cabinet Mountains of Montana, the Selkirk Mountains stretching into Canada, and Lake Pend Oreille lying majestically more than four thousand feet below them. The lake was formed during the last glacial period over twelve thousand years ago, which was when the U-shaped valleys around them were carved. It was a glorious, sunny day, blue sky, just under freezing, and snow conditions were excellent.

They started down a run suggested by a ski patroller they rode up the lift with, then turned off the slope, into the trees, when they saw the 'Double Jeopardy' sign with two black diamonds nailed to a tree. The spruce were nicely spaced and the fresh powder untracked as they descended to mid station. They stopped for a coffee and sat outside in Adirondack chairs, catching their breath. The run had invigorated them and they took time to enjoy the views of pristine mountains around them.

"Yesterday was interesting," Jake began. "I'm glad we went to the Mining Museum in Wallace. It had a lot of information on mining in the area. I'm a geologist and even I didn't know the Silver Valley was the richest silver district in the US and one of the top three valuable silver mining spots on earth. It's mind-boggling to imagine they pulled over a billion ounces of silver out of the area. It put the Silver Queen into perspective and made me more interested in a swap. I'd like a part of this history."

"The Silver Queen is relatively new though," said Libby. "When we drove into it, it looked pretty puny. The mine foreman was nice enough to walk us around and share some of the history, just because we're geologists. He was real careful not to share anything in terms of the operation."

"Yeah, but we did learn some things," Jake interjected. "The whole operation looked tidy, better than a lot of mines I've seen."

"I agree with that. Maybe because it's fairly new. The operator's not a big outfit so it's tough to get any real track record, but the equipment looked well-maintained and might not give us problems for a while."

"Did you notice anything about the staff?" Jake asked, clearing his throat.

"You mean all the Asians?"

"Yeah, I don't know if that's normal or not, but I didn't expect to see so many Asian workers here in the middle of Idaho."

"I haven't seen that before Jake. Maybe it's because the Lims own it, I don't know. You think it's a problem?"

"No idea, just thought it was odd. We need as much info as we can get on this thing."

"Peter's working on it and thinks he'll have something to review in a week or so. At least our visit didn't come up with anything bad, and that town of Wallace is cute. All the Victorian mining buildings. I love these old mining towns in the Rockies. Telluride. Georgetown. Aspen. I could buy a little house up here."

They finished their coffees and skied another couple hours before returning their rental equipment and heading back to Spokane for the evening flight to Denver.

PHILIP Lim sat back and let Bill Prescott handle the presentation from the end of the conference table. Prescott was the director of Lim Enterprises Inc, which handled the family's business in North America. He was using PowerPoint slides and a laser pointer. To Philip's right sat Liu Ling. Across the table sat Jake, Libby, Robinson, and Owens. Prescott was a mining engineer and had done a good job covering the geology, mining plan, and operational matters for the Silver Queen. He was near the end of his talk, summarizing the history and economics.

"The Silver Queen was staked over fifty years ago, had scratchings through the years, but went into full production only five years ago. The previous owner made the first serious attempt to mine, embarking on a production plan in the early eighties, when silver was above thirty dollars an ounce and spiked over a hundred. That silver bubble was created by the Hunt brothers, and it fueled a lot of dreams at the time. We took over the Queen in the late eighties when silver was just over ten dollars. When we started production in February of '93 it was $6.53 an ounce, and we lost money with every ton we took out. It's averaged $8.50 so far this year, which we figure is about break-even."

"You've run things on a shoestring," said Jake, "which is commendable from a cost-control view but dangerous from a compliance position. We'd need to spend money to get things on track."

Philip Lim had said little during the hours of presentation and question and answer session, but spoke up now. His English diction was perfect and he used words efficiently.

"I know what you would do," said Lim. "I know what it will cost. This mine will live or die on silver prices, like mines have done through the ages. It does not fit our portfolio and I would rather have the Egypt mine. Your position is opposite. So we will try to make this deal happen. The only thing left is to agree on a price for the exchange. I want you to consider one intangible. I want to discuss rare earths."

Jake's side had not yet brought up rare earths, although they had considered how these specialty commodities might fit into the deal. He and Libby were interested in hearing what Lim had to say.

"China controls a third of global rare earths production and within a decade will dwarf everyone else and will control prices. This strategy is not company-specific but is a national priority. Technology cannot do without these metals. We will dominate the supply chain."

"So you want to be involved in my California mine?" asked Libby.

"Not at all," replied Lim. "Your mine is insignificant. It makes little difference to me how much you produce. I am offering something else to sweeten our deal for you. I offer you an insight into pricing, with options for long-term contracting."

"You mean price-fixing? That is illegal," said Libby.

"I agree price fixing is illegal. But that is not what I suggest. We do not price fix. I am saying we can advise you on likely price trends, so you can decide when to lock in contracts with your customers."

"So you're not involving us in price-fixing. But you will tell us when you engage in it and give us details that might help us negotiate sales contracts? Am I understanding you correctly?"

"I don't think you understand, so let me explain it differently," said Lim. "What I suggest is that we meet twice a year and review Chinese production goals. You can then consider those goals against projected demand and decide on your own production goals and pricing. It is totally legal. The critical information here is Chinese state production goals, which are secret. We have a centralized planning system in our country, where setting production goals is legal and in fact the heart of our economic system. You can't get these figures, but we can."

Libby knew this information could help reduce risk and increase profits on her California mine, but was still not sure it would be legal.

"For example," continued Lim, "we know that you are presently deciding whether or not to spend significant money to increase production capacity. To go ahead you will sign long-term contracts to hedge your expenditure. Signing a long-term contract now would be the wrong thing to do based on what I know."

The conversation took a pause, with all parties considering what Lim had just said.

"Let's take a short break and reconvene in thirty minutes," said Jake.

Libby and Owens discussed the RE aspect of the deal and agreed it was worth quite a bit to her. On the other hand, it was no real cost to Lim. This might make price negotiation easier to achieve on the Muat – Silver Queen swap.

After they reconvened, negotiations continued into the early evening, with Owens taking over and hammering out details with Liu. Lim's assistant ordered an elaborate assortment of dim sum for a working dinner, with waiters rolling a cart through every few minutes with a new offering. By midnight they had the outline of a deal, but were still five percent apart on money. Each side committed to have something finalized within the month.

#

The next day they congregated in Jake's suite at noon. Robinson felt good about the geology of the Silver Queen, Owens was comfortable with the economics of the deal if they could meet halfway on price, Libby seemed excited by the potential reduction of economic risk to her California rare earths mine, and Jake was happy with the relationship they were developing with Philip Lim. There was still due diligence to perform and several small items to resolve, but it looked like GusCo would become the operator and sole owner of the Silver Queen. They would give the Lims full ownership of the Muat while keeping a ten percent overriding interest, basically providing them a check each year with ten percent of the profits.

The four Americans celebrated that night with a show on the West End, followed by dinner at The Fat Duck, a relatively new but highly rated restaurant west of town in a listed 16th Century building. The food was innovative and divine, and the wine free flowing.

THE RIVIERA lounge was Libby's second favorite dive in Denver. She sat with Jake at a table near the bar, watching the bartender feed raw hamburger to two piranha in a fish tank, while waiting for Stan Kawinski. There was an interesting mix of clientele in 'The Riv', including ranchers, lawyers, politicians, and tourists. Some business was getting done but it was mostly a fun crowd gathering for an early happy hour. Jake kept his eyes on the front door but somehow Kawinski entered the restaurant through another door and snuck up from behind, putting an arm around each of them. It was what you would expect from a man accustomed to hiding his whereabouts.

"Libby how are you?" he asked, giving her a peck on the cheek.

"I'm just fine Stan. It's been a while."

"Yes it has. Happier times than when we were last together. And Jake, how goes your war?"

"Mostly good. A few hiccups. Hopefully you're not bringing me new problems."

Stan was not an imposing man; in fact, Jake always considered him totally non-descript, which was probably a positive aspect for a spy. He could blend into a crowd easily and be forgotten even more quickly.

"I'm happy to bring only good and useful information this time, although most of it innocuous. Some of it interesting, none of it problematic. Are they serving dinner yet because I'm hungry?"

"They serve all day long," said Libby. "This is Jake's favorite Tex-Mex joint in Denver and one that has a special place in my heart. You've never been here?"

"No ma'am. But I like the looks of the place."

The Riviera was tucked behind a strip mall, in a building that pre-dated the restaurant by a generation. No corner was right, and few chairs matched the assortment of tables. Beer signs and bullfight posters dominated the walls. Lined up behind the long bar was every Mexican brand of beer Stan had heard of.

"You missed the daily feeding of the piranhas by just a few minutes," said Libby.

"Oh well, maybe next time. Let's get some food and I'll tell you what I've got."

Stan took a seat and looked at the menu. After ordering food and another pitcher of beer, Jake asked Kawinski what he had to share.

"I was with General Latif in Cairo last week. It was the NOFORTH group that sank your cores in the Red Sea, blew up that storage shed at the mine, and buggered up one of your gas wells. Latif has a dozen of them in custody, surprisingly half of whom are Bedouin. My guess is they'll all be in an Egyptian prison within the month. He's got a task force roaming the Sinai now so hopefully you won't be bothered again. It's pretty easy to watch people out there. Not as many people to hide among. The more interesting stuff I've got pertains to your Russian friend. This is not from Latif, although Latif knows the Russian and thinks he's bad karma. My info's from our man in Moscow. BFC is about to go down. Oblonsky got on the wrong side of too many important people and was declared a threat by those currently in power. I know he's out of your deal now, has transferred his interest to the Chinese, and has been busy divesting other assets. You'll have to wait for specific news on Oblonsky that I can't share, but he won't be in a position to hurt you soon. Have you heard the name Marat Bragin?"

"Yeah, I think so," answered Jake.

"Jake, that's the guy who gave me his business card in Moscow," said Libby. "Remember, he wrote on the back to contact him 'when shit happened'."

"He's the head lawyer for BFC," said Kawinski. "Apparently he's a numbers guy and knows everything about Oblonsky's businesses. Sort of a genius, and been with him for years. Anyway, Bragin's become friends with our man in the Embassy. Between information from him and a contact in the FSB, we think Oblonsky will be taken any day."

Jake asked a few questions about NOFORTH, Latif, Bragin, and the Chinese before dinner arrived. Kawinski chowed down on his Tex-Mex.

"So let me give you an Egypt update," said Jake while they ate. "The Seth Field has nine production wells online. Gas is flowing. We've had only one pipeline bombing, which is nothing if you've worked Nigeria. We've got long-term contracts in place, which was a good thing to do, since the first gas discovery just came in offshore Israel. No one knows how big it'll be, but now we'll have a competing gas source to contend with. The Muat shipped its first boatload of ore almost exactly one year ago, out of El Tor, bound for the smelter in Kenya. We just shipped boatload number nine. Things are not running smoothly yet but they're on track. The Chinese are doing a good job, and surprisingly have come back to us to review some of their plans, even though we're not involved from an equity point of view. That's what a good relationship can do for you."

"Sounds like all's good Jake," said Kawinski. "I'm happy things are going in the right direction. Enjoy it while it lasts, 'cause it never lasts."

"We're going to Marv's ranch in a few days," said Libby. "Gussie will be with us. You're welcome to come up Stan. I know both Jake's dad and Gussie would be happy to see you. A little R and R might do you some good. You seem to have a negative outlook."

"Thanks but I'm on my way to Columbia. Got a couple things brewing down there. I need the negative attitude."

CHICO Hot Springs, operating as a hotel since 1900, is located near Pray, Montana, thirty miles north of Yellowstone National Park. Springs emanate from geologic fault zones connected to the large Yellowstone Hot Spot; water flows out of the ground at 113 degrees Fahrenheit. Libby thought that Chico had the best chef in the Rockies, providing 'farm-to-table' meals with locally grown herbs and greens, fish caught in local rivers or flown in daily from the coast, and beef from ranches down the road. The main decisions each day were whether to soak in the pools before or after dinner, and whether to book a massage. The answer depended on whether one spent the day fly fishing, riding, hunting, or rafting.

Jake and Libby flew from Denver to Bozeman on her company plane then took a helicopter to Chico. Unfortunately, they would not have time to do any of the recreational activities. David Li had come over from Idaho. After the dust settled on the Silver Queen transaction, Jake had put David Li in charge. It was a huge step for the young man, but he had risen to the challenge. The Chinese American miners at the operation loved him, and Li's language skills brought him instant credibility and loyalty.

The three were in the main dining room, chatting over some of the signature cocktails on the menu. The historic old lodge was rustic but still comfortable and interesting. Some of the clientele came for the waters, but Libby loved this place for its culinary excellence. She looked at her Moscow Mule and urged David Li to give them an update on the Silver Queen.

"The whole operation's going well," said Li. "Our new safety procedures are in place, everyone's finished training, production is up and on schedule, and prices have improved. I'm just holding my breath, hoping nothing bad happens."

"Let's hope it doesn't," replied Jake. "Anything else David."

"Not really unless you want to dive into operational details."

The two partners trusted Li and did not feel the need for more detail. The conversation shifted to the Muat, with Jake giving the latest update.

"I've got news from the Muat. Last month the crew poked out of the main facies into an overlying rock layer when one of the miners noticed turquoise in the rubble. Seems we've got us a bit of that stuff as well, a really pretty blue strain. We've got no idea at this point how much we'll find, but we've put off any plans to follow it for now. They brought up a few samples and I was able to talk Liu into shipping some to Denver. I'm shipping some down to the Hopi in Arizona for fabrication into jewelry. Thought it would make nice Christmas presents for special staff. The Chinese loved the idea, all but the Hopi doing it. Liu said they could make the jewelry in China for less, but I said that wouldn't work for me. I'm making a belt buckle for Oblonsky. I wasn't sure if I'd be able to get it to him since Stan told me that Boris was convicted of tax evasion and is on his way to Siberia for fifteen years. I'm not sure he'll have a belt to put the buckle on."

"Well that's too bad," said Libby, sarcasm dripping from her words. "Couldn't happen to a nicer guy. Have you heard anything more about the BFC assets?"

"Liu told me her company will take over two joint assets. The Chinese aren't interested in much else. Why, do you think we should take a look?"

"Probably not. Would you want anything to do with Russians again?"

"That's an interesting question Libby. It's like the wild west over there now. Dangerous as hell but money to be made. We've got experience now so who knows."

Libby looked at Jake and wondered what he was thinking. She fell in love with his spirit years ago, and he had introduced her to a whole new world outside the US. She understood his passion for the exotic and his need to experience new things. She realized that she would not be satisfied with a more conservative man.

"Liu told me something else interesting," continued Jake. "Some BFC assets have become, in her words, 'inaccessible'. They think a few of Boris's old holdings have been tied up by someone named Putin. He's from St Petersburg but joined Yeltsin's staff last year in Moscow. Two months ago, he was named head of the FSB. Apparently he's got a degree in economics from the St Petersburg Mining Institute and is pretty business-savvy."

"OK, interesting. But that's enough business," said Libby. "I'm heading for the hot pool. Anyone joining me?"

The rest of the evening was fun but the signature after-dinner drinks and hot water took its toll and they retired early. Their helicopter lifted off the next morning at ten. It was a perfect day, with bright sunlight and a huge Montana robin-egg blue sky. The view of the resort was stunning as they circled a thousand feet up before veering off to the northwest, bound for Missoula. They left Li at the airport to catch a commercial flight to Coeur d'Alene via Spokane, while Jake and Libby stayed on the chopper for the short flight south to the ranch. Jake asked the pilot to circle the area slowly while he pointed out for Libby the hot springs where they first made love. As they landed, Marv and Gussie came out of the house as the helicopter blades slowed and then shut down. Marv helped with the luggage while Gussie hugged Jake and Libby for longer than usual. After they settled in with a bourbon and a Brown Cow, Marv suggested they take a walk.

Rather than stroll along the stream, he led them right down the driveway. A half mile down, they passed under the large stone and timber arch which marked the entrance to the ranch. He walked through, turned around, and pointed up at the large Bitterroot granite boulders which helped give the arch its substance. In the middle at the apex, the Bar J brand was etched into a circular disk of granite and the etching was coated with gold leaf.

"Do you remember when we built this arch Jake?" his father asked.

"I do dad. The gold was mom's idea. She loved to see it in the morning when it caught the rising sun."

"She got that gold leaf from somewhere," Marv went on. "I'm not sure where but it might have been that trip we took to China. You and she spent days rubbing it on there, do you remember?"

"I do. It's looking a bit worn dad. I think it could use more gold."

"That's also what I noticed son. We have some leaf left over. Haven't used it all these years. Maybe you and Libby want to do some patching while you're here. Come on Augusta, let's talk about dinner."

Marv turned and started walking back to the house with Gussie. Jake looked after them, his daughter holding his dad's hand, and felt a wash of emotions. He realized he had not been fair to his dad these past four years, since Gussie's accident, and his father looked older than he remembered. He put his arm around Libby and sighed.

"You were right. I think it's all good again."

KRASNOKAMENSK, a Russian town near Chita, more than five hundred miles east of Irkutsk, has a record low temperature of minus fifty-seven Fahrenheit and a record high of one hundred and five. It is the location of labor camp YaG-14/10, known for holding intellectuals and political dissidents throughout several decades. The earliest 'guests' were forced to work in the nearby uranium mine or processing plant, but that practice stopped when Russia caved to external pressure brought about by elevated death rates among prisoners working with those materials.

Boris Oblonsky was instead put to work in the prison's mitten factory. He had entered this prison two months ago when temperatures were near the hundred mark. They were still warm although today the first hint of autumn could be sensed. The other prisoners cautioned him to enjoy the season and to dread what was around the corner. Evidently their buildings were not well insulated and the heat poorly distributed. Ironically, the prisoners were not allowed to use any of the mittens they produced, but Oblonsky had already bribed guards to gain special privileges. For a man with his means, almost anything was possible even in the camps, except freedom.

The trial had been a farce, even though Oblonsky had the best lawyers money could buy. The initial charge of tax evasion was well documented, although some of the documents were created for the trial. The Oligarch had to admit the state did a good job explaining his creative accounting, although he thought they failed to make a case against him. Marat Bragin did everything Oblonsky paid him to do, and the numbers did not add up to evasion. Nevertheless he was found guilty. The follow-on charges of embezzlement and money laundering were handled even less fairly. Although the state did a reasonable job of 'following the money', they also fabricated a trail of data that had no relation to reality. Oblonsky knew enough about accounting to know which charges were fabricated, and Bragin did his best to prove so. Sadly, in the Russian legal system, it came down to 'he said, she said', and 'he' being the state always won. The tax charge carried a five-year sentence and the follow-on charges added another seven. His lawyers negotiated that down to eight total, and most importantly had secured a spot in a medium-security prison.

Oblonsky was outside in the central courtyard enjoying the sun, talking to another once prominent multi-millionaire he had befriended. They were careful to remain distant from anyone else, inmates or guards alike.

"Once the government decides you're a threat, you're screwed," said Yuri.

"I knew that, but believed it wouldn't happen to me," replied Oblonsky.

"Just because you were always able to buy your way out?"

"No, because I knew all the important people."

"Sometimes that's not enough. So let's speak honestly Boris. Are you guilty?"

"Of course I'm guilty Yuri. No one in positions like ours pays all their tax. That would be too much to pay. And money laundering is part of the business. Cyprus would not run without people like us pushing money through the place. I did not embezzle, however. That was made up."

"Who cares. It was going to happen. You were going to prison. They decided that way before they even started gathering data. What is the worst thing you did? You kill people?"

Oblonsky looked at the other man and gauged his earnestness. He glanced around and saw no one within earshot, no cameras trained on him, no danger to telling the truth.

"Didn't you? Oblonsky asked.

"Of course. I'm here, like you, for tax evasion. But it's part of the business to kill and torture. You do what you have to do."

"Yes, I know," said Oblonsky. "It's ironic that we've done all these things yet are not in prison for any of them. The funny thing is that some of the things I did were for the wrong reasons."

"What do you mean, the wrong reasons?"

"One example is the Chinese man Wang that I shot in my office. I shot him because I thought he sank a boat of mine, but it turns out it was sunk by terrorists. He was trying to screw me, OK, and he deserved to die. But really I had it in my mind that he sunk the boat and that's why I pulled the trigger."

"Who cares about a Chinese guy? You must have crossed a Russian VIP somewhere along the way."

"Sure, I've screwed partners. That's just how you do business. Looking back, I think one of my mistakes was crossing people in St. Petersburg a few years back. We were exporting metals from there and I pulled strings to avoid becoming entangled with a group who tried to extort us. They were skimming money from us and wanted more. It got nasty but in the end I won. I got to keep everything we had and keep exporting through the port. There was one guy heading up the Committee for External Relations, part of the Mayor's Office, who was a difficult and rough guy, and had to be threatened. He stayed in that post for quite a while and has recently moved up in Moscow government."

"You talking about Putin?" said Yuri.

"Yeah. Do you know him?"

"He's the reason I'm here."

#

Oblonsky was laying on his cot listening to Prokofiev's Peter and the Wolf, one of his favorite pieces of classical music. A guard pushed a small box through the opening in his cell door. It was not the normal time for mail to be delivered, and Boris cautiously approached the box. It had been opened but still had the original outside wrapping hanging off, which showed it had been mailed from the United States a month earlier. He took off the remaining brown wrapping and opened the box, within which was a smaller box and a folded piece of paper, which he read out loud.

"Dear Boris. We hope this finds you healthy if not wealthy or wise. A memento for you that we had crafted from a piece of ore recovered from the Muat Mine. Regards, Libby and Jake."

He opened the smaller box and pulled open the string tie on the deep purple velour sack. It was the same velour sack in which

Jake had been given the raw diamond. Reaching inside, Oblonsky took out a beautiful hand-crafted silver and turquoise belt buckle. Holding it up to the light that filtered in through the small window high up on his wall, Oblonsky chuckled.

"Well what do you know," he said. "There is turquoise there after all."

He put the buckle back in its sack and then its box. He would give it to his lawyer the next time he visited, for safe transport back to his house in Moscow. Until he was able to get back there, the Oligarch had no use for it.

JAKE and Libby saddled horses early in the morning, packed lunch, and rode west up into the mountains. They passed through fields lush with grass and cattle, past streams and aspen groves, and into forests thick with spruce and pine. Libby was better on a horse despite Jake growing up around them, but neither was afraid to push their limits, jump downfall, and climb slopes.

Three hours and three thousand feet of elevation gain later, they reached the same natural hot springs where they made love for the first time. After tying up the horses, Jake took Libby's hand and started to walk through aspens towards the spring.

"Jake, take my hand and lead me. I want to close my eyes."

The first time they came Jake asked her to close her eyes and led her in. She had no idea what was coming as they passed through the aspens, walked through evergreens, and approached the sulfur spring. The smell changed at every turn, along with the feel of the breeze, and the sound of the ground beneath their feet,

"I remember it so well," she said. "First I smelled the spruce, then heard the water splashing, and finally smelled the sulfur."

Jake could see the spring now and began to smell the sulfur. There was little wind and the sound of the tiny waterfall was like thunder in his ears.

"When I opened my eyes, I saw the most beautiful pool of water I'd ever seen. It was magical."

Jake told her to open her eyes when they reached the pool. The spring looked the same as it did five years ago. It had been improved years before that, with hot water at some higher elevation funneled into a PVC pipe that was positioned to shoot the water into a manmade rock tub. The resultant shower was refreshing and made a wonderful, soothing sound. Behind the springs sat Mount

Edwards, rising to 13,856 feet above sea level. From their vantage point they could see the glacial tarn, its turquoise water contrasting with green grasses and bushes around it and gray rock above, even now in August still harboring patches of snow from last season.

"What's your pleasure ma'am?" asked Jake.

"Oh, a gentleman. I remember everything from that first day you brought me here, but guess what my favorite memory is. I'm not interested in a gentleman right now. I want to see if sex can be as good as I remember."

Jake unbuttoned Libby's shirt and removed it along with her other clothes. He watched as she bent over to remove her pants and shoes. He didn't mind that it took a while as the pants got caught up in her boots. He did not play the gentleman and did not help her sort them out.

She glanced up at him watching her struggle and smiled. She stood up, naked, and walked towards him to help with his clothes. Soon they were rolling on the blanket Jake laid down. They made love slowly but not gently. After they finished, Libby started to rise and straddled his chest, pinning his arms on the ground above his head.

"It was as good as last time," Libby teased.

She kissed him again before plunging into the hot pool. Jake fetched the bottle of Zinfandel from the pack along with two glasses. They soaked and sipped, alternating between being in the pool and sitting on the edge to cool off. After the bottle of wine ran out, they made love again, soaked a while longer, then lay on the blanket with the picnic.

Jake had prepared the perfect lunch of cheese, pate, tapenade and French bread. Finally, he reached into the backpack one more time and took out a small box. Libby watched as Jake got closer and opened the box, holding it out to her.

"We should get married," he said simply.

Libby perched on an elbow and looked at the rock in the box. It was an unassuming dark rock the size of a golf ball, with a slightly frosted crystal jutting out the side.

"Is that what I think it is?" she said.

"I know you like gold Libby, but diamonds are a girl's best friend."

"Jake it's gorgeous. I've never seen a raw diamond except in pictures. Where did you get it?"

"It's from Mirny. It's not for a ring obviously. I'll get you a ring but wanted to propose with this. It's unique, don't you think? The geologist in me wanted to propose with this. So?" Jake looked at her. "Will you marry me?"

Libby stared directly at Jake. She loved him but she thought he still had unresolved issues. The thought of being his wife appealed to her but she needed him to fully commit to her. She had to believe that Jake had finally put behind him the deaths of his brother, mother, and wife, and the near-death of his daughter.

"Jake, I love you of course. You know that, right? But it's not time yet. I think it will be one day, but right now feels wrong. You still have personal issues, Jake."

"What issues?"

Jake felt let down and his ego was bruised. He felt defensive. He was sure Libby would say yes and was shocked by her response.

"If you don't know then you're not ready. Deal with your issues first."

Libby could tell Jake was stunned and offended by her assertion that he was not ready. He knew she loved him and he knew she was afraid of something. Jake waited for the moment, trying to sort through his feelings and trying to take in what Libby had said.

"Do I really seem that confused and messed up?" Jake asked.

"Jake, I just don't want to compete with anyone else. Time is on our side; I'm not going anywhere. You're just not there yet."

Jake closed the box and put the diamond back in the pack. He knew he had issues but did not know how to address them. He wondered if he needed counseling.

"Let's pack up lunch."

Libby smiled and grasped his hand. She reached over and softly kissed him.

"OK, I'll work on me," he said. "I can do that as long as you're with me."

They rode back, taking a route that Libby had never ridden. It had long, expansive views westward towards the Bitterroots and Mount Edwards and even more stunning views eastward across the valley. They stopped at an overlook and she saw the breadth of the Tillard ranch. It resembled a quilt, with patches of forest alternating with grazing land dotted with the solid black Angus that Marv loved. Two streams meandering through, and a jagged rock pinnacle perched in back of the ranch house. Jake explained that pinnacle on her first visit as the mostly eroded stock of an old volcano. As a boy he would climb to the top although the rock was jagged and crumbly. They continued their ride down, getting to the house just in time for dinner.

"Why not marry him?" asked Marv before dinner when he had Libby by herself in the great room. Marv had no idea Jake had proposed, but knew his son well enough to know he loved the pretty woman.

"He asked me today Marv, but he's not ready. I love him to death, and I hope the right time comes soon, but it's not here yet. He's re-engaged with his business responsibilities but he still has personal issues."

"I can't say I'm surprised, Libby. He's been through a lot. It pains a parent to watch their kids go through tough spells. But I think he's rounded the corner. He and I are pretty solid again; we can talk now. I'll always blame myself for Gussie's accident and I know Jake does the same."

"It was an accident Marv. We all carry some blame. Gussie depended on us and we let her down. But she's fine now. You of all people should know that growing up is a risky business. You make calculations, you make choices, you live life, and sometimes bad luck happens. At some point each of us needs to move on. Jake still dwells on his losses. Maybe it was the wrong time to give up operatorship of the Muat Mine. That would have kept him very busy. The Silver Queen is more or less on autopilot and won't require much. Maybe he needs another new business venture to change his focus."

Jake joined them as Marv poured Bourbons in the great room, under the huge logs that held up the roof. A bell rang out and they migrated to the dining room. She loved every room but especially this one, three walls draped in Navaho carpets, the fourth with windows looking out over the lawn to the creek. The sun was setting and the sky turning magenta. Dinner was served and Libby was not surprised it was steak. Jake never gave it a thought. What else would you expect on the Bar J.

"So what's next Jake?" asked Marv.

"I'm going to Egypt and Israel next week. We're in the final drilling phase and I want to make sure everything's lined up for full production by year-end. I'll get Israel to commit to the increased volumes we can deliver beyond our initial commitment. I'll try to extend the gas purchase contract as well. There's a gas discovery offshore, the first in Israel. That's concerning and I don't want it to knock my price down."

"So that's it then?" asked Libby.

Jake looked at her and saw the twinkle in her eye. He knew her better than he knew himself these days. He wanted this woman and pondered what she had shared with him.

"I've also booked a side-trip to Moscow," he said.

"Well that's interesting," said Marv. "I thought you'd had enough of the Russians. You sure you can stay out of prison there?"

"Yeah, Stan told me I'm good to go. In fact, I'll be staying with the Ambassador at his residence. What could be safer than that?"

"You're going to meet with Bragin, aren't you?" asked Libby.

"I am. Apparently he's looking for help in Siberia. There're a few opportunities still hanging around. It's like the Wild West there you know."

Marv and Libby looked at each other and smiled. Libby raised her wine glass and shook her head.

#

Early the next morning, as the sun was coming up, Jake slipped out of bed, careful not to disturb Libby sleeping beside him. She heard him dress and quietly leave the room. A few minutes later, Libby watched from the upper floor bedroom window as Jake walked across the lawn behind the house, towards the stream but veering right to the fenced-in area that contained a dozen or so

Tillard souls, buried under a beautiful, enormous Black Cottonwood tree that reached almost a hundred feet towards the limitless blue Montana sky. She saw Jake open the gate and walk to where Paula was buried. She could not hear what he said of course, but hoped it was something that would help him move on. Libby watched for a few minutes then got back into bed, thinking how nice it would be for Jake to bring her breakfast in bed.

Not long after, he did.

THE END

Acknowledgements

Thanks first and foremost to my best friend and wife Lesa, for tolerating another book project, for careful editing, for valuable suggestions, and for always being there. Thanks to Don Orsi, good friend and prodigious reader, for his ongoing encouragement and critical early suggestions.

Several friends read drafts and provided feedback which significantly improved the manuscript. Among these were Christine O'Leary, Laura Wray, Bob Lamarre, Sue and Bill Oehlman, and Bob Tremain. Others commented on excerpts or provided encouragement. Thanks, you know who you are. I am also grateful to the many people with whom I intersected in the past, who provided insights to the places and characters I described or created in the book.

Sarah Heller constructed great maps. Clare Lelek drew the artwork for the cover. Robert Etheredge created a stunning final copy, helping with the formatting, cover, and publishing.

While this book is pure fiction, it reflects my travels and experiences. Many places are real and I hope their descriptions in the book make them come alive for the reader. None of the characters are real except for obvious historical figures. Any errors are all my doing.

Jeff Lelek

Made in the USA
Middletown, DE
09 November 2022

14289274R00156